THE
SECRET
BOOK
SOCIETY

Also by Madeline Martin

The Last Bookshop in London
The Librarian Spy
The Keeper of Hidden Books
The Booklover's Library

THE
SECRET
BOOK
SOCIETY

A NOVEL

MADELINE
MARTIN

HANOVER
SQUARE
PRESS

HANOVER
SQUARE
PRESS™

Recycling programs
for this product may
not exist in your area.

ISBN-13: 978-1-335-01628-7
ISBN-13: 978-1-335-00115-3 (Hardcover Edition)
ISBN-13: 978-1-335-00176-4 (Canadian Exclusive Edition)

The Secret Book Society

Hanover Square Press
22 Adelaide St. West, 41st Floor
Toronto, Ontario M5H 4E3, Canada
HanoverSqPress.com

Printed in U.S.A.

To the book community that is such a network of strength, where readers can read what they like and never feel misunderstood or judged.

THE
SECRET
BOOK
SOCIETY

PROLOGUE

Lady Duxbury

London, England

June 1895

CLARA CHAMBERS, THE COUNTESS OF DUX-
bury, entered her drawing room and considered the urchin
who'd demanded to be seen at once. His urgency was evident
in the tap of his scuffed shoe upon the lush green-and-gold
Brussels-weave carpet. There was a leanness to the boy's cheeks,
with skeletal hollows visible beneath his collarbones, though his
face and hands were clean and his cap appeared to be new.

"My lady, your friend has been taken." A missing front tooth
showed when he spoke, one that likely wouldn't grow back due
to his age. He extended his hands and her gaze fell on the item
he offered.

Recognition crushed the breath from her: a single black kid-
leather boot with detailed rose embroidery stitched alongside
the lacings.

She knew that boot. And she knew its wearer.

"Taken where?" Lady Duxbury demanded.

"Leavenhall Lunatic Asylum." He shook the hair out of his

eyes with the jerk of his head, revealing an earnest brown gaze. "She called out as her carriage passed, asking me to tell you she was being took there and gave me your house number. She tossed me this boot out the window, so you'd know I was being truthful."

Panic hit Lady Duxbury.

The asylum.

This was her fault.

Everything had gone wrong.

What began with innocent intent had been manipulated into something ugly. Something dangerous.

She pulled in a fortifying breath and accepted the boot, the heft light in her hands despite the weight settling across her shoulders.

"You'll help?" The boy's brows pinched. "I know her. I didn't see her face, but I'd recognize that boot anywhere." His tone was soft, burdened with a sorrow that tugged at the fresh wound in Lady Duxbury's chest.

Could she help?

Her pulse thundered in her ears, and her stomach swam with a feeling she had vowed never to succumb to again. Fear.

After all this time, she thought she was stronger.

"I'll do what I can," Lady Duxbury said with a confidence she wished she felt.

After all, she was responsible. Not only for the woman now taken, but for the others as well. Women who had been repressed, who had been trapped, abandoned to their fates by those they loved. They were all at risk, exposed in ways that could be their downfall.

Lady Duxbury had offered the women sanctuary, opportunities that were never afforded to herself, and she'd failed them. That failure now sliced over a tangle of old scars deep within her.

She nodded to her butler. "Tip the boy generously for this

important message, Davies. He might well have saved a woman's life."

"I hope you're right, my lady." The boy's thin chest puffed out at her praise. Doubtless he was just as starved for affirmation as he was for sustenance.

"Give him some bread and cheese as well," Lady Duxbury added, unwilling to let him leave without a full belly. So many children in London these days were starving. "And more to take with him."

Davies's mouth drew in a hard line, the only show of protest in the middle-aged man's demeanor as he unlocked the small drawer where coins were held for such purpose. But then, he was diligent in his efforts to ensure her protection. The coins clinked into the boy's hand.

After so many painful years, she thought herself in control of her life. Insulated from the threats that once stalked her, surrounded only by those she trusted, shielded by Davies and the esteem and wealth of her position in Society.

Foolish.

She'd been foolish.

And now someone else would pay the price.

"Thank you for helping her." The boy held his cap reverently to his chest. "She's the only person who ever saw good in me."

An ache settled in the back of Lady Duxbury's throat, a vicious, stubborn knot that made breathing hard, let alone speaking. She nodded mutely with a small, reassuring smile that trembled more than she would have liked.

Davies led the boy from the drawing room, leaving Lady Duxbury momentarily alone.

She considered the boot in her hand. Mud encrusted one side, while the other was as pristine as the first day she'd seen it. Her fingers wandered to the smooth crystal cap of the brooch just over her heart where the lock of dark hair formed a crisscrossing pattern. A source of strength. A reminder of what she'd once had. There wasn't a day gone by that she did not miss him, that she did not recall her promise.

The solid stride of Davies's feet on the thick carpet announced his return.

Lady Duxbury hastily wrote out two notes. "Have these sent to the others at once."

Before he could depart, her gaze caught a new flower arrangement on the table by the book of herbs that had been so helpful in her past. "Wait—where did these come from?"

"There is a card, my lady." Davies bowed and departed to comply with her request, aware of its importance.

Once more alone, Lady Duxbury approached the flowers. The combination of blooms was a curious assortment she would never have commissioned. The waxy, bell-shaped foxglove rife with secrets, the promise of sorrow in the blue forget-me-nots, the violent red trumpets of petunias, and a mass of begonias, vivid pink and menacing. A warning hummed like a pitch in the back of Lady Duxbury's mind.

Who would assemble such a bouquet?

She gently set the boot on the table beside the wide vase and plucked the note from the verdant nest of stems. A single name had been printed in neat letters on the back of the card, and the muscles along Lady Duxbury's neck tensed.

Had the woman not done enough harm?

And how much did she know that might still be Lady Duxbury's ruin?

A lightheaded sensation washed over her, blurring the golds and greens of her drawing room into a nauseous palette. She leaned onto the table, drawing careful sips of air to set herself to rights. But how could she ever be right again with so much going so wrong, when she now realized that her strength was only a facade?

The room sharpened into focus once more, that horrendous bouquet, a threat in every vicious blossom. Quickly, she looked about to ensure no one had witnessed her moment of weakness.

Her gaze found the boot once more, catching a sliver of paper jutting from inside the tongue that she hadn't noticed before. Pinching the edge, she gently dislodged the note and unfolded it.

She exhaled a pained breath, immediately recognizing the stationery adorned with a crosshatch of heather and her own handwriting. The missive was one she'd had secretly delivered to the ladies two months ago. At the time, she hadn't considered that her endeavors to offer help might instead bring harm.

Even as she told herself not to, her eyes scanned the lines of the letter, reading the words she had put to paper at the start of it all.

You are cordially invited to the Secret Book Society . . .

CHAPTER ONE

Mrs. Eleanor Clarke

Two months earlier

London, England

April 1895

ELEANOR CLARKE PEERED OUT THE WINDOW where ivy curled around the perimeter. Gray clouds gathered on the horizon. A slight fog on the glass hinted at the day's chill despite the warmth in Eleanor's room. Every room in the expansive manor was heated, one of the many extravagances her husband insisted upon.

She turned from the window and lowered herself to the vanity seat, bending at the knees with her back perfectly straight to accommodate her heavily boned corset.

"The color of your gown brings out your eyes." Eleanor's maid smiled at her through the mirror as she used the silver-handled brush to sweep Eleanor's blond hair back into a fashionable coiffure.

"Thank you, Bennett." Eleanor barely glanced at the mirror to confirm that the pale blue did indeed enhance the azure depth of her eyes. She had chosen the color for its mood rather than its complement.

Her husband's foul disposition the night before had left her agitated. Every bump and creak in the house made her flinch, her nerves as hot as the delicate carbon filament in the light-bulbs glowing throughout their opulent London home. The pale, creamy blue silk soothed her, reminding her of the clear stretch of summer sky on her parents' estate in Sussex. Back from her girlhood days, when life was carefree and kind.

The color was one she found herself wearing more and more often of late.

The solid hue of her gown was broken up by the visible underskirt with vertical stripes in homogenous shades. There was comfort in the rigidity of those bold lines, in the unyielding strength to their structure.

"The sapphires will do nicely, my lady." Bennett held up the clamshell jewel case, revealing the costly blue stones glittering in a bed of ecru silk.

They were ostentatious, a gratuitous display purchased by a rich man making up for the newness of his wealth. Eleanor was part of that gratuitous display, a woman of noble birth to his merchant's status, purchased as surely as those gemstones.

Procured easily, no doubt, when Cecil caught the scent of her parents' financial desperation. Overdue taxes on their town-house in London, myriad bills extended far too long on credit, repairs to the summer estate she had so loved—they had become fate's shackles, binding her to this life.

She nodded to Bennett in the mirror and the encumbrance of the necklace settled over the tight, high-necked collar of her day dress. Next came the earrings, affixed to her lobes where they swung with the weight of Cecil's fortune.

She pulled open the middle drawer for a jar of hand cream, her skin always tight and dry following the winter months. Beside the small jar was a mysterious folded note with her name written in an elegant script.

"Bennett, what—?"

Bennett put her finger to her lips and winked.

Eleanor's pulse fluttered against the snug silk of her long, fitted sleeves.

A secret?

She never had secrets. Her entire existence was under scrupulous observation, her every word and action evaluated and measured by her husband to be deemed worthy or wanting. More times than not, he settled on the latter.

She was not allowed to have secrets.

Her shoulders lifted in a protective curl forward, despite being in the privacy of her own room. The stiff fabric and precise tailoring of her gown did not permit much movement, but still she pulled at its restraint to bend over the note.

A seal gleamed in a valiant stream of sunlight fighting through the gloomy day, illuminating a golden sprig of Queen Anne's lace impressed upon the hard green wax. Eleanor slid her finger beneath the seal, pulling the glossy disk from the parchment rather than breaking it, and read the message within.

You are cordially invited to the Secret Book Society.
Mrs. Clarke, I beseech you to hold this correspondence in the strictest of confidences. I often recall our encounter some three years past, not only with affectionate fondness at our similar literary interests, but also our circumstances. Alterations to my life have left me in the possession of an extensive library—novels written by women, stories with real heroines who endeavor beyond obedience to their fathers and husbands, books curated by my own assiduous efforts. I should like to share this collection—this freedom to read—with you and several of our peers who have been carefully selected for their intelligence

and discretion. More will be explained when we convene next Wednesday.

In addition to this private note, you will receive a formal invitation for tea, a pursuit your spouse will surely find customarily suitable. I do hope you'll accept.

With Consideration,
Clara Chambers, The Countess of Duxbury

The paper quivered in Eleanor's hand. "It's a secret book society," she breathed.

She recalled the encounter that the countess mentioned in her missive. They'd both been in attendance at the same charity event, raising awareness for housing for the underprivileged, when the often frugal Mrs. Colting spirited away the fine cobalt linen tablecloth upon the event's conclusion.

"I'm reminded suddenly of Mrs. Norris in *Mansfield Park* with the green curtain for the play that never happened," Eleanor had said, unsure what had possessed her to speak. Perhaps she'd only meant to think it, but the words had slipped from her lips.

Lady Duxbury had been beside her and suppressed a laugh politely behind her hand. "I've very much thought Mrs. Colting to be quite the real-life Mrs. Norris."

The kindred joy of having discovered someone who read the same book was immediate, a friend whose mind had once resided in the same fictional world.

"Have you read much of Jane Austen's works?" Lady Duxbury asked.

There had only been two other novels besides *Mansfield Park* in Eleanor's father's library—*The Picture of Dorian Gray* and *Wuthering Heights*, tucked between weighty tomes on law and the legal workings of parliament. Oh, and how she had read those novels, connecting with the characters in a way that made her soul ache. Those books were no longer in her possession, her limited freedom as a girl swapped for the restraining vows of marriage and the promise to obey her husband.

"I haven't . . . That is . . ." Eleanor had been saved from her stammering by Lord Duxbury's approach. Though his smile was warm, the possessive grip around his wife's wrist was as unmistakable as the flick of the countess's gaze to her feet in a show of yielding deference.

Eleanor sought out Lady Duxbury often after that encounter, but only ever saw her from a distance, Lord Duxbury at her side like a vigilant sentry.

Aside from those few novels unearthed in her father's library, Eleanor's education had been relegated to the edifying necessities for running a household and being a good wife and mother. That and the occasional literature on general knowledge, like *Goldsmith's History of England*. Most especially, she was familiar with the contents of *Debrett's*, which offered details on every titled aristocrat in England—first while seeking a husband, and then later to better associate with the peers Cecil needed in his milieu.

Never had she been at liberty to choose her own books. Not with her parents, her father a wealthy viscount of delicate reputation given his financial constraints, nor in her marriage to Cecil.

"Lady Duxbury's maid told me what the countess was on about when she delivered the note." Bennett kept her voice barely above a whisper. The walls had ears as well as eyes. "Perhaps this will help you through to June."

June.

Yes, June.

The simple, single-syllable word was mantra to Eleanor, a reminder of her impending reprieve. June was when her husband would travel to Peru, a priceless venture for them both. For Cecil, Peru was wealth, where his fortune originated in the droppings of foreign birds used to fertilize English soil. For her, Peru afforded an extra few inches in the confines of her life, to move without constantly looking over her shoulder.

Those precious few weeks allowed her to visit with their son whenever she wanted, without postponement or censure. A gift of days she did not have to tiptoe around Cecil's moods, a chance to finally breathe in this stifling prison.

Bennett saw what others did not, the tears Eleanor saved for when she was alone, the bruises hidden beneath fitted sleeves. She knew well what June meant to her mistress.

Eleanor needed only to endure this life until June when Cecil's journey would offer her enough of a respite to help her through the months or years to come after. Until his next departure.

The post lay on a silver platter later that morning at breakfast. Energy charged through Eleanor, making her want to jostle her leg under the table like a wayward child.

But ladies did not do such things, and so she sipped her tea with feigned patience while the seat across from hers remained empty.

What could be taking Cecil so long?

It was as if he knew the soaring height of her anticipation and sought to drag her back down to earth.

She peered at the envelopes, sorely tempted to let her fingers crawl through the stack of heavy cream stationery, seeking out Lady Duxbury's promised invitation. But Cecil did not like Eleanor going through the correspondence. As much as he stifled her freedom, he cherished his own.

She would never complain of such circumstances, of course. Doing so only led to more tightening, more squeezing, in a life that already left her with scarce room to breathe.

The familiar creak of Cecil's footsteps sounded overhead. Eleanor set her teacup on its small, gilt-edged saucer lest it tremble in her hands. He would be down in a moment's time.

Several agonizing minutes later, he entered the room, filling the space with the bulk of presence and the sharpness of his cologne, applied to indulgent excess. His gaze swept over her, coming to rest briefly on the sapphires at her throat and ears, before offering a nod of approval. Not for her—never for her—but for her intentional display of his wealth.

He sat down, setting the proud assortment of powder-blue hydrangea blossoms quivering. The servants rushed forward, draping his lap with a napkin and pouring a strong cup of tea. Goodness, but he took his time, reading through the paper, slurping his tea, crunching on the toast points after having slathered them with a gluttonous smear of butter.

Finally, finally, *finally*, he reached for the envelopes on the silver platter. He sifted through them in silence, pausing periodically to tear one open and cast it aside.

"This one is for you, Mrs. Clarke." He lifted his brows at Eleanor. "And from the Countess of Duxbury, no less." His brows inched higher, clearly impressed.

Rather than hand her the envelope, Cecil cracked the golden wax seal with a violent snap and withdrew the card with blunt, careless fingers. "Ho-ho, she wants you to attend afternoon tea next Wednesday." He sat straighter, as if the invitation was meant for him. "You'll go, of course, and I suggest you wear your new diamond necklace."

Everything inside Eleanor cringed at the order, but she kept her expression masked in pleasant amiability. "Diamonds would not be appropriate, darling."

Though she offered the protest gently, Cecil's face flushed, his eyes flashing with that mean glint that made her blood go cold.

"This is one of those fancy rules only nobility knows, isn't it?" he sneered.

Indeed, the rule was an unspoken one, known among aristocratic Society. Diamonds were for evening attire. Already, the many gemstones she wore during the day were considered vulgar. But Eleanor didn't say as much. She knew better.

"I'm too coarse a man," Cecil harangued. "Too common to know such things as my *esteemed* wife."

"Forgive me, darling, that isn't at all what I meant." Eleanor glanced at the servants, who stared impassively at nothing and yet saw everything. "Only I shouldn't like to show up my hostess when our wealth far surpasses her own substantial sum."

The high color dissipated from his fleshy cheeks at the stroke to his ego, and he sat back in his chair, appeased like a spoiled little boy who had been given a sweet. "Ah, how astute of you to consider, my dear. Yes, yes, wear whatever you think appropriate. I know how you are with your—" he swept his hand in a curling motion in the air "—fashion." He chortled in condescension.

She knew he found her sartorial taste silly, another banal quality of his vapid, noble-bred wife.

A man would never understand.

Especially not a man like Cecil.

He controlled with whom she was acquainted, where she went and what she did. He controlled the food she ate, the events she hosted and the mail she was allowed to receive. He controlled every halfpenny of his expansive fortune that passed into her hand despite his own profligacy.

He even controlled the single precious hour every other day that she was allowed to see their son, supervising the visit and admonishing her with sharp words when he felt she coddled their boy.

In all that Cecil controlled in her life, the limited time with her son caused the most pain, an ache that resonated from her empty arms into the depths of her soul.

But her clothing, her fashion—in such things she finally had autonomy. She ordered the garments she liked, decided which gowns and day dresses she wore and what hairstyles and reticules to pair them with. No matter how much Cecil denigrated that small square of freedom, it was hers.

June.

She only needed to endure this existence for two more months. And with access to the books Eleanor had been restricted from, that just might be bearable.

CHAPTER TWO

Mrs. Rose Wharton

ROSE WHARTON WAS SHOWN INTO THE DRAW-
ing room at Duxbury Place, a lovely townhouse three doors
down from her own in the fashionable area of Grosvenor Square.
Potted plants clustered becomingly throughout the room, their
leaves extended toward the windows, straining for the weak
light.

The sun was one of the things Rose missed most about America, where it seemed to shine in endless abundance. And while
England was lovely with its old-world elegance, she craved the
brilliant splash of light and warmth.

Lady Duxbury rose from where she sat in a great sage-green
armchair. "Ah, Mrs. Wharton, it is so good of you to come.
Please do have a seat."

Rose settled into a plush velvet chair beside a potted hel-
lebore, the leathery petals blossoming in shades of deep bur-
gundy and milky white. Small painted birds adorned the green
wallpaper, their feathers artistically rendered with such care, the
iridescent blue-green sweep of their wings caught the meager
light.

Accepting Lady Duxbury's invitation was no doubt a mistake,

another opportunity to be ostracized at a social gathering. In that way, London wasn't much different from Manhattan, where even women of Rose's own American nationality had put their backs to her, their heads tucked together as they whispered waspishly about the stink of new money.

However, there didn't appear to be any malice in the countess's smile.

She seemed too young to have already lost three husbands. Her rich raven-black hair was piled ornately atop her head, affixed with jet-black combs, her skin smooth over her high cheekbones. The delicate lilac of her gown indicated she remained in half-mourning for Lord Duxbury, who had been dead a full two years.

There was a difference to her countenance now, a self-assuredness she hadn't possessed upon Rose's first meeting with her. They'd been at a ball, one of the first in London Rose had attended after her marriage to Theodore. None of the other women had spoken to Rose and she had sequestered herself in the powder room with a book. Lady Duxbury entered some moments later, her narrow shoulders pinched together.

"Looks like you could use a moment alone as well." Rose had given her a conspiratorial grin.

A note of sadness had shone in the countess's large violet-blue eyes when they settled on the book propped in Rose's hands. "What are you reading?" Longing filled the countess's voice.

"*A Masque of Poets*. It's part of the no-name series, where authors are anonymous, so their work is judged on true merit rather than notoriety." Rose closed the book and extended it to Lady Duxbury.

The countess had flicked an anxious glance toward the door before accepting it, her touch a reverent caress on the black-and-red cover. Rose hadn't missed the way Lord Duxbury watched his wife with a predatory protectiveness. Some men were like that, controlling, restricting.

"Take it," Rose offered.

Lady Duxbury had stiffened, her brows furrowing together. "I can't."

"I'll have my maid find your maid to deliver it," Rose said. "I can always buy another."

That wasn't true, of course. The price of books was dear and funds were needed for items far dearer: marble, the contractors to lay the costly material and all the other bits and pieces necessary to reassemble a crumbling residence into one of admirable stature.

Still, she'd held out her hand, a smile of promise on her lips.

Lady Duxbury cradled the book to her heart before relinquishing it. "I shall never forget this kindness, Mrs. Wharton."

Rose had straightened a little taller then. Someone of note in that cold, unwelcoming Society remembered her name. Such consideration had been well worth the cost of the book.

There was no meekness cowing the countess now. There was only confidence, evident in the tilt of her chin, the squaring of her shoulders, her stature one of powerful wealth with a blatant disregard for the gossip hissed behind her back.

And with three dead husbands—two being young and virile until their deaths—there was gossip aplenty.

"Thank you for the invitation," Rose replied, aware as always of her American accent. Some found it charming; others found it grating. She was uncertain of Lady Duxbury's opinion, though her pleasant expression remained unchanged as she extended a hand to the other woman sitting on a stuffed chair the color of spring grass.

"You know Mrs. Clarke, I presume."

Mrs. Clarke.

Of course Rose knew her. The perfect Englishwoman if ever

there was one. And not simply for her beauty alone—though she was indeed beautiful, with her heart-shaped face, golden blond hair piled like a crown on her head and a fine figure in a perfectly fitted silk dress. She was the embodiment of poise and grace.

Their acquaintance had been made at a picnic months ago. Whereas Rose had looked like she'd been tossed about in the wind like a fish in violent sea at low tide, Mrs. Clarke had been immaculate, occasionally sweeping aside any loose locks of hair with graceful fingers. As if the move had been practiced to elegant perfection.

Mrs. Clarke always did the right thing, said the right thing and was exactly the right thing. No doubt even the lapis color of her gown was meant to enhance the brilliance of her lovely wide blue eyes.

If Rose was like her, she and Theodore would still be happy.

Mrs. Clarke had no idea how lucky she was.

"We have met." Mrs. Clarke offered a smile that was not too large as to be overeager, nor too small as to be unwelcoming.

The perfect smile on the perfect Englishwoman.

"Lovely to see you again," Rose replied cordially. "I simply adore your necklace."

Mrs. Clarke touched the strand of fat sapphires at her neck, as if one could forget having put on such an expensive bauble. "Thank you. I suppose it's a bit much for tea." A pretty blush blossomed over her cheeks.

"You know us Americans. We love a good string of jewels," Rose offered jovially.

The two women maintained polite expressions as the joke rolled over them like a square wheel. Rose always forgot English humor was different than that of Americans, that mention of wealth—even in jest—was vulgar.

But Rose *did* love jewels. Gorgeous sets of them—bracelets, earrings, necklaces, combs, brooches, rings, anything that could be set in gold to glitter and sparkle in a wash of unadulterated sunlight. Daddy had spoiled her with them when she'd been in Manhattan. Not that a vault of jewelry ever won over any Vanderbilt or awed any Astor. But they'd made her happy.

There weren't any new jewels now. Instead, the Wharton family townhouse on Grosvenor Square had been elevated to a presentable stature, no longer the tired, disintegrating shell it'd been upon her arrival. In that regard, at least her father's wealth was being applied to good effect.

And she had been genuinely happy with Theodore. At least in those early days.

Mother would have preferred Rose marry an earl rather than an earl's younger brother, to elevate their American wealth with an English title. But Theodore had been irresistible. From the charming way his mouth hitched higher on the right when he smiled to how he made her feel like she belonged with someone for the first time in her life.

Before that now-familiar ache in her heart could return, the butler entered once more through the open entryway. She realized suddenly that the door had never been closed behind her when she entered.

How strange.

Apparently, Lady Duxbury had the utmost faith in her staff to allow them to hear what was spoken in her drawing room.

The butler was a stocky fellow whose arms were thick as Christmas hams beneath the sleeves of his wide-shouldered jacket. His nose took up half his face and leaned hard to the right, as if it'd been broken a good half dozen times. Rather fitting given his past, or at least what Rose's maid had unearthed on Lady Duxbury's servants.

The butler was once notorious in the underground boxing circuit and—if word on the street could be believed—a few knocks shy of mortal retirement. Her maids were also pulled from a questionable past, having worked in one of those factories that puffed ghastly amounts of black smog into London's air.

The countess had an affinity for hiring from the base proletariat class.

Mother would have been shocked into an early grave at having such rustic laborers in her employ. Rose was of a more progressive generation, however. Not scandalized, but indeed fascinated.

"Lady Lavinia Cavendish," the butler announced, his tone bordering on snobbish for a man of indecorous background.

A petite young woman with auburn hair edged slowly into the room, appearing as if she'd rather be anywhere else.

"Lady Lavinia." There was a note of surprise to Lady Duxbury's tone.

"You invited my mother." Lady Lavinia's small frame tensed, and she cleared her throat before speaking again. "She thought I would benefit more than she."

The volume of her soft voice was almost inaudible, and Rose found herself leaning forward in her seat to catch the words.

"We're pleased to have you." Lady Duxbury welcomed her to join them and made the proper introductions.

Silence fell upon the small gathering, ripe with unspoken questions. Rose had been hopelessly curious since she'd received the invitation, secreted in the drawer of her vanity by her maid.

Nearly six months had passed since she'd been allowed to read what she wanted. After a lifetime of freedom, she now felt like a bird stuffed into a gilded cage. One she'd paid for.

How she longed to lose herself in a story, to let her heart meld with that of a character, to witness plights resolved by the final chapter. But more than enjoyment, she was starved for connection, for the feeling that she wasn't always so very alone.

A black-and-white cat slinked into the room and approached a wide, square vase on the floor that had been left empty. A strange notion until he slipped inside and tucked his paws into his chest. Happy as a clam, he gazed out with unblinking green eyes through the glass, the markings on his face giving the impression of a small white mustache.

"Oh, do pretend you don't see Otis," Lady Duxbury implored. "He's terribly shy. The only way to assuage his discomfort around others is with that vase, where he presumes he can see you, but you can't see him."

Rose didn't bother to hide her smile as they all hastily looked away. Her little pug had his own eccentricities that she readily catered to.

Lady Duxbury glanced at the large clock with its gleaming metal pendulum swinging tirelessly behind a crystal door. "There was another to whom I extended an invitation. I believe she may not be joining us after all." There was a note of disappointment in her tone.

The maid entered, a large tea tray in her hands, which she placed upon the low table between the women. The tablecloth was neatly pressed with delicate Queen Anne's lace and crosshatches of purple heather stitched around the scalloped edge. Lady Duxbury poured each woman a cup of tea while the maid returned with another tray filled with various cakes and scones and breads.

The women smiled shyly at one another as they approached the refreshment table. Rose considered the spread, hesitant to select anything. She hadn't been able to eat anything all day. Even now, her stomach turned, but she took a honey-spice cake molded into the shape of a rose and a slice of white bread, which she smeared with jam from a delicate venetian glass pot.

"I've been so very eager for today's tea," Rose prompted when they all returned to their seats. "What made you invite us?"

Lady Duxbury sat a little straighter, as though commanding herself to attention as she addressed them. "You see, my maid has informed me that your husbands—" Lady Duxbury nodded politely to Lady Lavinia "—and father are restricting what you read. Often when a woman's books are being restricted, so, too, are other aspects of her life. Such constraints can make a woman feel entirely alone."

Mrs. Clarke looked down into her lap where her slice of seed cake remained untouched. But Rose kept her head upright despite the way the countess's words resonated within her. She wouldn't be crushed beneath Theodore's subjugation.

"I am in the possession of an extensive library, as I said." Lady Duxbury absently set her teacup and saucer aside. "At one point in my life, I assumed owning such a luxury to be impossible. These books have been curated by my own hand, each purchase led by my heart. But such a gift is not to be kept away from others. It is my hope that you'll take advantage of whatever books pique your interest. And that we might discuss what we read. As friends."

Friends.

Yearning blossomed in Rose's chest, pushing up from a place of emptiness, of loneliness. She hastily took a sip of tea, intentionally breaking eye contact with the others. Not out of shame or remorse, but to refrain from gazing at them with the force of her desperation.

Two lifetimes had passed since she'd had true friends, before she came to England to be Theodore's wife, and even before her mother's insistence that they rise above the new money filling their vaults. Mother had shoved Rose in with the Vanderbilts and Astors and other "old money" in America, casting Rose to the desolate fringes of Society. Before Mother's ambitions, Rose's childhood had been filled with friends from the girls' school in Manhattan, one funded with "new money" where there was no prejudice at the age of one's bank account. In those precious days, there had been laughter, and fun and genuine joy.

For a while, Theodore had filled that gap of loneliness as New York's Society queens rejected Rose and her family. In a world of jigsaw pieces that never seemed to match her uneven edges, he had snapped into place, making her whole.

But that had been before.

"We are in a world where men have established a great power over us." The vehemence in Lady Duxbury's voice pulled Rose's attention back to the young widow. "I do not mean to imply that all men are wretched, of course." Lady Duxbury touched the strange hair-jewelry brooch over her heart, her fingers lingering like a caress. "But not all are good, either. Not that women are any more agreeable, especially when perceptions of one another are so often skewed by jealousy and fears of inadequacy."

Rose's cheeks burned as she recalled her assessment of Mrs. Clarke earlier.

"We're ignorant of one another's lives," Lady Duxbury continued. "I'd like to change that."

"Friendship," Rose said aloud. "I would be grateful for such a thing." All eyes turned on her. The weight of their attention altogether too heavy and uncomfortable. She gave a self-deprecating laugh, though it was likely the wrong thing to do. "Being American has left me feeling rather unwelcome in England. I'm too bold, too loud, too eager to speak my mind."

When the statement was out of her mouth, she realized she had parroted Theodore's exact complaints.

Their union hadn't always been so discordant, so broken.

Not when he'd been the mere brother of an earl, when the idea of his assumption of the earldom was practically impossible with his brother only one year older than himself and glowing with good health. But that was before the earl's lungs had been infected with cancer poisons, before the inexorable prospect of Rose becoming an English countess.

Now everything that made her American was unacceptable in the eyes of her brother-in-law. And subsequently in the eyes of Theodore. She had to be perfect. More subdued. More English.

More like Mrs. Clarke.

And nothing at all like herself.

The women's expressions following Rose's admission weren't ones of placid disinterest as she'd expected. They were soft with sympathy and made the hunger for friendship in her grow ravenous.

"We are more than keen on welcoming you," Lady Duxbury said with an insistence that fed the parts of Rose that were starved for acceptance. "We're glad to have you."

Rose took a delicate bite of the bread, reveling in the sweetness of the strawberry jam, and hoped Lady Duxbury was being genuine. Not only in her welcome, but in her wish that they might all become true friends.

CHAPTER THREE

Lady Lavinia Cavendish

LADY LAVINIA CAVENDISH HAD SPENT THE WEEK
dreading this afternoon tea at Lady Duxbury's. Her fingers wandered over the embroidery along the sleeve of her day dress, the neat stitches forming small, bell-shaped flowers that reminded her poignantly of belladonna, the flower of silence.

She'd worn that dress on purpose, to remind herself to remain quiet, to hold her secret close to her heart. To keep her family from shame.

Lavinia had begged her mother to go in her stead. After all, the invitation had been for her, not Lavinia. But Mama insisted whatever freedoms might be found in Lady Duxbury's drawing room would do more good for Lavinia than herself. And now Lavinia was here and utterly miserable.

At least the scones were delicious, crisp on the outside and buttery soft on the inside.

But then Mrs. Wharton had spoken up, her statement about being lonely blunt with unabashed truth. The honesty was refreshing.

How Lavinia envied Mrs. Wharton that freedom.

Lavinia wanted to say as much, to confess how she hated the

oppression she had been strapped into. How the more she resisted the bindings, the tighter they were tugged. How the fit of obligation had been too constricting for the whole of her life. How desperately she longed to burst from the confines, to shred them in an explosion of vitality and soar out into the world.

Before her father took away the books he deemed too emotionally taxing for her to enjoy, she had read the Greek tale of Icarus, of how he'd been given wax wings and flown too high despite countless warnings. Unable to resist the lure of the brilliant, golden sun, his wings had melted, and he'd plunged to his death. The story was supposed to present a warning against recklessness and encourage obedience.

To Lavinia, the story was cruel. To be offered such exquisite freedom, and then restricted with limitations. She had felt a kinship with Icarus, knowing she, too, would want to soar wherever her heart led her. Even if it meant being drawn to the sun.

Even if it meant plunging to her death.

The maid returned to refresh the teapot and placed the old one beneath a pressed cloth to carry away. The woman appeared to be at least five years younger than Lavinia's nineteen, the maid's youth as much of a strange choice as the brutish-looking butler was for his role.

And just as curious was the cat they weren't supposed to look at.

Lavinia glanced at Otis, who watched her with a confident stare. Quickly, she darted her gaze away, lest the little cat be made uncomfortable. She knew too well the burden of being constantly observed.

Mrs. Clarke took a sip of tea and set the cup delicately in its saucer. "I find your boldness rather enviable, Mrs. Wharton, if I'm entirely honest. Saying what is on your mind must be refreshing."

Mrs. Wharton blinked in surprise. "I don't know that my outlandish tendencies could ever be deemed enviable."

Lavinia should say something. Her heart galloped like a loose stallion, and she licked her dry lips before speaking. "They are."

Her words were too soft, likely drowned beneath even the quiet, rhythmic tick of the longcase clock. But they all looked toward her.

"Enviable, I mean." The words were thick in her throat. She brushed an embroidered purple bloom with her fingertip, wishing she'd just stayed quiet.

"It's so kind of you to say." Mrs. Wharton stirred her tea, not noticing as the spoon clinked against the china. "I think I'm often the butt of people's jokes. Circles of acquaintances tend to go quiet upon my entrance far too often to be coincidental. Now that I've said as much aloud, it sounds rather pathetic, but it's the truth. And is that not why you've brought us together, Lady Duxbury? So we might speak earnestly and share our lives as well as what we read?"

She paused and looked to Lady Duxbury, who nodded with encouragement. "Absolutely. Thank you for your candor, Mrs. Wharton."

"The genuine welcome here in your home is the first I've had since my arrival in England over two years ago." A relaxed smile graced Mrs. Wharton's lovely face, a quintessential beauty by American standards with her dark hair and large, dark eyes, her skin like porcelain.

"After we've finished our tea, I'll show you the library as I'd like everyone to be afforded sufficient time for their literary selections." Lady Duxbury lifted a pink frosted petit four from her plate. "In the meantime, would anyone care to share the authors you hope to read?"

Rose readily answered with a gush of praise for several American authors, Louisa May Alcott, Edgar Allan Poe and Mark Twain—ones Lavinia had not yet had the opportunity to read. But then, she'd only just begun to delve into novels before her father deprived her of the family's books, claiming her moods tangled too deeply with those of the characters. That the passion of her feelings might push her to the brink of madness.

Bur Lavinia had *felt* those characters in her soul, a link without shame or reticence, where nothing was held back.

Then the books disappeared—first from her room, then from the entire house. The loss had been impactful, cut from her life like a limb, like the very beating heart from her chest.

She yearned for the fictional stories that wound around her being, adroitly playing at her emotions as if they were the chords of a precious instrument. Be they poetry or epic tales, American authors or English, male or female, she was desperate for them all.

When Lavinia returned from Lady Duxbury's tea that afternoon, she had a copy of *Jane Eyre* tucked neatly in the large reticule her mother had insisted she bring. Not just any copy of *Jane Eyre. The* copy of *Jane Eyre*, the very one that had been her undoing. How had it fallen into Lady Duxbury's possession?

Lavinia wished to be alone with the book, to stroke its familiar back, now scorched from that horrible incident, to reclaim the stories that had been taken away.

Lavinia's brother and father entered the foyer, preparing to depart just as she returned. Papa's top hat rested on the crown of his head while Robert's was tilted at a rakish angle.

"I'm sorry to miss you, Livi." Papa smiled at his childhood name for her. "Did you have a pleasant afternoon with Lady Duxbury?"

Lavinia nodded.

He lowered his gaze in a look bordering on chastisement. "You behaved yourself, didn't you?"

She nodded again, eager to please him. Always so eager to please her father.

He beamed at her, loving her best when she was compliant.

How she craved those expressions, ached for the assurance of his love. The more he doled his affection out like a reward, the more she yearned to receive more. To be the girl he wanted her to be. Only she wasn't quiet and demure. The appearance of being so was merely a shell slipped over her real self, masking what lay vibrant and explosive within.

But he knew how deeply she could feel. And he despised her for it.

"I heard Lady Duxbury killed her husbands." Robert lifted his heavy brows.

Her brother always did try to incense her, especially after his spectacular success the year prior.

She ought to remain silent. Robert's bait held a sharp hook. Except that the urge to protect Lady Duxbury surged through Lavinia, a need to shield the countess who had brought together women who had no one to help them, noble in her efforts to offer learning and friendship.

"It's all gossip." Lavinia's voice carried an edge, one perfect for slicing the conversation off at the head.

"Gossip usually holds truth in my experience." There was a perpetual ruddiness to Robert's cheeks that burned brighter when his hackles were up. A match ready to burst into flame.

Lavinia's contradiction was always enough to strike a spark with him.

"Yes, I've heard," she added coolly. Despite his own lofty arrogance, he was not above inspiring the gossips. The women he'd debauched, the gambling halls that emptied his pockets, the poor boy he'd beaten over a miscommunication.

"Enough now, Livi," Papa scolded. He nudged Robert with his elbow, offering a cordial chuckle, as though the rumor was indeed good sport they could share a laugh over.

Lavinia looked at the floor rather than witness her brother's smug expression. Heat seared her cheeks, blazing at the unfairness of how a son was treated versus a daughter.

"We're off to White's," Papa announced. "Now that my boy can officially join me there." She looked up in time to see him gaze at Robert with glowing pride.

"It must be a joy as well as a wonder." Lavinia plastered a bland smile on her face, knowing the flight of her cynical words had nowhere to land on Robert's hubris.

For truly, it was a wonder that White's accepted him at all. The elite gentlemen's club was notorious for blackballing applicants for the slightest infraction. Gaining Robert entry into the club must have cost Papa a fortune.

Papa tipped his hat at Lavinia and headed out the door with her brother, just as a crack of lightning streaked across the darkening sky.

Once in her room, Lavinia settled by the rain-spattered window and withdrew the copy of *Jane Eyre* from her reticule. A brown burn streaked the bottom, marring the green back and singeing some of the pages. The odor of smoke still clung to the text, recalling that night in the library a year ago.

She'd been reading peacefully when Robert entered, his words slurred, his ire roused. He'd been looking for a fight and knew the right words to elicit one. Already, Papa had expressed his qualms with Lavinia's reading and how it might put off suitors. Already, he'd threatened to keep her from her books. Lavinia's dear younger sister, Delilah, had secretly promised to share her books should that happen. Delilah always worked so hard to keep the peace in their home, to ensure everyone was happy, an endeavor that was becoming more and more difficult.

Recently Papa's anger had been stoked by Lavinia's refusal of the one offer of marriage she'd had. Mr. Brightly was only several years older than her, but his countenance reminded her of Heathcliff from *Wuthering Heights* and she refused the proposal despite Papa's approval. Robert found her reasoning hilariously preposterous and took to teasing her mercilessly about it that night.

She'd swallowed her rage at Robert's pecking, continuing to ignore him. Finally, he grew bored with her lack of response and threw her book into the fire.

He'd been in his cups and his aim was off, thank heavens. The book landed close to the flames, scorching rather than burning. Once she'd safely retrieved it, he'd struck her, open-palmed against her cheek.

"You're mad." He spit into the flames, sending up a menacing hiss. "You're mad like *her*."

She'd punched him then. Square in the nose.

Her satisfaction had been short-lived and her punishment swift. All invitations previously accepted to balls were canceled, which she hadn't minded. And all her books had been taken away. Which she had minded very much.

As she recalled that horrible night, she absently caressed the damaged cover. How fitting that the book of her downfall now be the onset of her rebellion; like the phoenix, rising from the ashes anew.

But how had Lady Duxbury obtained this copy?

A soft rap sounded on her door several moments later, and Lavinia's mother entered. "How was the tea?"

Lavinia sighed and pressed her brow against the cool windowpane. "I was rather awkward, I'm afraid." The raindrops melded together outside and dripped down the glass.

"Did you not feel welcome?" The pillow along the broad seat shifted as Mama joined her.

"How can I be when there is so much to conceal?" If Lavinia had her brother's ruddy complexion, she would doubtless be a livid red. "My state of sanity, any prospects for marriage, our good name, even Delilah's coming out in June. I put everything at risk every time I enter Society, even for a simple tea. Even a secret gathering." Her emotions swelled, rolling over her like a wave she was powerless to stop.

Precisely how it had been for Grandmother.

No, Lavinia wouldn't think of her, or her unwanted legacy.

Especially not when her younger sister would have her debut soon. Delilah selflessly put aside her wants for everyone in the family without complaint. Any misstep on Lavinia's part would damage Delilah's prospects, ruin her before she could even come out.

Of all the people in the world, Delilah did not deserve such a fate.

"You will become more comfortable as you grow acquainted with the other women." Mama settled a reassuring hand on Lavinia's forearm.

Lavinia pulled away. "What if I'm not? What if the madness grows worse? What if I can't control it any longer?"

Suddenly, the pressure building in Lavinia's chest was too much. The weight spread across her shoulders, nearly crushing her.

A sob erupted from the depths of her very soul. Mama's arms were around her in an instant, surrounding Lavinia with the familiar, warm sandalwood fragrance of Hammam Bouquet.

"Be patient with yourself," Mama's voice soothed as she released Lavinia and handed her a handkerchief.

Lavinia wiped her eyes as the ragged gasp of her breaths calmed enough to regale her mother with details of the afternoon.

Mama's eyes sparkled as Lavinia spoke, lit with love.

They had the same green eyes, which Lavinia cherished. But while Mama had thick, dark hair, Lavinia's tresses were fiery red, bestowed upon her by an ancestor on her father's side from the time of King Henry VIII, when auburn hair had been *en mode*. Or so her father told her. Lucky for the distant aunt, but unfortunate for Lavinia, who had missed her fortuitous time in history by over three centuries.

"Mrs. Wharton is the American woman you met last year," Lavinia went on. "And she says precisely what she's thinking. I know it should be shocking, but I found it refreshing. And Mrs. Clarke has always seemed so perfect, I've been afraid to speak to her, but she's really quite agreeable. Lady Duxbury's library is exquisite, and she seems intent on us being friends, which I very much like." Even if allowing others to know Lavinia did rather intimidate her.

"I'm pleased to hear it." Mama smiled.

"I was even allowed to select a book to bring home." Lavinia turned *Jane Eyre* over to demonstrate the scorch mark. "It's *ours*."

Mama's brows knit together and her fingers ran over the singed cover. "Your father said he sold our books." Her expression softened. "But now I understand how Lady Duxbury knew to reach out to me." She opened the inside flap, revealing where her maiden name was written in a looping script at the corner. "Lady Duxbury has always been kind to me. She will be just as kind to you."

Lavinia gazed at the faded ink, marveling over her mother's neat handwriting, which she hadn't noticed before. The conspiratorial look Lady Duxbury had given Lavinia as she left now made sense as well. "A fitting book," the countess had said of the slightly burned copy of *Jane Eyre*. "You may keep it if you like."

Lavinia had always wondered what happened to the stores of books her father removed from their home, a fortune in literature with embossed leather covers and gilt designs. Now she knew what had become of them, and how this particular one had made its way back to Lavinia's hands and heart.

"I ought to ask if you can join the tea, Mama. There was another woman who was invited but did not attend, so there would surely be accommodations for you."

But Mama was already shaking her head. "Let this be something of your own, my darling girl. Without concerning yourself over my opinion. Give these women a chance to befriend you."

In a world where Lavinia was always judged, the idea of having freedom to speak and act away from her mother's eye brought a surprising sense of relief. "You can borrow the books when I'm done."

Mama's smile cleared the worry from her lovely face. "Now, that offer I will happily accept."

In this way, Lavinia could repay her mother's generosity while having a second chance at easing her way back into Society.

This time, Lavinia would not let her mother down.

CHAPTER FOUR

Mrs. Eleanor Clarke

ELEANOR STOOD BY HER HUSBAND AS THEY welcomed the last attendees to arrive at their ball. Impatience chafed her raw nerves. Mrs. Wharton and Lady Lavinia had both arrived earlier, but while she was eager to join them, she did not dare leave Cecil's side until they'd greeted all their guests.

The invitations to her new friends had been sent on short notice, but Cecil insisted they be invited when he discovered they'd also attended Lady Duxbury's tea.

The countess had been invited as well. But though Cecil expected her imminent arrival, Eleanor knew Lady Duxbury wouldn't come. Balls were prime grounds for fortune hunters, and Eleanor suspected Lady Duxbury was entirely done with matrimony.

"Do excuse me, darling." Eleanor set a gentle hand on her husband's arm. Heavy diamond bracelets shackled her gloved wrists. "I should go speak to our new guests who were kind enough to overlook our late invitations."

"Yes, yes, do what you must." There was a flush to his cheeks from whatever was in the flask at his breast pocket. She has-

tened her departure before his bored indifference shifted to
something spiteful.

The incandescent glow of the costly electric lights was on
full display, igniting the ballroom with more light than hun-
dreds of candles, and at far more expense. The luxury escaped
no one's notice and was whispered about by more than one
guest. The brilliance of those lamps highlighted the many vases
of amaryllis flowers adorning every table, the red blooms set
haughtily atop their tall stalks, bold and proud.

Eleanor spied Lady Lavinia and Mrs. Wharton amid the
crowd. The two had already connected, and both turned to
smile in welcome as she approached.

"Lady Lavinia, how lovely you look," Eleanor said as she joined
them. The Brunswick green gown brought out the young woman's eyes. "And, Mrs. Wharton, you are practically glowing with
good health. I believe dancing with your handsome husband has
left you in fine spirits."

Mr. and Mrs. Wharton had been quite the pair swirling
across the dance floor, their movements confident and fluid,
moving together in a way Eleanor envied. At no point in Eleanor's own marriage had she and Cecil ever been in sync in
any aspect of their lives. Certainly, he never made her blush or
giggle the way Mr. Wharton did his wife.

"Your gown is stunning," Mrs. Wharton complimented.

Eleanor ran a hand down the buttery-yellow silk that shimmered in the golden glow of the electric lights. Yellow was not
something she wore often. It was the color of hope, which she
had not possessed in quite some time. However, she now found
herself holding on to it with a tentative grip.

Not only for the potentially budding friendship with the
ladies of the Secret Book Society, but also from the book she'd
borrowed from Lady Duxbury.

Sense and Sensibility was a novel Eleanor had heard mentioned often, one she'd never had the opportunity to read.

Once started, the story had been impossible to put down, and she found herself repeatedly drawn back every moment she had to spare, a moth to a flame.

"It's unfortunate Lady Duxbury couldn't be here," Mrs. Wharton said with a sigh. "She's so young to be a widow. No doubt eligible bachelors will be pleased when the final few months of her half-mourning have concluded."

"I'm not so certain she would be inclined to wed again," Eleanor hedged.

Mrs. Wharton tilted her head in quiet consideration. "I wonder at the hair brooch she wears."

Eleanor recalled the piece of jewelry that revealed a crisscross pattern of dark hair. Strange indeed, for the former Lord Duxbury had gone completely white in his advanced age.

Whose hair was in the brooch?

"I want Lady Duxbury to be happy." Lady Lavinia's delicate voice was nearly lost in the din of the ball. "She's kind."

"Did you know she hired a set of sisters and their mother as her maids and cook to keep them out of the workhouse?" Mrs. Wharton flicked open a vivid purple fan and swept air toward her flushed face.

"Did she?" Eleanor recalled the remarkable youth of the woman who had brought in the tea tray, the one whose hands were lined with deep scars.

Mrs. Wharton leaned closer. "And her butler used to be a famous pugilist, forced into retirement after a great defeat. His father was apparently a butler, but no one would have hired him with such a background."

"How on earth did you learn this?" Eleanor asked.

"I had my maid seek out information before our first meeting." Mrs. Wharton lifted a shoulder, as though her foresight was nothing to be admired. "I wanted to see what I was getting myself into."

It was so like Mrs. Wharton to confess her maid's inquiry in a manner that was openly frank.

"Lady Duxbury gives chances to those others have abandoned." Lavinia's softly spoken words fell among their little group with weighted poignancy.

From across the room, Cecil met Eleanor's gaze, a sharp lure that caught at a place within her that he always knew how to reach.

"Please excuse me," Eleanor said quickly. "I must attend my other guests. Do enjoy yourselves and I hope to see you both at tea tomorrow."

Regret pulled at her as she left her friends.

Yes, friends.

Despite such a brief encounter at tea, she already considered them closer than the host of acquaintances she'd known over the years. Some of whom she saw weekly.

But the women of the Secret Book Society were drawn together by exactly what Lady Lavinia had stated so succinctly. They were women who had been abandoned in some way.

Eleanor suspected the more the bond between them grew, the more they would learn about one another.

Suddenly, she felt fiercely protective over the women, and threw one last look back at them before giving herself over to the mercy of Cecil. His face had reddened with drink, the way it did when the dregs of the flask had been tipped back, and the glint in his eyes told her she had been away from his side for too long.

She knew with a sickening twist deep in her gut, there would be a price to pay.

CHAPTER FIVE

Lady Lavinia Cavendish

LAVINIA STOOD BY THE LONG REFRESHMENT table, the lemonade in her crystal glass tepid from the heat of her palms.

Mama had insisted she attend when Mrs. Clarke's invitation arrived, and Lavinia had acquiesced to avoid causing offense to the woman she hoped might become a friend.

The invitation on such fine, thick card-stock stationery would have delighted Lavinia when she was a girl. The young Lavinia had anticipated these social events, imagining herself spinning on the dance floor the way Mrs. Wharton was now as she danced with her husband, the American woman's smile evidence of her joy.

That had been before Lavinia was plagued with onslaughts of emotional weakness, her words held captive in her throat, the walls around her closing in. Before Lavinia had lost the confidence of her dearest friend.

You aren't like everyone else.

Even the memory of Jane's statement at their parting held malice.

Lavinia brought her thoughts to the present, recalling the

three invitations to dance she'd received that evening and readily turned down. How could she accept when the dance floor
put her on a stage to be observed and judged?

"You'd be prettier if you smiled."

Lavinia stiffened as a middle-aged man frowned at her in
disapproval. The Earl of somewhere she didn't care about.

She cared even less for his opinion but didn't have the teeth
to bite back. If only she possessed Mrs. Wharton's temerity, she
could issue forth a scalding reply without a lick of guilt or regret.

Or fear.

Somehow, word always got back to Papa.

"And you'd be more of a gentleman if you were actually polite," a masculine voice stated curtly from beside Lavinia.

The Earl of something sputtered indignantly and stalked
away.

Lavinia turned to her savior to find he was likely only a year
or two older than herself.

"That was inordinately kind of you," she said with gratitude.

He stared after the departing earl. "What you women have
to endure is a travesty."

What did he know of being a woman?

Though she didn't voice her words aloud, she must have
blinked in surprise, because he deduced her trail of thinking
and replied, "I have four sisters. All lovely, and all vexed by men
such as him. The lovelier the woman, the more beastly these
types seem to be."

Heat warmed Lavinia's cheeks at the sideways compliment.
"Your sisters are fortunate to have a brother who cares for them
so well."

"It's a brother's duty to protect his sisters." He straightened
with stalwart determination. "I'm sure you have a brother who
looks after you, do you not?"

"Evidently, you are not acquainted with my brother." Her
mirthless laugh came out with a jagged edge.

He frowned. She had said the wrong thing.

"I . . ." The man started, then gave a sheepish grin. "Do forgive my being so forward, but would you care to dance?"

There was an awkwardness to his demeanor, his delivery slightly stilted. But rather than put her out, his evident discomfiture set her at ease.

His hair was not smoothed back with pomade as was the fashion. Instead, his dark curls were longer and tossed messily about, like a hero from a Jane Austen novel, and the lines of his face were almost too sharp in the absence of a mustache or beard. And yet, despite his unconventional appearance, she found herself captivated in the most wonderful way.

"I don't believe we've been introduced," she stammered.

After all, there was still propriety to consider.

"Ah, yes." He chuckled and shook his head, as though reprimanding himself. Suddenly, he scanned the ballroom, the corner of his lip tucking downward. "Our chances of being formally introduced this evening may be against us. Mrs. Clarke is engaged with the ever loquacious Lady Welton."

Lavinia smothered a laugh.

"Actually . . ." He narrowed his eyes, a soulful hazel fringed with dark lashes. "I do believe we have been introduced before."

Lavinia considered him curiously. Surely, she would have remembered having met this man with his endearing ungainliness and his refreshing perspective on women.

"At a picnic, I believe," he said thoughtfully with a conspiratorial wink.

Oh.

"Ah, yes, I recall now," Lavinia replied, following the charade.

"Forgive me, but I seem to have forgotten your name." He played his part well with an embarrassed smile.

"Lady Lavinia Cavendish."

"Yes, yes, yes." He shook his pointer finger as though his

memory had been thoroughly jostled into place. "And I'm sure you remember I am Mr. William Wright."

"But of course I do." She blinked innocently, and he laughed with a good nature that delighted her.

"And now that we remember having been introduced . . ." He arched a single brow. "Will you consider dancing with me?"

"I've said no to every other gentleman this evening," she admitted.

"Then I'll be even more pleased if you say yes."

She bit her lip to keep from grinning. "Except that doing so would be terribly rude to those I've declined."

"As considerate as you are beautiful." He put his hand over his chest, atop his heart. "I will honor your wishes. But I am compelled to ask . . ."

She stepped closer, drawn to him with curiosity and an undeniable anticipation.

"When we meet at the next ball, now that it's been ascertained we have, in fact, been introduced, will you save the first dance for me?"

She hesitated. "If I dance with you, I'll have to dance with others." The answer was honest, surprising even her.

"Then you shall have to lie effectively as you tell your suitors I tread upon your toes so terribly that you cannot dance another set."

She laughed at that.

A gentleman in the distance caught Mr. Wright's attention with a nod. Mr. Wright waved in reply, accidentally upsetting a debutante's feathered hair adornment and earning him a look of annoyance. But he scarcely noticed as he turned back to Lavinia. "Forgive me, Lady Lavinia." He lifted her gloved hand in obeisance and pressed his lips to the back. "It was delightful to—" there was a wry lift at the corner of his mouth "—to see you again."

"And you as well, Mr. Wright." She smiled as he straightened, feeling in that moment absolutely radiant.

He turned, gracelessly bumping into a couple, and headed toward the man who had summoned him.

No sooner had Mr. Wright slipped away, than the crowd of people seemed to crush in, as though his presence not only captivated her, but also held the mass around them at bay. The alarming number of attendees now made themselves known in the push and jostle of warm bodies against her as they swept by.

Whatever joy lingered from her conversation with Mr. Wright dissolved, washed away with the rise of *that* feeling. The one that consumed her, threatened to drown her.

Her pulse quickened in that horrible way it did when she found herself overwhelmed, unable to maintain her composure.

No.

Not here.

Not now.

She edged back, seeking the fringes of the room, away from the bustle of so many people, where the air was easier to breathe.

In the distance, Mr. Wright caught her eye and cast her a grin before his attention was pulled by one of his friends. He laughed at something they said, engaged in the conversation at hand, comfortable in the very space that she was now desperate to flee.

If he became better acquainted with her, he would quickly learn of her inability to control her emotions, how readily she fell prey to her capricious nature. He would be horrified. Disgusted.

Sweat prickled at her brow and her breath came faster.

When he saw her next, he wanted to claim a dance with her. In front of everyone. On display, all those stares crawling over her like ants, prickling at her skin. Even imagining it made her flesh feel too tight.

Then he would know her true self, and he would cast her off as Jane had. Even her dearest friend could not tolerate how she teetered on the edge of madness. One hysterical episode away from being sent to an asylum.

Lavinia's heart slammed in her chest, pounding as though it might crack her ribs. She could never be with Mr. Wright; she understood that. Not him or any other man.

The emotion charging through her was too complicated to name, but ravaged her nonetheless, robbing her of breath, of control. She continued to back up, as if she could physically escape what now crashed upon her. The wall hit her back, but the sensation pressed on, boxing her in. There was nowhere to go.

She was trapped.

Panic swept over her as the room squeezed inward and the urgency of her breathing failed to draw in air.

A hand touched her forearm. "Lady Lavinia, I'd like to show you the painting I mentioned earlier."

Lavinia snapped her head toward the voice and found Mrs. Clarke at her side with an agreeable expression on her pretty face. Without waiting for a reply, Mrs. Clarke took Lavinia's arm in hers and led her from the ballroom.

Lavinia blinked rapidly as she tried to orient herself. There had been no conversation about a painting. At least none that she could recall. She followed regardless, eager to be free of the oppressively crowded ballroom.

As soon as they entered the empty hallway, she drew in a long, discreet breath. This time, the air reached her lungs and the spots dotting her vision faded.

"Right this way." Mrs. Clarke led her to a door on the right and clicked on the electric light, immediately illuminating the space like magic.

The room was adorned in lovely shades of blue and wonderfully, gloriously, empty of people.

The door closed behind Lavinia. "Please do have a seat and take all the time you need," Mrs. Clarke said in a gentle voice.

Lavinia lowered to a cushioned chair and breathed in long, careful breaths until the racing of her heart began to ebb.

Mrs. Clarke sat in the chair opposite her and issued a wistful sigh. "The quiet in here is blissful after the noise of the ball."

Lavinia nodded weakly and swallowed, trying to find her voice and summon her manners. "Forgive me. I don't recall you having mentioned a painting."

Mrs. Clarke smiled. "I didn't."

Lavinia's stomach clenched with mortification. "I imagine I looked quite a sight out there."

"Not at all," Mrs. Clarke reassured her. "I'm attuned to people's moods more than most." A strange look crossed her face, and for a moment Lavinia thought she might add more.

When she did not, Lavinia examined the walls where several paintings hung in gilded frames. Now that she had scraped together her wits, she was genuinely curious. "Is there an art piece here that you favor?"

"Indeed." Mrs. Clarke rose gracefully and approached a painting of a cloudy beach, the subtle hues of blue and gray blending perfectly with those in the well-appointed room. The woman in the painting stared out at the sea while the wind pulled at her cream-colored dress and the single ribbon tied in her hair.

Mrs. Clarke studied the artwork in quiet contemplation. "This is a piece titled *Miranda* by a painter I've come to admire. John William Waterhouse. His pieces always carry a touch of whimsy."

Now recovered, Lavinia joined her and considered the painting. Darker patches of clouds behind the woman were offset with a lighter area where she looked off in the distance. "She's longing to be swept away by the ocean, away from everything she's put her back to."

Mrs. Clarke tilted her head. "It appears she does." Her musing tone held a note of sadness.

Lavinia regarded her in a new light, wondering at the woman behind the polished veneer.

There was a reason Mrs. Clarke had been invited to Lady Duxbury's. A reason that they each had been selected. And perhaps in time, all those reasons would be revealed.

CHAPTER SIX

Mrs. Rose Wharton

ROSE WAS THE LAST TO ENTER LADY DUXBURY'S the following day for tea. But then, she'd been out of sorts ever since Mrs. Clarke's ball.

The women of the Secret Book Society all greeted her warmly, and Lady Duxbury exclaimed, "Mrs. Wharton, your boots are perfection."

Rose glanced down at her new footwear. The black kidskin leather was butter soft with bold roses embroidered in variegated shades of red and pink down either side of the laces amid brilliant green vines and leaves. Not only were they stylish, they also held a secret.

A small pocket was sewn inside the tongue of the boot, for a stash of money or even a note. Rose had slid the invitation to the Secret Book Society there, enjoying the thrill of the secret tucked so close.

The boots made Rose smile when she received them from her father. Not just for the pretty extravagance, but for what they represented. They were a reminder that she was loved dearly by her father, that there was an opportunity to return home. Even if doing so meant admitting to her mother that she'd been wrong about Theodore.

Divorce would be unlikely, but at least the separation of an ocean might help heal her heart.

She would have to make her mind up soon one way or the other. She was running out of time.

"Thank you for inviting us last evening," Rose said to Mrs. Clarke. "Mr. Wharton and I had a lovely time."

They had, too. Theodore swept Rose onto the dance floor and they'd shared an enchanting night of banter and play like they had in their days of courtship.

Then they'd gone home, and the fairy tale shattered into reality as her many shortcomings were noted. She had lingered too long with her friends. Her interaction with other men might be perceived as flirtation, and why did she have to be so very *American*?

All examples of how Rose would never be enough for the countess role she would soon fill.

With that unfortunate determination, she took a scone from the refreshment table and absently moved to close the drawing room door.

"Leave it open," Lady Duxbury exclaimed.

There was such desperation to the countess's plea that Rose snapped her attention to the woman, finding her face pale, her posture stiff.

"Please," Lady Duxbury added in a softer tone as the corners of her mouth flicked up in an unconvincing smile.

Rose hastily opened the door, hot with embarrassment at having clearly offended their generous hostess and friend. "I'm terribly sorry."

Lady Duxbury visibly relaxed and waved a hand as if the entire incident had been of no consequence.

Plate in hand, Rose settled into the same green chair as before, noting a frothy spray of Queen Anne's lace flowers spilling over the edge of a round blue vase. They weren't the opulent bouquet of a grand home, but a cluster of flowers a little girl might collect in the countryside. Charmingly quaint.

"It was my pleasure to invite everyone to our ball," Mrs. Clarke said, smoothing over Rose's misstep with redirected conversation. She reached for her teacup, then paused to tug at the sleeves of her dark gray gown.

"Perhaps next time we can persuade Lady Duxbury to join us," Rose teased, desperate to maintain the lighter tone, as if doing so might erase her folly.

Though, truly, why would a closed door have been so upsetting to Lady Duxbury? The more Rose gleaned about the countess, the more she realized she didn't know.

Otis entered the room, silently padding his way toward the empty vase.

"Perhaps." Lady Duxbury gave an affectionate smile at her cat, seeming fully recovered now, then slid her gaze away from the little mustached feline. "I hope you enjoyed the books you borrowed last week."

"Very much so." Mrs. Clarke straightened with an unaccustomed eagerness. "I read *Sense and Sensibility*—" Her hand disappeared into her reticule and reappeared with the book. "I've been longing to read more of Jane Austen's work, as I'm sure you know." The two women shared a look, suggesting a prior conversation. "I enjoyed how the practicality of life was balanced with the importance of feeling."

"Which of the Dashwood sisters did you find the most agreeable?" Lady Duxbury pressed. "Elinor or Marianne?"

"Both, I think." A flush spread over Mrs. Clarke's cheeks and she suddenly appeared uncertain she had given the correct answer. "Elinor is the more sensible sister and Marianne the more passionate one. I feel as though these women are the split of me. You see, I act like Elinor, but I *feel* like Marianne."

A hint of pride sparkled in Lady Duxbury's lovely eyes. "You saw into the heart of the story."

"The story saw into the heart of me," Mrs. Clarke said and then shyly ducked her head.

"Don't be embarrassed to say such things, please," Lady Duxbury encouraged. "This is precisely why I've started this society."

Otis's tail twitched from where he lay in his observation vase on the floor, and Rose caught Lady Lavinia glancing at the cat, then snapping her gaze respectfully away.

"I should very much like to read that if you're done." Lady Lavinia's words were quietly spoken and her shoulders curled forward, drawing into herself.

She wore her reticence like a tightly wrapped cloak, as if she could hide from the world. Even at the ball, Rose supplied the conversation for them both. When Lavinia was left on her own, the poor thing hovered near the wall, like a trapped rabbit.

There was something powerful lingering beneath that fragile exterior, and Rose was suddenly determined to win the shy young woman's trust.

"Did you enjoy *Jane Eyre*?" Lady Duxbury asked.

Lady Lavinia nodded. "I haven't quite finished it yet." She rubbed her slippered feet against one another, a childish and yet endearing show of unease. "I find it fascinating that she doesn't always do what is expected of her."

"And you admire that?" Lady Duxbury pressed encouragingly.

Lady Lavinia nodded again in reply. Mrs. Clarke handed her the copy of *Sense and Sensibility* and received a timid smile of thanks as Lady Lavinia hugged the book to her chest.

"I've been reading *The Female Quixote*," Rose said in an effort to spare poor Lady Lavinia from having to speak further. "I find it terribly ironic that the heroine has been addled by all the books she's read."

Lady Duxbury smirked. "Indeed. Women are denigrated for reading, as though we're committing moral sin. Books, after all, distract a mother and wife from her duties to her family. An informed wife might be disagreeable when she dares have opinions that differ from her husband." Bitterness laced the countess's statement in a rare display of emotion. "And we women are, after all, too frail to handle the excitement of a novel. Why, that might lead to bouts of hysteria."

Lavinia shifted in her chair beside Rose.

"Though this does present an ideal opportunity for discussion." Lady Duxbury lifted her teacup and spoke carefully. "Why do you believe your reading materials are being restricted?"

Rose wasn't sure if Lady Duxbury meant to ask her specifically, but replied regardless. "My situation is a byproduct of circumstance. I had the freedom to read anything I wanted up until several months ago."

She paused, aware that the discussion of familial matters was likely an egregious *faux pas*.

Yet, this was intended to be a private setting, one where women were to open their hearts as well as their minds.

"You don't need to divulge any information you aren't comfortable sharing," Lady Duxbury offered.

The lack of pressure compelled Rose onward.

"I want trust with this group," she insisted. "It's important to speak of these restrictions, to know they are wrongly imposed and not due to deficiencies on our parts." The force of her statement left her heart pounding with indignation. "My brother-in-law, the Earl of Amsel, is gravely ill and likely will not live out the year. He has been preparing my husband to assume the earldom and has expressed concerns at my ineptitude to perform in English Society. In his opinion, I will make a terrible countess. The pressure he exerts on my husband about my comportment has resulted in my oppression. Never in my life have I been so constrained, especially regarding my reading materials, which my brother-in-law assumes is where my wild notions take root."

"That's rubbish," Lady Lavinia stated abruptly, startling them all. "You are gracious and considerate with a wonderful ability to set others at ease. And you're an exceptional dancer. Those are all qualities to be admired in a countess." Her face went red and she shrank back into the green velvet settee. "Sorry, I shouldn't have spoken out of turn."

"You should," Lady Duxbury insisted. "It warms my heart that you should defend one of us so ardently. Thank you." She looked from Lavinia to Rose. "And thank you for being forthcoming."

"It's very brave of you." Mrs. Clarke put aside her teacup, tugged the edges of her sleeves down and opened her mouth as if to say more.

Perhaps to share as Rose had.

Rose edged forward in her chair, anticipating another woman revealing her heart as she had.

CHAPTER SEVEN

Mrs. Eleanor Clarke

ELEANOR'S LIPS PARTED, THE CONFESSION OF her own unpleasant marriage rising in her throat.

But then she glanced down. Her right sleeve had slid up, revealing the discoloration of a bruise visible beneath a delicate strip of lace. A reminder of Cecil's wrath.

He'd been displeased when she'd taken Lady Lavinia to the parlor during the ball. Still, even knowing how she would be punished, that he would brutally grab her, that he would issue threats in a low growl that stank of whatever spirit had poisoned his disposition—given the chance, Eleanor would help Lady Lavinia again.

An underlying warning prickled at the back of her mind.

What would Cecil do if he found out she revealed his secrets, if she admitted her utter misery?

Her mouth snapped closed, and she instead fell back on the benign expression she had mastered. A look of profound disappointment crossed Mrs. Wharton's features, pinching at Eleanor's guilt.

But Mrs. Wharton was brave, and Eleanor was a coward.

"I think perhaps we ought to retire to the library," Lady

Duxbury said, mercifully filling the ensuing silence. "Please feel free to take any book you like."

"What if we are still reading our previous book?" Mrs. Wharton asked.

"Well, you'll need another for when you finish," Lady Duxbury replied.

As they rose to adjourn to the library, Eleanor considered Lady Lavinia, who still cradled *Sense and Sensibility* in her hands. The way she had adamantly defended Mrs. Wharton earlier had been a lovely surprise, as had the emotional layers she'd described in the painting in Eleanor's parlor. And Mrs. Wharton's admission of her concerns with her marriage had been so revealing. Mr. and Mrs. Wharton had appeared the ideal couple at the ball, beautiful and graceful and deeply in love.

They all had secrets.

Before Eleanor could follow the other two women into the sunlit library, Lady Duxbury stopped her with a gentle touch to her forearm. "Mrs. Clarke, may I have a word?"

"Of course."

Lady Duxbury's gaze followed Mrs. Wharton and Lady Lavinia as they departed before speaking quietly. "I'm aware of your . . . complications."

Before Eleanor could question the cryptic statement, Lady Duxbury gently lifted Eleanor's arm, baring the mottled discoloration of pale yellows and greens of old bruises mingling with the vivid red and purple stains of new.

Eleanor drew her arm away, tugging at her sleeve so hard, she feared she might rip the stiff slate-colored silk.

Blue had not been sufficient for her mood today. There was no calming the turbulent sea of her misery with subtle cerulean shades. No, today wanted sorrowful gray, to wallow in her despondency.

Lady Duxbury locked her gaze on Eleanor. "You are not at fault."

The vehemence of her words took Eleanor aback. "I beg your pardon?"

"What your husband does—this . . . No transgression on your part warrants this punishment." Lady Duxbury spoke gently, but fire showed in her eyes.

Eleanor pulled at her sleeve once more, hating the rawness of her vulnerability. The conversation was one she was not ready for. She might never be.

Yes, what Cecil did was wrong. But she also pressed and pulled at the sway of his mercurial moods. Even knowing what tipped his temper, she still spoke and acted in ways that fueled his wrath. Like when she spirited Lady Lavinia into the drawing room.

Lady Duxbury nodded with a somber expression, and Eleanor realized the countess truly understood. And there was only one way to truly understand.

A connection knit between them in that moment, bonded in the empathy of shared pain.

Lady Duxbury started to turn away and then stopped abruptly. Her mouth opened and she hesitated before finally saying, "Please do remember, *anything* you find in the library is yours for the reading." She tilted her head as if sharing a secret. "Be mindful of the knot in the bookcase near the door. It appears to be loose and in need of repair."

Eleanor thanked her and joined the others in the library, wondering at the curious mention of the bookcase. She paused, admiring the freedom she had in that moment, appreciating the beauty of the room before her and what it offered.

Books lined every wall but one, which was filled with rows of windows, splashing light on the bookshelves extending from floor to ceiling. While most libraries were oppressively dark with polished mahogany and oiled leather, this one was open and airy. The ceiling overhead was brilliant white with a cornice scrolling the perimeter like curling ribbon, and the lovely pastel French Savonnerie carpet and blond wood shelves practically gleamed in the sunlight. Several delicate pink velvet chairs were placed about the room, and every window offered a bench with a thick cushion. This was no masculine space.

This was a lady's library.

Eleanor tugged at her sleeves once more, ensuring her secrets were properly hidden.

Mrs. Wharton sat at one of the window seats, cast in a beam of sunshine with a book in her lap. Lady Lavinia was bent over *Sense and Sensibility* in one of the overstuffed velvet chairs across the room.

Rows of multicolored spines lined the shelves, offering more than Eleanor could ever read in a lifetime. A true gift if ever there was one. She approached the shelf nearest the door, determined to read her way from one end of the wall to the other, and scanned the titles.

Lady Duxbury's cat padded into the room. Much to Eleanor's surprise, Otis swept his tail around her skirts as he passed. She bent to pet him, but he arched away from her, leaving her hand skimming the air just above his fur.

That was when she noticed the slight discoloration in the wood paneling, a carved whorl that appeared slightly different in texture and makeup than the others. She ran her finger over the defect. The knot moved slightly, and a soft click sounded. A narrow section of the shelf paneling slid up, revealing a secret pocket that housed a single book.

Eleanor glanced about the room. Neither woman appeared to have witnessed what had transpired. Lady Lavinia was still hunched over her book, oblivious to the world around her, and Mrs. Wharton had her face tilted into the sunlight, her eyes closed.

Pulse whooshing in her ears, Eleanor reached for the hidden book.

The vibrant blue leather cover offered no hint as to the title or author.

Eleanor opened it to the first page to find neat, slanted handwriting, scored over many times in a slash of black ink.

The Diary of:
   ~~*Clara Howell*~~
   ~~*Clara Howell Edwards, Viscountess Morset*~~
   ~~*Clara Howell Edwards Ashdown, Countess of Esterly*~~
   Clara Howell Edwards Ashdown Chambers, Countess of Duxbury

Eleanor's breath caught.

This was Lady Duxbury's diary.

The widow's words repeated in Eleanor's head. Not only that *anything* found in the library could be read, but also the caution she'd issued on the loose bit of wood.

Had Lady Duxbury meant for her to find this? To read it?

Eleanor glanced about the room again, to ensure no one had looked her way. Did they not hear the hammering of her heart at this discovery? Did they not sense the excitement practically vibrating off her?

The book remained pinched in her fingertips, her curiosity about the young widowed countess blazing. Eleanor longed to understand more of the enigmatic woman who hired servants from the poorhouse, who spoke with passion as she insisted Cecil's actions were not Eleanor's fault.

And, yes, Eleanor was interested to possibly learn more about the three husbands who had met such untimely deaths.

Still, Eleanor hesitated, overwhelmed by the sense that she might be violating Lady Duxbury's privacy.

Perhaps just a peek at the first line.

Eleanor turned the page.

February 1878

I was compelled to run away, to abandon my wealth and my family, and start life beautifully anew.

Eleanor paused, the scales of guilt and curiosity teetering opposite one another. Had Lady Duxbury *truly* meant for her to read this?

Eleanor understood the appeal of wanting to run away, to abandon her wealth, the esteem of her name—everything—in the pursuit of freedom. She would sacrifice everything for a fresh start. Everything, that is, except her son. He was at once the buoy in her life and the anchor.

But why would Lady Duxbury want to run away from home? Had she been in a situation similar to Eleanor's? And if she had run away, how had she been welcomed back into Society?

The questions nipped at Eleanor's thoughts as she did a quick calculation. Lady Duxbury was likely in her mid-thirties now, which put her around seventeen or eighteen when the entry was written.

Before Eleanor could change her mind, she pushed the knob on the secret door, closing the panel so it fit seamlessly against the smooth back of the bookshelf. If one didn't know where to look, the secret would be nearly impossible to locate.

Selecting a random book that was taller and wider than the diary, Eleanor carried both to a comfortable chair on the opposite side of the room as Mrs. Wharton and Lady Lavinia.

She opened the larger book, the collected works of Edgar Allan Poe, nestled the diary into the generous fit of the spine and began to read. Just one entry, then she had to return the diary before anyone else noticed.

CHAPTER EIGHT

Lady Duxbury's Diary

February 1878

I was compelled to run away, to abandon my wealth and my family, and start life beautifully anew.

My parents have been most insistent on a marriage to the Viscount Morset. He is young, unlike the ancient baron my poor cousin was forced to marry, but there is an arrogance to the curve of his lips that casts a condescending air. What's more, he's an impoverished, pompous viscount who is merely seeking access to my father's wealth. Unfortunately, it is undeniable that his elevated rank would improve my family's standing in the eyes of Society.

The latter is what propels Mama to pursue this marriage for me so ardently.

Escape was the only alternative I could see. Though it was admittedly poorly conceived, and I very nearly found myself in the clutches of a woman intent on procuring me for her brothel.

I was ignorant to my own ignorance, it would seem. I stared doe-eyed around at the train station in my borrowed maid's clothing, attempting to deduce where to go and how best to acquire a ticket. Unwittingly offering myself as an easy target.

The sky opened with a crack of thunder and a deluge descended. As I pondered my plight, the woman approached with a gentleman at her side, informing me the tickets had been sold for the evening. Their offer that I might join them at their home if I had nowhere else was generous. Having no wish to return to my father's estate, I gratefully accepted.

We had only just departed the train station when a young man ran after us, asking if I knew the couple I followed.

The rain assaulted us like ice shards. I was eager to put him off and quickly explained their generous offer. Before I could understand what was happening, he inserted himself between me and the couple and swore to defend me from their disreputable intentions.

What then transpired leaves me still in shock. The couple argued with the man at first, but when they realized his insistence, the gentleman became apoplectic and lunged at the man. This led to fisticuffs, right there in front of the train station.

The man was not so skilled as the gentleman and took rather an unfortunate walloping, inspiring in me a great sympathy for him for so stupidly putting himself between me and the couple. The power of my empathy worked to my favor. I always do find myself cheering on the weaker party. Perhaps because I have been at similar disadvantage in life, crushed beneath the heels of my betters.

I bid the couple a fervent farewell, refusing their apologies and imploring offers of a dry bed and hot meal—though they did indeed entice as the rain continued.

Instead, I tended to the man whose name I learned to be Elias, the owner of a quaint bookshop near Threadneedle Lane. He divulged the notorious couple to be brothel owners who scoured train stations for young women to abduct and force into unmentionable labor.

When I asked how he knew of their perfidious endeavors, he blinked at me in surprise and stated that everyone knew. Everyone, it would seem, except for me.

I admit my life has been sheltered, oblivious of penury save for what I have glimpsed through the windows of our carriage. I was raised to never know that women of sordid endeavors should even exist in this world. To think I might have fallen prey to such a scheme leaves me reeling.

And Elias saved me.

He asked for no reward, but instead offered to escort me anywhere I wished to go. His solicitude demonstrated how poorly I'd assembled my escape. I endeavor to be more fastidious in strategizing my next escape. Which meant I had to return home.

I could not tell Elias that I was an heiress, especially as I was dressed as a maid. And so, I allowed the falsehood to linger as he escorted me home.

When the townhouse came into view, he gave a long, low whistle of appreciation at my incredible luck to work in such an esteemed household. His reverence had me grateful to have lied.

After all he had done for me, I did not wish to put him out by eliciting feelings of inferiority.

He asked if he might receive my permission to call on me sometime. I ought to have declined, but I could not bring my lips to form the words. Instead, what emerged was a yes. Though I informed him I would meet him at an agreed upon location rather than have him approach the house.

When I returned home, no one had even been aware of my absence.

The lack of notice at my prolonged disappearance was not surprising. I am not the future heir as my brother is, educated at Oxford and prepared to assume the family business and wealth management. And I am not my younger sister, whose grace and obedient manner make her a prize in my parents' eyes.

In fact, it was on behalf of my sister that I am being pushed toward a swift marriage. An earl has fallen in love with her. Of course he has. She is beautiful and perfect and amenable. But though she loves him, she cannot wed until I have been bound in nuptials.

Despite the blatant desires of my family, despite my knowing what I ought to do and what I ought not, I have seen Elias.

Not once, but a dozen times.

Enough to know every fleck of black and gold in the velvety brown of his eyes. Enough to have learned the silkiness of his hair as it passes through my fingers. Enough to be fully, unequivocally and completely in love.

CHAPTER NINE

Mrs. Rose Wharton

ROSE STOOD ALONE AMID A CLUSTER OF TWO dozen women, waiting for luncheon to be announced. She only accepted Mrs. Baskin's invitation to please Theodore. Just as she had likely only been invited at Mr. Baskin's behest, being that he was the brother of an earl, the same as Rose's husband.

The other attendees huddled together, bound by gossip and friendly chatter, relegating Rose to the fringes of the gathering. How she abhorred being alone in a crowded room, her every attempt at conversation buffeted away by barely concealed contempt.

Mrs. Baskin played the role of hostess and approached Rose. "Thank you for coming, Mrs. Wharton." Her smile did not reach her eyes.

"I appreciate the invitation." Rose opened her mouth to say more, but Mrs. Baskin quickly turned away, having duly seen to welcoming her unwanted guest.

Left to her own devices, Rose stared at an uninspired painting of a landscape with a blocky blue sky over a field of plain green. She preferred fascinating art, like the surreal images by Odilon Redon, or even the beauty of Auguste Toulmouche. Particularly

Le Fruit Défendu—*The Forbidden Fruit*—depicting sisters stealing into a library to read. The image of young women conspiring to sneak books reminded her of the ladies in the Secret Book Society.

Though the luncheon had not yet begun, she already longed to be home with her little pug tucked in her lap and *The Female Quixote* in her hands.

"What a divine gown, Mrs. Wharton." A friendly female voice pulled Rose from the bland landscape.

She turned to find Mrs. Clarke smiling prettily at her. "I must have the name of your modiste."

"Then you'll have to travel to America, I'm afraid." Rose slid her hand down the blush-pink panel draped over the front of her silk gown. "The frock was made there before I left for London."

Several women shared peevish glances with one another. Rose had said the wrong thing again.

"That explains why you have such uniquely beautiful items in your wardrobe," Mrs. Clarke interjected, her praise smoothing over Rose's rocky reply. "Especially your lovely rose embroidered boots I saw the other day. I do so admire your keen fashion sense."

Rose's face flushed with warmth. For a woman of Mrs. Clarke's immaculate taste to praise her attire—and in public no less—was quite the success.

Rose thanked her cordially, anticipating Mrs. Clarke would spirit away to the company of the other women.

But she remained at Rose's side and inquired, "I trust you're well?"

Thus began the litany of colloquial English topics—the health of one's family, the mention of the marriage of an acquaintance, the anticipation for the treacle pudding at luncheon for which Mrs. Baskin's cook was known for and, of course, the weather. Under normal circumstances, entirely unexceptional.

To Rose, however, the conversation was extraordinarily exceptional. Not only for the public acceptance, but thus marking the first time she'd been spoken to by a true friend rather than an acquaintance adhering to the basics of propriety.

"Have you been introduced to Mrs. Edwards?" Mrs. Clarke indicated a woman standing nearby.

Mrs. Edwards turned warily toward them. The skin beneath her eyes was puffy and she wore a long-suffering expression that pulled even lower when she saw Rose. Mrs. Clarke did not appear at all put off by the woman's obvious lack of enthusiasm.

"Have you recovered from the headache that kept you from the ball yesterday evening?" Mrs. Edwards asked Mrs. Clarke with solicitude. "Have you seen a physician? I was plagued with them before, but Dr. Livingston has helped considerably."

"Much recovered, thank you." Mrs. Clarke addressed Rose. "Mrs. Edwards heads the Society for the Advancement of the Poor alongside Mrs. Baskin and is always enlisting others to help her cause."

"I suppose I am," Mrs. Edwards stammered, apprehensive as she considered Rose.

"Mrs. Edwards is one of the kindest women I know," Mrs. Clarke effused.

Mrs. Edwards reddened at the praise.

While Rose appreciated Mrs. Clarke's intent to ingratiate her into the circle of women, working with the Society for the Advancement of the Poor did not hold great appeal. Rose no longer possessed the wealth to donate heftily as she would have done before. Her assistance would have to come in the form of labor.

And truly, if the poor had insufficient income, couldn't they simply work harder to improve their lot?

Her grandfather had been a coal miner who saved every coin to invest in a new railway line. Such foresight was admirable, but a feat anyone could have accomplished.

And yet this was an opportunity Rose could not squander.

She forced a pleasant expression on her face. "I should love to be of assistance."

This time, the smile Mrs. Edwards offered appeared genuine, almost relieved. "I would be grateful for the help."

Luncheon was announced then, and Mrs. Clarke looped her arm with Rose's as they entered the dining room. A long table was adorned with a brilliant array of hothouse zinnias, cheerful with the promise of amity amid the formal place settings.

As they entered the room, several women clearly noted Mrs. Clarke's favor toward Rose and approached to compliment Rose's American-made gown. When they sat, Mrs. Clarke took the seat to the right of Rose and the one at her left was quickly filled by a young woman who mentioned she also assisted the Society for the Advancement of the Poor.

Through the meal, Mrs. Clarke was perfectly sociable, generous in her compliments and persistently pleasant, yet she never once divulged personal information. Any questions directed toward her were gracefully flipped back to the person who'd made the inquiry. Given how many of Society's women enjoyed talking about themselves, the tactic was effective.

Effective, and unnoticed. At least to everyone except Rose. But what Rose perceived that day in Mrs. Clarke made her long to discover more about the woman with whom everyone was acquainted, but whom no one actually knew.

CHAPTER TEN

Mrs. Eleanor Clarke

ELEANOR WAS THE FIRST TO ARRIVE FOR TEA with the Secret Book Society, followed by the white-mustached cat, who carefully slipped into the vase, assuming his ostensibly unseen perch.

"So lovely to see you, Mrs. Clarke," Lady Duxbury said as she joined Eleanor.

"I'm a bit early, I'm afraid. I hope I haven't put you out." Eleanor plucked at her gown, a rich salmon velvet that was as close to red as she ventured these days. Red was a bold color, one of fearlessness. She was not strong enough to wear red.

But she did need courage to bolster her resolve.

Lady Duxbury waved off the apology. "Not at all. Meeting with the three of you is the joy of my week. You are welcome here anytime." Her smile made her appear younger, and Eleanor recalled what she'd read in Lady Duxbury's journal. How at only seventeen, she'd fled from an unwanted engagement.

Eleanor had been curious about the young girl Lady Duxbury had been, but before she could even fathom what to appropriately ask, the maid entered with a tea tray.

"Thank you, Mary." Lady Duxbury smiled at her with maternal affection and the young maid beamed back.

Eleanor once more noted the scars gnarled across the young woman's hands as she deftly set the drawing room table for tea. For all the wealthy women of England offering their assistance in various societies to the poor, none had accomplished what Lady Duxbury had in saving girls from factories and poorhouses through employment.

Mrs. Wharton arrived exactly on time with Lady Lavinia following only seconds behind her.

Eleanor shifted in her seat, her body restless with nerves as she reached for her teacup, a delicately painted set with chamomile flowers on both the rim of the cup and along the edge of the saucer.

After the last Secret Book Society meeting, she chastised herself for not having been forthright about how Cecil limited her reading. And everything else in her life.

She had been anxious for this meeting, her nerves stretched taut with anticipation.

Mrs. Wharton caught Eleanor's eye. "Thanks to your support at Mrs. Baskin's luncheon, several women have already extended invitations to tea, and I've been enlisted to assist with the Society for the Advancement of the Poor." She lifted her teacup. "I'm eager to start."

"The pleasure was all mine," Eleanor replied with sincerity, grateful to have had some influence in the improvement of Mrs. Wharton's social standing.

Lady Duxbury nodded approvingly at their exchange. "Seeing your interactions extend beyond our teas is heartening. This is what women ought to do for one another, help and befriend."

"Mrs. Clarke helped me, too," Lady Lavinia offered in a small voice. "At the ball. Sometimes I become—" she rubbed the toes of her slippers together "—overwhelmed." She gave a tentative smile. "I think you saw that when you invited me to your parlor for a moment of peace."

Eleanor tilted her head sympathetically. "I believe we have all been overwhelmed with Society on one occasion or another."

"The ability to sense another's feelings is a special talent." Lady Duxbury's perceptive gaze settled on Eleanor. "I wager it is a skill that has been hard-won."

Eleanor's heartbeat quickened at the countess's implicit understanding of so much more than what was said out loud. As if she had witnessed the countless times Eleanor gauged Cecil's temperament and adjusted her own actions in accommodation. The ability had been fine-tuned over the years in response to his mercurial nature, helping her skirt his rage and protect herself, until the skill had indeed become second nature.

"Yes." Eleanor's acknowledgment came out in a breathy whisper. Her mouth was suddenly dry. She took a sip of her tea and glanced down at the salmon-colored velvet in an attempt to reclaim her confidence. She ought to have worn red. "My husband, he is . . ."

Her words faltered.

Was she truly going to do this?

If Cecil found out, what would he do to her?

Her heartbeat thundered in her ears. The room was suddenly too small, the temperature too warm, the air too thin.

A hand settled over hers.

Eleanor blinked at the slender, delicate fingers and looked up to find Mrs. Wharton offering her support. "You are among friends."

"Take all the time you need," Lady Lavinia said, echoing the words Eleanor had said in the quiet space in her parlor during the ball.

Lady Duxbury nodded in understanding.

Eleanor exhaled, slowly releasing her held breath. "My husband possesses a terribly erratic nature that turns bilious at a moment's notice. He is . . . often unkind. I confess, my ability to understand what people are feeling despite their words and actions stems from my constant need to read him. I . . ."

There was so much she wanted to say that teetered on the tip of her tongue. How she hated her circumstances. How the iniquity of her restrained life compared to her husband's freedom made her burn with an impotent rage. How every time he berated her and laid forceful hands on her, she wished he would die so she might finally be free.

The last thought came in a maelstrom, unexpected and shocking, even to her.

"I am unhappy," she said instead. "Intolerably so. My life is one I would not wish upon my greatest enemy."

"Does he strike you?" Mrs. Wharton asked in a quiet voice, her hand still cradling Eleanor's.

Eleanor looked away, too embarrassed to admit how the force of his wrath left her bruised, how she did not retaliate and instead waited until he left to allow her tears to flow.

"Are your parents aware of your treatment?" Lady Lavinia's innocence was evident in her wide green eyes, a child wrapped in the protection of her parents' love.

"My father was a good man." Eleanor ran her finger around the rim of her cup, following the chain of painted chamomile flowers. "He died this past October, and my mother cares only about her place in Society. I endure my life for the sake of my son."

"There is much a mother would do for her child." There was conviction in Lady Duxbury's words. As if she, too, had been a mother.

Had she?

If so, when? And what had become of her child?

Eleanor's thoughts trailed back to Lady Duxbury's diary. Contemplating someone else's life was preferable to focusing on her own.

"It is kind of you to offer your library, to have this place of friendship and acceptance to speak openly," Eleanor admitted. "I've only ever had one opportunity to venture outside the etiquette books I was instructed to read. *Mansfield Park* was part of that exception. I'm grateful for the prospect to read more." She presented the large copy of the collected works of Edgar Allan Poe that she'd borrowed, the one she'd used to hide the diary behind. "Where *Sense and Sensibility* was about the need for passion, this book is the embodiment of such expression. Emotion flew from the pages, the longing, the regret. It was dark and powerful."

Lady Duxbury touched the curious hair brooch over her heart, her lips pressing together as if she meant to protest Eleanor's pointed shift of conversation from Cecil to books. Then her expression cleared and she turned to Lady Lavinia. "Did you finish *Jane Eyre*?"

"I did," Lady Lavinia said. "She's such an inspiring character."

"I think I shall like to borrow that one next." Eleanor reached a hand out and accepted the book from Lady Lavinia.

"Well, I would not recommend *The Female Quixote*," Mrs. Wharton said bitterly. "The ending was wretched."

"I wondered if you might think as much." Lady Duxbury set her teacup aside. "The conclusion was rather disappointing. Still, I found the story up to that point a refreshing perspective. Let us adjourn so you may select your next books."

Eleanor brought *Jane Eyre* with her into the library, contemplating the size of the book and wondering at the slight scorch mark at its back. Surely, the cover was large enough to conceal Lady Duxbury's diary.

"Mrs. Clarke."

Eleanor turned to find Mrs. Wharton behind her.

"May I borrow that one?" She indicated the collected works of Edgar Allan Poe.

"You won't find the endings much happier," Eleanor warned lightly as she handed her the large book.

Mrs. Wharton accepted the heavy collected works and hesitated. "I'm sorry to learn of your circumstances." Concern pulled at her smooth forehead. "I'm aware it's vulgar to discuss such topics, but if there's ever a way I can offer assistance, please let me know."

Eleanor offered a weak smile. "Thank you."

With that, Mrs. Wharton took her place, settling on the cushion of the sunlit window seat once more, Edgar Allan Poe propped in her lap. Lady Lavinia, however, perused the shelves, pausing periodically to lift a book for consideration. This lasted something of an eternity before she finally selected one.

Book in hand, she headed for the chair she'd occupied last time, leaving Eleanor to select the book she'd been most desperate to return to. She bent, as if scanning a row of books, and pushed at the small knot of wood, gratified at the familiar click as the panel released.

Eleanor withdrew the diary and opened to the second passage to sneak a peek at what was written next.

May 1878

I have been captive for fifty-two days.

With *Jane Eyre* offering a snug shield for the diary, Eleanor assumed her place away from the others and let her curiosity of Lady Duxbury's life get the better of her.

CHAPTER ELEVEN

Lady Duxbury's Diary

May 1878

I have been captive for fifty-two days.

Mama's endeavors to compel me toward a union with the Viscount Morset have been unsuccessful. In her contempt for my stubbornness, I have become a prisoner in my own home, the door to my room locked until I agree to marry.

Every day, Mama attempts some new method of persuasion. Initially, there were promises of an auspicious future if I gave in readily. Then came the threats as she raged with vicious censure. This was followed by tears at my lack of propriety and lamentations of my contumacious nature.

I have always been a disappointment to her.

I am indifferent to the antics she summons in her bid to sway me.

Perhaps the worst punishment of all has been the removal of my books until such a time that I agree to this unsavory marriage. This punishment is particularly cruel, robbing me of my one comfort.

In my confined state, I am allowed one privilege, the opportunity to see Alice, my dearest friend. Though I swore I'd keep my affections for Elias close to my heart, circumstances have prevailed upon me to confess to Alice so that she might seek out my beloved to explain my absence, to enlist his aid.

She agreed to go to him and disclose my transgressions, promising to return with his response. It was solicitous of her to help. But then, Alice understands what I have with Elias, for it is all she's ever desired. Perhaps such a longing stems from the way her parents eschew any interest in her or how she is readily passed over for her prettier cousins, but she has spent a lifetime desperate to love and be loved.

Those days until Alice's next visit were interminable.

When she arrived, I begged her to be expedient with every detail. She did not disappoint . . . and yet she did.

My heart aches in my breast with such agony, I can scarcely breathe as I lift pen to page.

Elias, my handsome, loving, compassionate Elias, was appalled at my deception. Through Alice's lips, he suggested I marry one of "my kind."

I am unsure if by my kind he implies one of considerable wealth, or one of comparable moral turpitude.

Either way, Elias is gone. There is no one to come to my rescue.

Alas, that was not all the unfortunate news bestowed upon my household by Alice that afternoon. She has betrayed my confidence, and shared my deepest secret with my parents, providing them with the motivation to gain my acquiescence.

I am cut to my core.

In the end, I have agreed to marry the viscount. Not because of Mama's daily pontification on the qualities of an advantageous union or the maelstrom of her fulminations. Certainly, not on account of whatever tears her mean heart spits out in transparent manipulation. Nor did my decision have to do with *my beloved books that were promised to be returned upon my capitulation.*

Sadly, I was induced into agreement of the much unwanted union by the cessation of my courses, and by the new life growing within me.

CHAPTER TWELVE

Lady Lavinia Cavendish

THERE WERE MANY PLACES LAVINIA WOULD rather be than at Mrs. Baskin's dinner party where she knew she would see Jane.

Chiefly, in her window seat at home in a comfortable dressing gown, returning to the world of *Sense and Sensibility*. But at this point of the evening, any one of Dante's nine circles of hell would still be preferable to where she was.

She was seated between two stodgy earls, both of whom glanced at her with interest until they deemed her conversation laconic and did not deign to turn in her direction again. The first course arrived, revealing an appetizer of prawns. Lavinia's stomach lurched at the prone creatures staring up with beady black eyes, their bodies boiled to a reddish-pink.

The earl to her right tore in with gusto, shredding a thin exoskeleton to access the meat within.

How awful to consume something as it watched you. The earl jabbed a fork into his next victim and bile rose in Lavinia's throat.

"Afraid they're still alive?" Jane asked from across the table, a condescending clip in her tone.

To think they had once been friends . . .

In past years, Lavinia spent considerable time in this town-house and in their summer residence in Essex where the Baskins neighbored Lavinia's family's estate. With such proximity to one another and being the same age, their acquaintance was inevitable. As girls, they'd found a common interest in languages, in books, in the world around them and the people who moved within their circle. As women, Jane saw Lavinia as competition, especially when the very man she had fixed her sights on only had eyes for Lavinia, who had not sought his attention. A fact that did not matter to Jane. The incident marked the end of their friendship, and all the secrets Lavinia had confessed to Jane became like bullets, loaded into a hunter's rifle, waiting to be fired.

"They do seem to be staring at us, don't they?" Mrs. Wharton prodded a prawn with her fork, earning her a sharp look from the man at her side.

Jane didn't even glance at Mrs. Wharton. Instead, her eyes narrowed to malicious slits. "Don't become upset, Lady Lavinia. I know how you can be."

Lavinia's heart skipped to a petrified stop.

She swallowed, but found her throat dry as ancient parchment.

Jane knew how impassioned Lavinia could become when distraught. After all, Lavinia had foolishly confessed Papa's concerns at how deeply Lavinia connected with books, and how desperately frantic she became when he suggested she stop reading. All those admissions came rushing back now. How she cried when she read, how she laughed aloud, how she admitted developing an intense fondness for fictional characters like Mr. Darcy.

Oh, Mr. Darcy . . .

And how when Lavinia realized her fervent protests upset her father, she immediately calmed, resorting to begging. Her change of moods too fast. Capricious. Mercurial.

Mad.

Was everyone looking at Lavinia now, or was she imagining the weight of their stares?

Her heart hammered back to life in great galloping beats and heat flooded her face.

She didn't move her head, remaining perfectly still as her gaze swept from side to side. Sweat prickled at her armpits and palms.

This dinner party transcended any circle of hell Dante could create.

Jane casually picked a bit of lint off the sleeve of her gown, the crimson silk embroidered with bright yellow tansy flowers. "How *is* your maternal grandmother?" Her voice was louder this time.

Unease crawled over Lavinia's skin.

Jane knew her grandmother was dead. The question was a threat, layered beneath a seemingly benign social inquiry.

"She behaved in an odd fashion, did she not?" Jane looked about, her lips curled in a hard smile.

Mama was watching the exchange, her face white. Everyone truly was turned in Lavinia's direction now, drawn by the elevated volume of Jane's voice.

Lavinia looked down, desperate to escape the weight of so much unwanted attention only to find the sightless black eyes of the prawn staring helplessly up at her.

"Well, whose grandmother doesn't behave in an odd fashion?" Mrs. Wharton asked with a laugh. "My grandmother collected every lost button she found and would insist on keeping her old clothes to remake into new ones. Such curious behavior."

She chuckled. No one else did.

Lavinia ought to offer some comment in sympathy, the way Mrs. Wharton had just done for her. But her mind was a whirl of thoughts, too frenzied to form anything coherent.

Instead, she mumbled an excuse and slipped from the table while the focus remained on Mrs. Wharton.

The act was cowardly, a decision Lavinia knew would vex her later. For now, she could not maintain her composure in the wake of Jane's attack. Sequestered in the solace of the water closet, and blissfully alone, she splashed water from the tap on her face. Her image stared back in the mirror, cheeks stained scarlet with humiliation.

Lavinia scrunched her eyes shut, embracing the relief of solitude, and recalled Mrs. Clarke's quiet parlor, the subtle blues of the decor, that wistful painting.

Her face cooled and her pulse quieted, allowing her to draw in deep, even breaths until the roiling sensation in her stomach ceased.

The click of heels on the marble floor in the hall outside indicated she no longer had the luxury to take her time. She stiffened and pressed back against cold tiled wall, wishing for nothing more than to simply disappear.

"Lady Lavinia?" a voice asked gently from the other side of the door.

Lavinia's shoulders relaxed somewhat. The intruder wasn't Mama, whose inevitable concern was its own burden to bear.

"Lady Lavinia," the voice repeated softly. "It's Mrs. Wharton."

The wash of relief was so great, tears burned in Lavinia's eyes. She blinked them away and opened the door.

Mrs. Wharton gave a friendly smile. "May I come in?"

Though the space was small, Lavinia stepped back in invitation. Mrs. Wharton entered and closed the door once more, thoughtfully joining Lavinia's privacy rather than dragging her out into the open.

"Miss Jane is horrid," Mrs. Wharton whispered of their hostess's daughter. "And I know you probably wish you could stay in here for the rest of the night."

"But I can't," Lavinia confirmed miserably.

Mrs. Wharton shook her head. "Doing so will only make the gossip worse. Trust me, I've tried."

"You have?"

"Unfortunately." Mrs. Wharton rolled her eyes in her self-deprecating manner. "At one of my first dinner parties in London, Lady Meddleson was immensely rude. Later, I overheard her with several other women laughing at my expense. It was all I could do to remain at the table. And then . . ." Her cheeks colored and Lavinia imagined she was recalling the moment vividly, as one does when reliving a painful memory.

"What happened?" Lavinia pressed.

"Well, I went to dip my strawberry in a bit of cream and the dratted thing rolled off my fork, leaving a red trail over the tablecloth. The women began whispering to one another behind their fans, staring at me all the while. I fled to the washroom, determined not to leave until my face was no longer red from crying."

Lavinia grimaced. "How long did that take?"

"Long enough for everyone to think my American stomach found the food disagreeable and assumed I was in the washroom for . . . other reasons."

Lavinia clapped a hand over her mouth in horror.

"You should come back." Mrs. Wharton leaned closer. "Not only because you don't wish people to be left to their assumptions, but also because Miss Jane choked on a prawn." A genuine smile broke out on Mrs. Wharton's face. "She rallied with a little belch that made everyone frown fiercely." She laughed. "I do love when miserable things happen to miserable people."

Lavinia joined in the laughter, imagining Jane making such disagreeable noises at the table.

Mrs. Wharton offered her arm to Lavinia. "Let us defy the miserable, my dear. Together."

Lavinia threaded her arm through Mrs. Wharton's. "To-gether."

They separated as they entered the dining room, each with the fortifying strength of knowing she wasn't alone. That strength helped Lavinia through the evening, no matter how many spiteful comments Jane volleyed her way, or the number of times Mama glanced over with concern.

Mrs. Wharton offered support Lavinia had not felt in a long time. All the women of the Secret Book Society did. Suddenly, Lavinia regretted having not been candid in sharing her secrets as the other women had.

While she had been betrayed by Jane, a woman she once trusted implicitly, these women were different. Not spoiled and self-centered, but women whose pasts were marred by hardship, whose futures were as flimsy and bleak as Lavinia's. Each woman had shared and been vulnerable while Lavinia remained silent.

But she was done being silent. She'd spent too many years suppressing her voice. If her friends could share their secrets, so, too, could she.

CHAPTER THIRTEEN

Mrs. Rose Wharton

BY ALL ACCOUNTS, ROSE HAD CONSIDERED THE night at Mrs. Baskin's dinner party a success, as much as was possible when hosted by such an odious woman.

Theodore's disposition, however, suggested otherwise. He aggressively paced Rose's bedchamber as her maid pulled the jewels from Rose's dark hair. Pluto sat by her feet, his soft body warm against her toes. His liquid brown eyes followed Theodore's agitated gait from one wall to the other and back again.

The weighty silence was broken only by the plink of discarded hairpins as Rose's maid worked as quickly as possible. An undercurrent of frenetic energy ran through the room, a storm brewing. One of ire and vexation.

When all the pins had been hurriedly plucked from Rose's hair, she dismissed her maid and turned to Theodore with a sigh. "I've displeased you."

He spun on her, his smooth-shaven face crimson with disapprobation. "You only just gained the good graces of Mrs. Baskin and now you've ruined it."

Pluto scrambled to his feet, putting himself between his mistress and his master.

Rose leaned down to pat the little pug to soothe his ruffled state. He was always disquieted when she and Theodore argued. She straightened and addressed her husband in a calm voice she hoped put her dog at ease. "I'm offering enough time to the Society for the Advancement of the Poor that I would imagine one small joke would not put me out of her favor."

In the past week, Rose had attended the society house nearly every day. The location was wretched, crammed with tenement houses leaning into one another, where costermongers and odd men yelled at her to buy their wares, and filled with a permeating odor she could not quite place—nor did she want to.

She had never witnessed abject poverty before. Newspapers and books mentioned starving children and she'd heard of the dismal state of penury in less polite conversations, but she'd never witnessed it with her own eyes. Even now, her heart cramped as she recalled the endless line of people outside the society. They came for clothes that Rose first mistook for rubbish. They came for food—runny stews with more fat than meat, and coarse bread—and Mrs. Edwards said they came for hope, though Rose found none there in Whitechapel.

The children were small as dolls, their skin clinging to bone-thin limbs, faces gaunt like old men beneath a layer of grime, young backs hunched from hard labor at the factories. Some didn't even have shoes. Their mothers were overworked and fragile, too tired to mind their children, leaving the task to older siblings. The men who bothered to see to their family's aid did so with an air of heartbreaking futility.

"Your efforts with the charity are commendable and have been noted," Theodore conceded.

By *have been noted*, Rose was certain he referred to his brother, who watched her with a scrupulous eye.

"But your conduct at the dinner party . . ." Theodore shook his head, dislodging that dark curl that was wont to fall over his brow.

Rose longed to smooth the strands back with her fingers as she so often did in the past, to set the endearing curl back into his parted and pomaded hair. Instead, she turned away, regarding him from the cold glass of the mirror's reflection.

"What you said about your grandmother's behavior was entirely lacking in thought," he continued. "Rose, are you mad?"

"Am I mad?" She spun around to face him, mouth falling open in outrage. "Perhaps you'll recall that my grandfather was the one whose gold mine propelled my family into wealth, that before such abundance, they had nothing. My grandmother was raised in a life of poverty and never stopped worrying they would fall to financial struggle again."

Pluto barked when she stopped, punctuating her statement with one of his own.

"And you'll recall that Miss Jane is Mrs. Baskin's daughter, and your comment was made without a thought to propriety. Have you lost all sense?" There was a harsh quality to Theodore's tone, the one he'd recently adopted from his brother, authoritative and saturated with judgment.

What would life be like when Theodore *was* the earl?

Pluto growled low in his throat, shifting the weight of his small, rotund body from one foot to the other. Rose set a calming hand at his side.

"I only sought to help Lady Lavinia after Miss Jane's slight." Rose patted Pluto a final time and pushed to her feet. "The only person deserving of censure here is Miss Jane."

Theodore rubbed at the center of his brow as he did when his head ached. "And then you were gone so long in the washroom. Do you not recall—"

"Of course I recall." Rose cut him off before he could delve back into that awful memory.

What she'd laughed about with Lady Lavinia only hours before now made her cheeks blaze with indignation.

Pluto gave another sharp bark, backing his mistress in this battle.

"You have a headache," Rose surmised. "Come, I'll fetch some of the lavender oil I know you like and—"

But Theodore shook his head once more, that curl still stubbornly lying across his brow.

"I know you're displeased with me, but things will appear brighter without a headache," she cajoled.

How weary she grew of this constant war at home, and how she longed for the happy, carefree days of their marriage when they reveled in one another's company.

The stiffness in his shoulders did not soften, and the frost in his blue eyes chilled her.

"Are you truly so displeased with me?" She sighed again. "You are even more vicious than usual tonight."

"I read your mother's letter." He spoke low and even.

Trepidation scraped down her spine. "You read my correspondence?" she demanded with great offense, as if ignorant to the contents of that letter.

Clearly sensing the tension vibrating in the air, Pluto's hackles rose.

"Apparently, your mother is most pleased you'll finally be a countess, as she desired." The ice in Theodore's voice now matched that of his eyes.

"That is my mother, not me." Rage pressed against the dam Rose had erected months ago when all this began. "I never wanted to be a countess. I only ever wanted to be your wife. If I had wanted to marry for a title, I could have had a duke. But I wanted *you*, Theodore Wharton."

Memories rushed at her, the way he'd swept her off her feet the night of the New Year's Eve ball of 1891 in New York, stealing a brazen kiss at midnight when no one was looking. How he'd sent her a bouquet of red roses every day until she agreed to see him again. His earnestness when he proposed and promised her a life of happiness.

"I wanted you," she repeated, her voice breaking.

His expression softened, dulling the edge of his fury. But before a wisp of hope could flare to life in her breast, his countenance shifted, going hard and unyielding once more.

"That is not our life now, Rose." He shoved a hand through his hair, missing the piece on his forehead. "We have expectations we must meet. We have responsibilities. You need to realize that. You need to do better." He stormed into his room, slamming the door behind him, followed by the sharp click of the lock.

Pluto growled in the wake of Theodore's departure.

For Rose's part, that locked door was symbolic.

Yes, this was their life now.

But she did not have to acquiesce.

Her father would whisk her back to America in the blink of an eye if he knew the depth of her misery. She'd kept that knowledge tucked against her heart, unable to give up on Theodore and the life—the joy—they once had.

As much as she longed to flee this miserable life, she longed even more to see her marriage restored. Her fingertips grazed her lower stomach, which had not yet begun to swell. It would soon, though, with their child growing inside her.

No, she was not yet ready to give up hope.

CHAPTER FOURTEEN

Lady Lavinia Cavendish

LAVINIA'S FEET SEEMED SHOD IN LEAD BOOTS when she arrived at the Secret Book Society's next meeting.

Her resolve had been securely in place the night before. Indeed, her determination to share her fears with the other women had been so great, she scarcely slept as she rehearsed what she would say.

Now that she was being led to Lady Duxbury's drawing room, her hands were damp and her thoughts scattered in her brain like a sack of upended marbles.

She entered the room to a chorus of welcomes. The reception was one she still had not grown accustomed to. Not when people ordinarily looked through her.

Here she comes, that odd girl. Don't look her way lest she try to join us.

But not the women of the Secret Book Society. Their warm smiles and dulcet tones made her feel like she belonged.

Would they still be so agreeable once they were privy to her secret?

Lady Duxbury opened their meeting in the usual fashion with delicate cakes, perfectly baked scones and a decadent Victoria

Sponge, her hand steady as she served them all tea. Discussion flowed in its usual fashion as well with mentions of books read and opinions expressed.

Mrs. Clarke loved Jane's temerity in *Jane Eyre* and Mrs. Wharton found the works of Edgar Allan Poe simultaneously distressing and compelling. Lavinia could scarcely concentrate on what was being said, and quickly glossed over her own feelings of *Sense and Sensibility*, which truly had been an excellent book. Especially as never once in the novel was Marianne's behavior described as *hysterical*.

The conversation fell into a comfortable lull. Now was the time.

Lavinia took a breath. But rather than speak, she let out a feeble exhale.

Wordless.

"I believe Lady Lavinia has something she'd like to say." Mrs. Clarke nodded in encouragement.

She truly was skilled at reading people, even what civility and fear masked. Though Lavinia didn't know whether to be relieved or distressed at being announced.

"I haven't shared why I'm here." The air was suddenly difficult to draw in, and her words came out breathless. "That is, why my books were taken away."

"You are not required to do so," Lady Duxbury said gently, offering Lavinia an opportunity to abandon this reckless endeavor.

"I know." Lavinia swallowed, willing her wild heartbeat to calm. "But I wish to. You see, the restriction of my reading material is entirely my fault."

Lady Duxbury's brows pulled down in confusion. Or perhaps concern?

Lavinia was not as adept at reading people as Mrs. Clarke.

They were all watching Lavinia now.

Her mouth was far too dry. She took a hasty sip of tea and set the cup back in its saucer with an unladylike clack. Mrs. Wharton caught her eye and offered a patient smile. Lavinia nodded. She could do this.

"You see, I become too engrossed in books, and am affected in a way my father perceives as destructive. What I mean to say is . . ." Frustration tensed at Lavinia's muscles. She was explaining this wrong. "I feel things too deeply," she tried again. "Especially in novels. All my emotions are too exaggerated. It is not anger which consumes me, but rage. It is not melancholy, but a deep despair. It is not joy, but euphoria. Every feeling is . . . is out of my control."

She paused and everyone remained silent, as though knowing she had not concluded with what needed to be said. "My grandmother behaved in a similar fashion." A lightheadedness sent spots of light dancing in Lavinia's vision. "My grandmother is . . . was . . . in a lunatic asylum."

Their gazes took on a tenderness Lavinia could not bear. She looked at her feet where the tips of her boots peered out from the hem of her white gown. "I'm afraid I, too, will end up in a lunatic asylum."

"Oh, Lavinia." Lady Duxbury said her name softly, pulling Lavinia's attention up to the young widow. Her expression wasn't one of horror or even pity, but instead reflected sympathy, possibly even understanding.

"There is nothing wrong with you, my dear." Lady Duxbury edged forward on her chair, bringing herself closer. "You have passion. That is something to cherish. Something to be celebrated."

Disappointment flooded Lavinia. They didn't understand.

Yes, praise was better than horror, but Lavinia did not want to be placated.

"Will you indulge me for a moment?" Lady Duxbury asked.

Lavinia nodded reluctantly.

"Close your eyes," Lady Duxbury instructed.

Lavinia hesitated only a moment before complying.

"Now, think about your anger and explain what that feels like to you," Lady Duxbury said.

A frown pulled at Lavinia's mouth.

What it feels like?

What a curious request.

"I want you to detail every moment of your experience with anger," Lady Duxbury continued, her smooth voice mesmerizing. "How the emotion starts, how it builds, what happens when you *feel* all that rage. Describe every layer."

Lavinia remained quiet a moment as she objectively analyzed her feelings.

"My chest draws tight, muscles tense, like a vessel prepared for the ensuing storm," she said, focusing on the darkness behind her lids and the memory of the last time anger had consumed her. "The burning starts in my breast, embers that catch like kindling, flaring to life and swelling with flames that whip into a wicked conflagration. That force is trapped within me, a wild thing confined, clawing to be freed, writhing in desperation that is both helpless and powerful. My throat aches as the rage scorches up before emerging from my mouth in a scream that leaves me raw and yet, to the rest of the world, the sound falls completely silent."

As the final detail left Lavinia's lips, her heart pounded at the memory, her words fast and choppy, delivered as they came to her.

"Now describe sorrow." Lady Duxbury's voice startled Lavinia from a strange trance she had somehow fallen into.

Before Lavinia could question the request, her mind was already stirring the depth of despondency, of such sadness as she had ever experienced.

"My sorrow is a flat lake in the middle of the darkest night, the water like ink, so black it absorbs the light, refusing to reflect even the moon. The water is cold as ice yet does not freeze. There is no movement in the water. It is still. Dead. Hopeless.

A pebble tossed into its depths is swallowed as readily as the reflection of the moon, trapped for all eternity. A prisoner in a bottomless well of despondency."

Her heart slowed as she spoke, her words reflecting the very emotion she described.

"That's what I wanted to hear." Lady Duxbury's voice made Lavinia slowly blink her eyes open.

There was a jarring moment of realization that she was still in Lady Duxbury's drawing room with the others, their eyes wide, their mouths slightly agape.

In shock.

Horror?

Fear prickled at Lavinia's scalp. What had she done?

They had been ready to accept her only moments before, and now she had shown them her madness, illustrated with damning details that left no room for questioning her lunacy.

She had erred in a most egregious way.

CHAPTER FIFTEEN

Mrs. Eleanor Clarke

ELEANOR COULD NOT STOP STARING AT LADY Lavinia. No, not staring—gaping, entirely enraptured.

The reserved young woman who scarcely said more than a sentence had transformed.

Lady Lavinia's voice had been strong when she spoke of anger, her words filled with a power that made Eleanor experience the emotion, her own voice joining that scream the rest of the world did not hear.

The scream of obedience.

The scream of being a good daughter, a good wife.

The scream of a woman's plight.

Lady Lavinia's eyes darted around the room and filled with tears. "I should not—"

"That was beautiful," Eleanor whispered.

"Exquisite," Mrs. Wharton echoed in agreement.

Lady Lavinia blinked. "I . . . I beg your pardon?"

"You aren't plagued with madness, my dear," Lady Duxbury said. "You are gifted with passion."

Lady Lavinia's lips twisted with doubt.

"'Strange fits of passion have I known . . .'" Lady Duxbury began.

Mrs. Wharton smiled. "William Wordsworth."

"Precisely." Lady Duxbury jabbed the air with her forefinger. "Lady Lavinia, if you were a man, you'd be lauded as a poet. Like Wordsworth. Or Lord Byron."

"Or Edgar Allan Poe," Mrs. Wharton added.

"But because you are a woman . . ." Lady Duxbury shook her head, her mouth tucked down at the corners.

A vast emptiness opened in Eleanor as she finished Lady Duxbury's thought. "She is relegated to madness."

"Madness. Hysteria. Lunacy." Lady Duxbury smirked and let her fingers play over the top of her brooch. "But that doesn't mean you cannot write poetry. I dare say, I think you should. You have an artist's soul. What you are feeling is the fire of creativity burning to be free. Stop suppressing what you need. Put your pen to page the next time you experience the stirring of emotion and liberate your passion."

Lady Lavinia's delicate neck muscles strained against her skin, and her eyes shone with a brilliance that filled Eleanor with undeniable envy.

"Will you do it?" Lady Duxbury asked.

Lady Lavinia nodded, the motion tight, but vigorous. "I will."

"I'll follow you to the library." Lady Duxbury pushed elegantly to her feet, the lilac silk of her dress rustling as she led the way. "I know I do not normally make suggestions, but you may wish to consider *Aurora Leigh* by Elizabeth Barrett Browning. She was a poet who published under her own name."

She entered the library and scanned a row of spines before plucking a book with a light blue cover from the shelves.

Lavinia accepted *Aurora Leigh* with reverence. "She published in her own name?"

For decades—possibly centuries—female authors and poets assumed men's names to be taken seriously and have their works printed. Authors like George Sand and George Eliot, and even Jane Austen, who simply published under the title: "by A Lady."

"She did." Lady Duxbury handed the book to Lavinia. "Ironically, the work is about a woman's pursuit of a career as an author. I think you will find the story inspiring. Or, at the very least, edifying."

"You certainly have the talent," Mrs. Wharton added. "I *felt* your words when you spoke. You have a gift."

Lady Lavinia's face went red as she murmured her thanks. But despite her apparent embarrassment at being the focus of so much praise, her back was straighter, her shoulders squared with quiet confidence. She was a woman coming to realize her gifts and learning to embrace the beauty of her true nature. The first tentative steps upon a path that might take a lifetime to tread.

The young woman's passion was inspiring. And what she said was astonishing, to know that beneath the surface, other women were experiencing the same deep feelings. For of the two emotions Lavinia stated with such poetic eloquence, Eleanor most understood anger.

Those embers had been glowing in her for the whole of her life, first as a dutiful daughter and then as a biddable wife. Her experiences with the Secret Book Society stoked new flames to lick at the injustices of her world: her husband's sharp words of reprimand, his rough hands administering punishment, the nightly duties of a wife who was never allowed to say no, the pitifully small world to which she was confined.

She had tried to speak up. A single shake of her head when she dared deny Cecil. Even now her skin throbbed with bruises that resulted in her absence at Mrs. Baskin's dinner party the night before.

The understanding that other women felt as trapped as Eleanor was one of relief and frustration. For how long would women be held under the thumb of men? How long until they broke free?

Eleanor hovered near the bookshelves while Lady Lavinia carried *Aurora Leigh* to her chair as the countess departed the room, lilac skirts swishing elegantly behind her. With Mrs. Wharton similarly occupied, Eleanor pressed the little knot in the wood.

In Lady Duxbury's previous entry, she was in a delicate way, agreeing to marriage only to protect her child.

Though Eleanor had wanted to ask after Lady Duxbury's child among acquaintances, doing so would have been unseemly. Especially when the tenor of her three dead husbands always remained in the chorus of London's gossip.

Diary in hand, Eleanor sank into the chair she regularly occupied and opened the cover to read the next entry.

CHAPTER SIXTEEN

Lady Duxbury's Diary

January 1879

I never knew how deeply I could love.

Not my husband. He's a profligate and a philanderer. If nothing else, his nightly endeavors keep him from my bedchamber.

No, my effusions of love are for my son.

George Edmund Edwards, the future Viscount Morset, has absolutely stolen my heart.

I am enamored of every aspect of my child to the point of losing hours gazing at his small face. The way the gaslights play off the rounded tip of his nose, how his diminutive hand can grip my own with such ferocity, as though he is as loath to let me go as I am him.

He latches on to my heart every time I stare into his eyes, the most beautiful velvety brown, flecked with black and gold.

I never thought I could love so truly. I never thought I would experience affection in such ineffable quantity.

Edmund, my husband, sees our son only as an heir, useless until George is of age to begin education in his duties. I am grateful

Edmund does not question the healthy weight of a child born over a month before his time.

My husband is not so indifferent to me. He is quick with his censure, heaping his disappointment at our unfavorable marriage at my feet. Despite my mother's promises, this union has not facilitated the return of my beloved books. Austen and the Brontë sisters, Dickens and Poe, all my dearest friends denied to me once more.

I endure the abasement and abject misery for my son.

For where there is love, I can survive any amount of hate.

And despite that hate, I have never in all my life been happier.

CHAPTER SEVENTEEN

Mrs. Rose Wharton

ROSE HAD FOUND HEAVEN ON EARTH.

She lay against a sumptuous wall of pillows with Pluto snoring softly in her lap and *Jane Eyre* propped in her hands. The story was entirely worth the wait for her turn to read it. A plucky heroine with the boldness to speak her mind—Jane was a protagonist Rose could cheer for.

A bowl of grapes sat on the table beside Rose, and she indulgently reached for the plumpest one, popping it into her mouth. The book dipped slightly in her hand as she did so and Pluto's ear flicked at the disturbance.

"Rose." Theodore's voice boomed on the other side of the door connecting their rooms.

Before she could even consider secreting her book under Pluto's round body, the door flew open and Theodore stepped in, distractedly pinching the starched cuffs extending from his jacket sleeves. "Have you seen the cuff links you gave me for—"

Rose went still, the book frozen in her hand.

"For our wedding," he finished slowly as his eyes narrowed. "What is that?"

The grape was barely chewed, but she swallowed it down

with an unladylike gulp and pointed to Pluto with her free hand. "This sweet thing? Why, husband, surely you are well acquainted with our dashing little pug, Pluto."

Pluto's soft snore ended abruptly at the sound of his name, but he did not open his eyes.

"I don't mean Pluto and you well know it." Theodore jabbed his index finger to the book. "I mean *that*."

She gave an aggrieved sigh. "Well, if you must know, it's *Jane Eyre*."

"That isn't from our library."

"How very astute of you." She casually turned the page and devoted her focus to the book once more.

"You know you aren't supposed to be reading those novels."

"Those novels," she repeated slowly. "Do you mean ones where the heroines have actual thoughts that extend beyond what a woman should put upon the table at night, or how best to please her husband?"

Theodore's chin angled downward in irritation. "Don't be cross. You know Byron thinks those novels are rubbish, filling women's minds with nonsense."

"What Byron thinks." Rose scoffed at her brother-in-law's words coming out of her husband's mouth. Pluto shifted grumpily off her lap, sensing her irritation. "What do *you* think, Theodore?"

He ran a hand through his hair in a way Rose had once found endearing. Now the action was reminiscent of all the times he'd done so in frustration at her shortcomings. "I think we both have a long way to go until we can properly represent the family as earl and countess."

His neatly pomaded hair jutted up slightly.

Perhaps it *was* still endearing.

"I know you find the restrictions disagreeable," Theodore continued, his tone gentle in a way she assumed he meant to be persuasive. "I've endured restrictions as well."

She clamped her mouth shut on an argument about her own unhappiness. Because he was right. His entire world had flipped when the terminal nature of Byron's cancer was pronounced, leaving Theodore with the burden of the future earldom. *Their* entire world. She was not the only one who was unhappy.

Gone were the languid days traipsing through museums together and the evenings whiled away at Covent Garden. Gone were the shopping holidays to prepare the townhouse precisely how they desired rather than how decorum dictated. Gone were the easy smiles and lack of concern for what transpired in the world and Society around them.

Rose wished she'd known then how very ephemeral those moments would be. They wouldn't have been squandered so carelessly but savored, to cherish in these hard days.

"I don't share my mother's feelings," Rose said softly, referring to the letter that had precipitated his ire in their last argument, from which they had still not fully recovered. "I never wanted to be countess. I still do not."

Color flushed Theodore's cheeks. "And I don't want to be an earl, but we don't have a choice, Rose. Byron will likely not survive the year." There was a catch to his voice that snagged at her heart. "We have to play by the rules," he continued, rallying. "Which means you need more allies among the women in Society. This would all be so much easier if you weren't so set in your ways, if you didn't perpetually displease Byron." He gestured to *Jane Eyre* still propped in her hands. "It's just a bloody book."

"My ways?" She set the book aside and Pluto grumbled, hopping off the bed. "You fell in love with me for my ways, and now I'm forced to become someone I never wanted to be." Her voice climbed higher as her composure crumbled. "I wear the clothes you tell me to wear. I engage in the dullest conversations about the weather and gossip about people I don't know with those you wish me to impress. And yet, no matter how diligently I apply myself, I say the wrong thing. I do the wrong thing. I *am* the wrong thing."

"I'm asking you to try harder, not to be someone different." Theodore's voice rose in mutual frustration. "Stop filling your head with that rubbish." He flung his hand toward the book, the movement crisp with anger.

"It's not rubbish," she shot back. "It's an escape from this wretched existence."

Pluto growled on the floor below.

"Those books are the catalyst for your foolhardy thoughts," Theodore bellowed. "Those women in novels who aren't obedient, they encourage you. I *demand* you stop reading at once."

Rose leaped to her feet, her spine snapping ramrod straight. "Absolutely not."

Theodore's brows shot up. "I beg your pardon?"

"I said absolutely not. I will read what I like despite how often you regurgitate your brother's words to me."

"Now, see here . . ." Theodore moved forward, his manner aggressive.

He hadn't gone half a step when Pluto darted forward with a savage growl unlike any Rose had ever heard from her coddled lap dog. His lip curled, baring his small teeth amid a low, menacing snarl.

He'd been the runt of the litter, and though plump, he still weighed less than half a stone. And now he bravely put the whole of his body in front of her. To protect her.

His intrepid spirit and selfless love squeezed at her heart.

Theodore was not unaffected and paused, mid-step, setting his foot down gently. The rise of color in his face dissipated and he sighed, the sound heavy with defeat.

"Come, Pluto." He knelt and reached tentatively toward Rose's brave little warrior, whose hackles were still up. "I didn't mean to be frightening." Theodore's softened gaze lifted to Rose. "To either of you."

Rose pulled the book to her chest and wrapped her arms protectively around the cover, her chin tipped up in defiance.

Pluto acquiesced to his master's affections, felled with a scratch behind an ear that set his stocky back leg kicking.

Theodore offered one final stroke on Pluto's head and stood. "Please direct your reading pursuits to more wifely endeavors." He cast an imploring look at Rose, one she'd been powerless to resist early in their courtship. "Please."

"I'll simply reread my copy of *Mrs. Beeton's Book of Household Management*," she offered sweetly.

He smirked, clearly aware of her sarcasm. They both knew she'd never read that ridiculous book. But rather than continue to fight, he slowly walked toward his room, his cuffs loose without the missing links, and closed the door between them.

Rose stared after the door for a long moment, thoughts racing with all the things she could have said. All the things she had not.

Because she knew her husband beyond his preference for beef over pork for dinner parties, or the exact way he liked his shirts starched, or that he read *The London Journal* before any other newspaper in the morning. She had at her disposal an arsenal of weapons she could have used against him, each sharpened to a razor's edge with knowledge. His sensitivity toward his family's financial straits and the necessity of Rose's fortune to save them from ruin. The feelings of inadequacy he faced with the looming assumption of the earldom. His fears over his intellectual shortcomings and his inability to quickly acquire the necessary skills for the role.

Yes, she could have taken any one of those daggers and slipped them into the parts of him that were the most raw and tender, for she knew those, too.

And yet, she did not.

Because despite the disagreeable turn of their marriage, and despite her husband echoing her brother-in-law's displeasure, Rose still loved her husband.

Wholly. Completely.

Unfortunately.

A fluttering sensation in her womb interrupted her thoughts. She put a hand to her stomach, uncertain if she'd imagined it. Curious if she might experience the feeling again.

She did, though this time the movement was like the flick of a small fish inside her womb. She exhaled a shaky breath.

Their baby had quickened. No longer was the quandary of her future an invisible problem.

Pluto leaped onto the bed and flopped beside her.

She lowered the book to the mattress, absently petting her brave dog with one hand, while resting the other on her stomach in a moment filled with a maternal elation, and the undeniable taste of fear.

She was running out of time.

CHAPTER EIGHTEEN

Mrs. Eleanor Clarke

ELEANOR WAITED IN THE LIBRARY FOR HER SON to be brought down from the nursery, her body tense with an anticipation that wound tighter every hour since she'd last seen him. Her pale yellow day dress was light and hopeful. The way she felt on the mornings she was allowed to see William.

"This best not take long," Cecil groused from behind a spread newspaper. "I have an appointment in half an hour."

"Oh, Cecil, do be patient," Eleanor ventured delicately. "He's our son."

"He can't even speak properly yet. You mark my word, he won't remember a moment of this as an adult." Cecil lowered the paper and gave her a sardonic smirk.

Before she could reply, he snapped the paper upright once more and spoke from behind the wall of print. "I don't care for that gown on you. The color is unflattering."

His criticism tore through the joy she'd clutched onto only moments ago, but still she held tight to those shreds, desperate for any scrap of happiness she could salvage.

The door swung open, and the nurse carried William in on her hip.

"William." Eleanor rushed to her son, pulled forward on a wave of light and love and everything wondrous.

Her son squealed in delight, his chubby hands lifting for her to take him into her arms, the same way he did before Cecil insisted she coddled the boy and restricted her time with him. She pulled her son's familiar weight against her and he immediately wrapped his small arms and legs about her, clutching to her with every part of himself.

His hair was silky against her cheek and smelled of soap and that precious, ineffable fragrance toddlers somehow possessed. She breathed him in, her soul at peace.

Lady Duxbury's diary entry came back to Eleanor as she held her son, reminding her of how great a mother's love for her child could be. And how that love could give her strength to survive any amount of hate. Such words were perfectly stated, especially in a situation Eleanor knew far too well.

She hugged her son to her, rocking slightly, wishing she could hold him like this forever.

June.

In June, when Cecil left for Peru, she would see William every day. Multiple times a day.

She would savor that rare time with her son, harvesting memories to sustain her through Cecil's return, when the grip of his control over her life turned to iron once more.

Quickly, she brushed the thought aside. Cecil always seemed to sense when she anticipated something. Hope was yet another tool he used against her, wielding it to ensure her submission.

William lifted his hand, revealing a blue spinning top in the cradle of his palm. "Look."

"Shall we spin it?" Eleanor asked, settling onto the floor with him. The corset of her day dress was more forgiving than those of her finer garments, but was still by no means comfortable, and she sat at an awkward angle beside him.

"Mrs. Clarke, you are the lady of the house," Cecil said disparagingly. "Not some pet flopping onto the ground."

Eleanor ignored him and spun the small top, so it twirled round and round on its thread-thin spindle. William watched in wide-eyed wonder.

Though Eleanor's time with him was woefully short, these were the moments she loved best, when she could see the world through his eyes.

To her, the top was a bit of carved wood that required altogether too much effort to keep spinning. But to William, there was magic in the rapidity of the revolution that drew the top up from its side to dance in circles across the glossy hardwood floor. He was delighted, and therefore, so was she.

When the top eventually slowed and tipped back to the earth, Eleanor was already picking it up before William could shout "Again!"

This was repeated thrice more, and each time Eleanor and William laughed with shared pleasure as the top set off on its course. The moment was simple and beautiful and left Eleanor's heart feeling almost too large for her chest.

Cecil abruptly lowered his paper. "That is damn well enough."

The top tipped to a clattering stop, as if commanded by Cecil's mood.

He nodded at the nurse. "Return William to the nursery. I have a meeting I must attend, and Mrs. Clarke must prepare for her luncheon."

"My luncheon is not for three more hours," Eleanor protested. "We've only been here several minutes. Might I stay longer? Please?" She pulled her son into her arms in a feeble curl of her body around him, a subconscious act of protection.

"So you can spoil him?" Cecil snorted derisively. "The boy will grow up weak."

That familiar anger prickled at the back of Eleanor's mind, sharp jabbing needles of indignation; the unfairness of a woman's lot in life.

She should remain quiet—the burgeoning fear inside her told her as much. But she was tired of being quiet, tired of being obedient, of quelling the rage burning in her, exactly as Lavinia had described.

Though the moment of Cecil's criticism was no different than before, Eleanor herself was no longer the same.

Her time with the Secret Book Society made her see the world in a different light, that other women suffered as she did, that they were relegated to a lower rung on the hierarchy of man, that their opinions not only did not matter, but were also seen as a threat.

Cecil pushed to his feet, busying himself with folding the newspaper as he turned away. The matter settled in his mind.

"I thought you said William wouldn't remember these days when he grew to adulthood," she retorted.

Cecil stopped and turned slowly to her.

"What did you say?" His voice was low, dangerous.

Eleanor's heart was a drum, her panic banging in wild crescendo. "I'm pointing out that if he will not remember these days, then my staying longer with him will be irrelevant. I . . . I should like very much to stay. Please." There was a tremor to her voice.

Fear.

Cecil could smell it, taste the metallic tang of it in the air like a snake.

Eleanor tightened her grip on William.

Cecil stepped closer, bending over her, his face florid as he issued a single word in a low growl. "No."

Bravado had led Eleanor into unchartered waters, tossing her about in a torrent of emotions with no certainty but what lay on the other side of his wrath. She knew well the consequences waiting for her when she was alone in her room later with Cecil.

And yet, desperation pricked at her, urging her onward. She'd waited a full day to see William and had scarcely spent a quarter of an hour with him. "Please, Cecil, I—"

He leaned over where she sat on the floor, holding their child in her arms, and jabbed his pointer finger at her face, stopping just before the tip of her nose. "No." His voice was a boom of unquestioning finality.

Humiliation burned in her cheeks, at the nurse witnessing his treatment of her, at her son seeing his mother so demeaned. In the end, her fear of Cecil was not what quelled her arguments; it was that scorch of mortification.

"Nurse, take the boy upstairs," Cecil said sharply, not bothering to call the young woman by her name.

Eleanor struggled to her feet with William still cradled against her. "Please, Nurse Susan."

Cecil scowled at Eleanor and stomped from the room.

The nurse leaned toward Eleanor to extract William from her embrace. Though Eleanor tried halfheartedly to dislodge his grip on her, he refused to go with the nurse.

"Mama." His cry muffled against Eleanor's sleeve.

"I'm sorry, ma'am." Nurse Susan pulled gently at William, clearly flustered.

An ache knotted in Eleanor's throat as her son was wrested away. The warmth where his body had lain so comfortably against her own seeped away, leaving her cold and bereft.

She wouldn't see him for two more days, and that seemed so terribly long. The threat of tears tingled in her nose and stung her eyes. Being separated from her son was too painful, the stretch of time too great.

But she had to push away such thoughts. She had to be brave for her boy.

William twisted and writhed in Nurse Susan's grasp, reaching for Eleanor with shrieks of protest.

"Come now, William, we must go upstairs." The young woman's patient voice wobbled with the effort to contain her thrashing charge.

All at once, William ceased his struggle and turned to Nurse Susan, his sweet face hardening into a hateful expression. He jabbed a finger toward the young woman and forcefully expelled a single word. "No."

Horror washed over Eleanor.

She stood motionless as the nurse carried William away, too stunned to issue an apology on behalf of her son.

No.

The word resounded in Eleanor's mind, echoing between father and son.

If left to Cecil's influence, would William become like his father? Those ready smiles growing ugly and cruel, the warmth of his affection chilling into apathy?

No matter how desperately she wanted to believe William's sweetness would last forever, he would surely learn Cecil's behavior. Today it was his nurse, but how soon until he turned his disapprobation upon Eleanor, his own mother?

A visceral ache clenched in her chest.

She could not bear for her darling William to become like Cecil.

But was there a way out?

CHAPTER NINETEEN

Mrs. Rose Wharton

ROSE HADN'T TOUCHED THE SCONE ON HER plate. Usually, the scones at Lady Duxbury's were among her favorites. So, too, were the rose-shaped honey-spice cakes.

She hadn't touched those, either.

Her stomach dipped with an anxiety that had grown familiar since her babe quickened. When the sands of time began to sift between her fingers.

Would remaining with Theodore be best for the child?

Having a father was important.

But to be consigned to the life of an earl's offspring would be suffocating. A daughter born to become a dutiful wife, or a son sculpted for a noble role.

In the days since the babe moved within her, she had sought to distract herself, throwing any spare time she had toward the Society for the Advancement of the Poor. Her frequent visits allowed her the opportunity to become acquainted with those who appeared often for whatever help could be procured.

Most were under the age of fifteen, ill-fitted in coarse hodden gray, and she'd come to know too many of them. Bess, who collected food for her entire family on Monday, her nails blue from helping her mother with laundry that took days to wash and distribute to clients. Simon, whose small body bent over like an old man when he coughed and whose eyes shone with gratitude when Rose brought him a draught to help. A draught that would likely only offer temporary comfort to a fatal infection.

And Sam. Sam was perhaps her favorite. He was a spritely boy of around twelve, missing his front tooth and eager to do any chore for a spare shilling. When he wasn't in line for food, that generally meant he was running about shining shoes with the other boys of the Boot-black Brigade who wandered the streets. That, or he'd picked up work as a ladderman, climbing impossibly high scaffolding to paste bills onto advertising boards. While dangerous, the task paid more than any other pasting role and most grown men refused to go up that high. He'd told her this with a note of pride, grinning without a care for his missing tooth.

He saved every penny after paying rent for him and his mother, intending to buy a pair of horses, hire a cart and obtain a license to drive a Hansom. When he did, he wanted to paint roses on the carriage's side that matched those embroidered on Rose's boots.

The boy was a charmer.

She always set aside a meal for him on the days he did not arrive in time for the food line, and came up with small tasks he might do for a few coins.

Never in Rose's life had she seen someone more determined to elevate themselves from their lot in life. And truly, the lives they led in Whitechapel were trying indeed. The air was choked with smog and the streets squelching with mud and filth. There was not enough food, not enough housing. Not enough love.

Rose blinked herself back to the Secret Book Society, realizing with a start that everyone was staring at her. She pulled her hand from where it had been resting on her stomach. "I beg your pardon?"

"What are your thoughts on *Jane Eyre*?" Mrs. Clarke tilted her head as if assessing Rose's countenance.

"I didn't finish it," Rose admitted with a sigh. "Unfortunately, my husband found me reading. When I didn't heed his order to set the book aside, it disappeared from my nightstand." Rose worked to keep the anger from her voice. "After three days of scouring our home, I located the book in one of his office drawers. But what I have read, I've enjoyed. I also now understand why men think books are so dangerous to women."

"Oh?" Lady Duxbury raised a brow.

Rose lifted her chin as she replied, "Jane reminds us that we have a choice. That we are not relegated to the paths men carve for us but can forge ahead on a road of our own making."

Her palm had somehow wandered to her stomach. Quickly and without thought, she snatched her hand away.

"Not all men," Lady Lavinia said with a wistful smile.

"Is there someone in particular you have in mind?" There was a coy tone to Lady Duxbury's question, and Lady Lavinia's face went pink.

"A gentleman I have recently met." Her eyes sparkled.

Ah, to be young and in love.

A pang of jealousy echoed through Rose. No, not jealousy— sorrow, for the way her own romantic notions had been so turned on their head by reality.

Whoever the gentleman was had better treat Lady Lavinia with care, or he would have Rose to answer to. And likely the rest of the Secret Book Society as well.

"He defends women, standing up for them," Lady Lavinia continued. "He . . . empowers me." She gave a soft exhale of a laugh with her shy admission.

"Not all men are narrow-minded," Lady Duxbury agreed, her gaze staring into the distance as she was clearly gripped by a memory. Her fingertips swept over the hair brooch at her breast.

Rose found herself wondering about the curious piece of jewelry for the countless time, driven to distraction as to whose hair could be so neatly crisscrossed beneath the crystal cap.

Mrs. Clarke lightly massaged her temples, wincing slightly.

"Are you well, Mrs. Clarke?" Rose asked.

"Forgive me." Mrs. Clarke gave a shy smile of apology before pulling at her sleeves, easing them perfectly into place. "I have a bit of a headache today."

Lady Duxbury's fingers fell from her brooch. "Actually, before we adjourn to the library today, I have something I've been meaning to share." She rang the bell to summon the maid. "Herbs for various remedies. Beyond what many of you already know, of course, from the general curatives detailed in *Notes on Nursing*. And far more effective than the ostensible 'cure-all' blue pill every chemist advertises. Heaven knows what's truly in them."

Like every woman in England, Rose had a copy of Florence Nightingale's *Notes on Nursing* in the library and referred to the text regularly. Her interest was piqued.

The maid entered the room, and Lady Duxbury addressed her as Otis watched them with his unabashed stare. "Mary, be a dear and bring me my book of herbs, please."

The young maid bobbed an agreeable curtsy and disappeared, but not before Rose caught sight of the scars twisting over her small hands. Rose recalled what her own maid had said about the girl and her family.

Mary was the eldest at thirteen and had worked at a cotton mill the last five years. Her sister, only two years behind, worked there as well. A third sister had not survived the ordeals of their brutal employment. For when nimble hands fell slow with exhaustion from sixteen-hour days, machines did not stop the steady grind of their gears.

Last summer, Mary, too, had fallen prey to those machines. While she had escaped with her life, her hands paid the price, so mangled, she was unable to work. The loss of two incomes threatened them with the poorhouse before Lady Duxbury happened upon them.

Mary returned with the book in her scarred hands and Lady Duxbury thanked her with a grateful smile. Most parents did not treat even their own children with such benevolence.

Lady Duxbury had not only taken in the small grieving family, she had also paid for the extensive care for Mary's hands, restoring them as well as could be with the advancements in modern medicine.

While Rose once found Lady Duxbury's choice of employment a curious notion, the many hours spent in Whitechapel cast the situation in a new light. Lady Duxbury's generosity kept the family from being one of the many lining up daily for food, while enabling them to retain their dignity and pride.

"Herbs may seem provincial among the plentiful offerings at the chemist," Lady Duxbury continued. "But many pills and tonics sold contain substances that can prove unreliable and harmful." She wrapped her fingers around the massive book in her lap. "Arsenic, phosphorus, mercury and so many more. Oftentimes the water used to make these medicines is not clean, exposing one to further dangers."

Rose recalled the murky water at Whitechapel, used for drinking, cooking and cleaning.

"But what comes from the earth can be quite efficacious." The book creaked as Lady Duxbury drew it open, revealing rows of neat penmanship and the occasionally drawn flower or herb. "Everything from headaches to sleeplessness to pain from one's courses." She paused with a smile. "Such things ought not be mentioned, but how can relief be found when secrets are kept? Forgive the vulgarity, but any number of woman's issues might be addressed within these pages. Without embarrassment or scorn or judgment. Amid the list of general ailments, you'll also find a section on woman's courses and afflictions."

They all leaned forward collectively to see a carefully hand-written index.

"There are aids for everything from being with child to caring for children," Lady Duxbury pressed on, still turning the pages with apparent reverence.

Rose went still.

Why was Lady Duxbury mentioning the book now of all times? Was it because of Mrs. Clarke's headache? Or had Lady Duxbury seen Rose touching her stomach?

Perhaps Rose's secret was beginning to show.

She clasped her hands in her lap to refrain from the temptation of touching the small curve of her belly. Her child fluttered about within her, beckoning the embrace of her palm.

Lady Duxbury set the book on the table. "I'll leave this here for anyone to peruse in private while we adjourn to our reading."

Rose followed the other two women into the library, but her thoughts remained in the drawing room. Not only was her curiosity piqued by Lady Duxbury's words, but a new concern for her child's well-being lingered in her mind as well. Were the pills from the chemist truly so bad?

And what of arsenic?

What woman did not take an arsenic wafer from time to time, letting the bitterness melt upon her tongue in hope of a clearer complexion? And if blue pills were disagreeable for the body, how did they continue to be so effective?

Or at least so popular . . .

Rose hesitated at the doorway to the library. Lady Lavinia sat in her chair with *Aurora Leigh* in her lap, still enchanted with the idea of a woman publishing poetry under her own name. As well she should be. Such aspirations ought to be attainable for women, especially ones with her talent.

Mrs. Clarke hovered near her usual spot by the bookshelf

as she so often did. Rose had wandered by there once and saw nothing of note, yet the location continued to draw Mrs. Clarke. How strange.

Mrs. Clarke regarded Rose suddenly from across the room and gave a cautious smile, the kind one gave when they did not wish to be the object of someone's notice.

Perhaps she'd found a scintillating book? If so, Rose hoped she would share the title.

Rose turned from the library, leaving Mrs. Clarke to her secrets.

The drawing room was blessedly empty, save for the numerous potted plants around her and the partially cleared table of refreshments. Rose sat on the settee beside a particularly lovely pot of daisies and lifted the weight of the book into her lap. Her gaze skimmed the list: agues, blocked digestion, fever, pimples, plague of the nerves, pregnancy.

Her finger settled on *good health for the unborn child*, indicating page twenty-seven. Rose flipped to the page and found a list of herbs alongside a drawing of fenugreek with a considerable amount of information written beneath in neat print. Just as she wished she could write down the information, she noticed a stack of paper and fountain pen nearby.

Lady Duxbury had thought of everything.

Hastily, Rose wrote down the ingredients for a healthy mother's tea, as well as the formula for pimple curative, and vowed to never touch another arsenic wafer again.

She was grateful for the advice on her health and that of her baby. She was equally appreciative for Lady Duxbury's discretion, for clearly she suspected Rose was in a delicate way.

And though she'd tried not to notice, there were strange items of note in the index of herbal remedies, including a tincture of belladonna and how to crush foxglove safely. Rose could not stop herself from wondering that with such a book, what secrets the countess herself might be keeping.

CHAPTER TWENTY

Lady Duxbury's Diary

August 1883

I fear for my son's life.

His inheritance most certainly, but foremost, his life.

Threatened by his own father. Or rather, his perceived father, Viscount Morset.

Alice—my false friend—has edged her way into my life once more. I note false friend as her perfidious nature was revealed to me after her confession to my parents of my affair with Elias, and she continues her assault on my life even now. She sought my forgiveness then and I grudgingly gave it. After all, with such knowledge, she could ruin me.

Worse, she could ruin George.

And now she has.

Two years prior, she married the Earl of Meddleson, a man of great influence. From what I understand, the union is not a happy one and Alice—Lady Meddleson—remains barren.

Claiming to be burdened still by my secret, she approached my husband, informing him of the truth of George's origin.

After Alice's visit, he accused me of deceiving him, and laid

*hands on me with such violence, I worried I might not survive
to protect my son. As our marriage began, I am once more under
lock and key, immured in the prison of my home.*

*Though on this occasion, I am more concerned for my son than
my own well-being.*

*My husband's rage is savage and knows no bounds, which his
treatment of me today has proven. But the wounds he inflicted
upon me can be tended to by my maid, a gentle soul whose book
of curatives has been passed down to her through the hands of her
mother and grandmother.*

*Beyond the brutality against my person, Edmund has at-
tacked my beautiful library, one I have never even been able to
access. I am disconsolate as I recount his fiendish delight when he
tossed my books into the hearth. The lot of them, kept under lock
and key like beautiful songbirds, were liberated for a scant second
only to be tossed into the flames. The characters whom I love like
friends and whose authors spoke to my heart, the adventures I
once journeyed and meant to revisit, were consumed in a conflagration of bibliocide.*

*If Edmund has visited such violence upon both my library and
my person, what will he do to my child?*

The very thought leaves me tremulous.

*I am shaking at my overwhelming enmity toward Lady Med-
dleson. I do not understand how a woman can turn so on another
woman. Let alone someone who is a friend. Should we women
not help one another in this world where we have so little power?*

*I must find a way to stop Edmund before George suffers at his
hand—in any number of ways. Even broken, bruised and bleeding, a mother will do anything to protect her child.*

Anything.

CHAPTER TWENTY-ONE

Lady Eleanor Clarke

ELEANOR LOWERED THE DIARY, HER BREATH coming fast, pressing her expanding ribs uncomfortably against her corset. A terrible fury vibrated within her.

How could a man be so cruel as to threaten a child?

Quickly, she turned the page to sample what was to come next.

January 1886

If my mother were still alive, she'd be immensely pleased to find I am no longer a viscountess, but a countess.

There was not time to read another entry, not if Eleanor wanted to keep the diary a secret. But a quick skim confirmed what Eleanor suspected: Lady Duxbury's first husband had died.

No details were presented.

There had been many rumors about the countess and her three dead husbands, suspicion of foul play.

No one believed the gossip, of course, or the countess would be a pariah. In reality, she was highly sought after for social engagements, likely due to her infrequent attendance.

But even if the whispers of her husbands' untimely deaths were true, Eleanor would not blame Lady Duxbury if such drastic measures saved her son. Especially after suffering such abuse.

Eleanor could not help but appreciate the immense relief the countess must have felt upon her husband's death.

To never be held prisoner again, to never be restricted from life again. To never be struck again.

Eleanor shifted her hold on the book, her right wrist aching and weak from where Cecil had roughly yanked her arm. Her head throbbed despite having taken one of the blue pills before coming to the Secret Book Society. Perhaps she ought to consider Lady Duxbury's book of herbs after all.

Except that Mrs. Wharton had gone to explore its contents.

Before the other woman could join them in the library, Eleanor took the opportunity to return the diary to its secret location, her thoughts tumbling over the familiar name.

Lady Meddleson.

Eleanor knew the woman well. Tidy blond curls, wide blue eyes like a China doll, blinking and sweetly innocent. She was a woman of great importance, for her husband was by far the most appealing earl to be found in the pages of *Debrett's*. Her acceptance or disapproval could make or break a woman's reputation.

And there had been many broken by a single word from the esteemed Lady Meddleson.

Eleanor had never trusted the woman whose overly delicate voice seemed even less genuine than her insincere smiles.

Mrs. Wharton appeared after the diary was once more concealed behind the hidden door. She gave a quick, secretive lift of her brows before assuming her place by the window.

The book of herbs in the drawing room was now free to peruse, and Eleanor could not deny she was curious. Knowledge of herbal remedies could be beneficial in the event William fell ill. Certainly, a few herbs were a far cry better than the barbaric act of bloodletting. There might even be a curative for Cecil's foul mood.

That thought caught in her mind and led to another consideration.

If Lady Duxbury knew ways to heal, might she also know ways to harm?

The diary entry remained with Eleanor through the day and carried her into the evening. When she finished speaking with the cook to accommodate a last-minute guest Cecil invited, she returned to her room to prepare for dinner.

A vibrant magenta gown lay out on the bed.

She looked to her maid in surprise. "This isn't what I chose to wear."

When Eleanor had been younger, she'd enjoyed brilliant jewel tones. Now they were too bright for the dullness of her spirit.

But even when she wore those vivid colors, she'd always avoided magenta. The bright purple-red color had been named for Napoleon's victory over the Austrians after a battle in Italy, the color said to represent the blood spilled. She would never have ordered something with such a macabre history.

Before her maid could answer, the adjoining door between her room and Cecil's flew open. He wore only his white linen shirt buttoned up over the great bulk of his belly. "Ah, you've returned." His hand flicked to the gown on the bed. "I had that made for you. Wear it tonight."

She stared at the dress, the final scrap of her autonomy being snatched away.

"That was generous of you," she demurred. "But unnecessary. I already had something selected."

"That gray monstrosity?" He scoffed. "One would think you're in mourning with all your somber colors. Add life to your wardrobe, Mrs. Clarke."

The walls pressed in, closing around her like prison bars. "I wore the yellow dress the other day," she protested.

"Hardly an improvement." Cecil curled his lip. "That paste-colored frock bled the color right out of you."

Eleanor said nothing, staring down at the gown in that hideous color that was named after an oppressor's victory.

"If you knew what that frock cost, you wouldn't act so bloody downtrodden," Cecil threw out crossly. "I'll have something else made for you soon for an important soiree in two weeks' time. I want you at your best."

So this was to be a recurring practice, his dressing her. Her one freedom lost.

Eleanor squeezed her hands into fists, nails biting into flesh as she tried to maintain her composure. "I have many gowns—"

"This will be the event of the season. I cannot have you looking like a widow."

"But there's the red velvet—"

"I already have an appointment with your modiste." Cecil threw his arms out, effusive in his delight. "The event of the season, Mrs. Clarke!"

She didn't care if the garment was for a visit with the queen herself. Eleanor wanted a say in what she wore.

"Come now, chin up." A warning tone tinged Cecil's words, the underlying threat skittering down her spine. "Don your pretty gown and I'll meet you downstairs to greet our guests."

She gathered her wits, which had been scattered to the ends of the earth, and gave him the smile he loved best, her eyes wide with adoration, her mouth stretched to the point of cracking. As she did so, she thought of Lady Duxbury's book of herbs and what forbidden knowledge she might find within. Herbs to heal . . . and possibly herbs to harm . . .

Cecil grinned in return, his chin tucking back in pleasure against the fleshy folds of his neck. "There now." He turned and strode from her with the confidence of a man who ruled his kingdom with smooth efficiency. A man who had won.

"And don't worry about the new gown," he called over his shoulder. "Everyone will love it, including our esteemed hostess, Lady Meddleson."

CHAPTER TWENTY-TWO

Lady Lavinia Cavendish

LAVINIA STOOD MISERABLY AGAINST THE WALL in a spring-green ball gown. The silk was of the highest quality, sumptuous and run through with gold thread so the reflecting light sparkled like magic. She'd been enamored of the fabric when she saw it at the modiste, thinking that in such a garment, even *she* might crawl out from behind her bashful shield.

How wrong she had been.

A gown couldn't make her more inclined toward idle small talk or build her courage to dance. The frock might look fantastical, but in the end, it was just a bit of costly silk. In fact, were the gown two shades darker, the color would match perfectly with the wall covering in the ballroom of whoever's home she was in. She couldn't recall their name now.

In her dreams, she hoped she'd be the belle of the ball. In truth, she was barely a step above the wallpaper.

"I trust you saved a place on your dance card for me." A man's voice broke through the fog of her wretchedness.

She cringed inwardly, a ready refusal on her tongue. More than the misery of attending balls, she hated the pity-based requests to dance.

Go on, be a good lad and see to the one blending into the wallpaper,
the poor dear.

"Thank you, but I don't—" she looked up, the last word
faltering "—dance."

Mr. Wright gazed down at her, his brown hair even longer
than last time, just unruly enough to lend him a roguish air.
Mirth danced in his hazel eyes. "Still swearing off dancing, I
see."

"I've never much enjoyed it," she admitted.

The flutter of nerves low in her belly was not as intense
as with their last encounter. But then, she had written in her
diary before readying for the ball. The entry had been filled
with the poetry Lady Duxbury had suggested, expelling the
force of Lavinia's anxiety in words that jangled and hummed as
she scrawled them, her brain moving faster than her hand, her
thoughts frenzied.

Putting those feelings to paper had soothed her nerves, emp-
tying her of restless energy and leaving her drained in a most
satisfying way. Even now, she continued to feel the effects in
the strength of her voice, her pulse ticking at a blessedly normal
pace.

Mr. Wright was not put off by her awkward reply. "Perhaps
you should prefer a turn about the room, then?"

She hesitated. Walking around a room was such a silly notion. But then, they would attract attention standing too long
in one place without chaperones present.

"That would indeed be preferable to dancing," she answered
slowly.

He offered her his arm and she accepted. After all, she *had*
resolved if they should meet again, she would be painfully honest with him, no matter the outcome.

Unless, of course, his attentions were drawn by pity. Likely,
he didn't even recall her name.

"Pray tell why the prettiest woman in the room finds dancing so deplorable," he prompted. Then, as if he'd been privy to the cynicism of her thoughts, added, "Lady Lavinia."

Her name on his lips was far more agreeable than she'd expected. Perhaps his interest wasn't due to pity after all.

The truth, she reminded herself. Speak only the truth. "I don't care to be the center of attention."

"I find that must be difficult with hair such as yours."

Heat rushed to her cheeks.

Her hair was more copper-red than reddish-brown, making it decidedly not *en mode*—at least, according to more than one conversation she'd overheard about herself.

An unfortunate garish red.

The hair color of someone with a delicate disposition.

Or . . .

The hair color of someone with a fiery temper.

Or, worse yet . . .

Ugly.

Only when Mr. Wright accidentally tugged her forward did she realize she'd slowed her pace.

He looked down at her. "Your hair stands out from all the rest, you know."

"I'm painfully aware, yes."

"Painfully?" He drew to an abrupt stop. "You don't like it?" His mouth opened and closed as if he was trying to find the words to say. "Your hair is . . . well, it's like burnished copper, or a flame burning in the night. Absolutely mesmerizing." He shook his head at himself. "That sounds overly poetic, and I don't mean it in that way. Only . . . your hair is beautiful, Lady Lavinia. *You* are beautiful."

There was no malice in his tone. No mockery.

A flush crept up his neck and he gave a sheepish smile.

She ducked her head and offered a quiet murmur of thanks at the compliment, afraid to give it any weight. Too afraid to trust.

"I'm happy to see you tonight." He resumed walking, leading her beneath the balcony where the musicians played above them. Their conversation lulled for a few moments, the silence between them washed away by the volume of skillful strings and an energetic flute.

"I'm pleased to see you here as well," she answered when she did not have to fight to be heard.

He chuckled. "I wouldn't miss it. Mother would be bereft if I skipped her ball."

This was his home?

Lavinia had always been a poor actress, her emotions written on her face as surely as if they were ink upon a page.

He gave a good-natured grin. "You didn't know?"

She bit her lip and shook her head.

"My father died soon after my youngest sister was born." He glanced across the room to where the hostess chatted with a young woman, presumably one of his sisters given the way her mouth curled in the same manner as Mr. Wright's. "For years it had been the six of us until my mother met Mr. Wilcox."

Ah, yes. Mr. and Mrs. Wilcox. They were the hosts of the ball.

Lavinia covered her face, wishing to disappear. "I didn't realize. Do forgive me."

His hands rested on hers and gently pulled them from her face to reveal his smile. "There's nothing to forgive." He led her round the dance floor. A couple bounded past in a country reel, leaving the scent of perfume and sweat in their wake.

For a fraction of a moment, she could imagine being on the dance floor with Mr. Wright, their faces alight with joy, eyes locked, souls joined. She studied his profile, admiring the curve of his chin, slightly too large to the point of appearing stubborn, and the bump at the bridge of his nose. His gaze slid toward her, catching her staring.

It was a dream, all of this. A farce.

Souls joined, indeed.

The conversation was moving too slowly. She had to warn him off her before she could let false hope take root.

"There is, actually." She stopped walking and looked up at him. "Something to forgive, I mean."

A grin played at the corners of his mouth. "Have you done something egregious?"

"No."

Not yet.

"But you must understand." Lavinia swallowed. "I am not a woman to warrant your affections."

His brow quirked up, and she wished it did not make him appear so handsome. "Oh?"

Lavinia inhaled and admitted the horrible truth about herself. "I don't care to dance, I abhor social events, I'm not at all fashionable, I find small talk the ultimate form of misery, I sometimes feel so overwhelmed at social events that I want to scream, and . . ." She hesitated only a moment. In for a penny, in for a pound. "And my grandmother was mad, and I write poetry."

He tilted his head, as though studying her. "Are you a reader as well?"

She drew back at his question. Had he not heard the whole of her confession? "I am."

"You remind me very much of Jane in *Jane Eyre*."

She blinked. "I beg your pardon."

"There's a frank quality to your demeanor. I find it refreshing. Very much as Jane is portrayed in the book."

His words left her stunned.

"You've read *Jane Eyre*?" she stammered.

"I have." He offered her his arm again. "Several times, in fact."

She accepted his arm, and they began to walk once more.

"I have a particular affinity for the work of the Brontë sisters," he added.

"In that case, I can honestly say that is the most flattering compliment I've ever received." A new sensation tickled up inside her, effervescent and entirely delightful. "What else do you like to read?"

He chuckled. "You'll find it dull."

"Perhaps I will not."

He gave her a skeptical look. "I enjoy reading books on law."

"Perhaps I will," she amended.

He laughed, open and warm in a way that made her join him.

"I want to be a solicitor," he explained. "I see so many people in need of help, women who have no rights."

She studied him, intensely curious. "You can give women rights?"

"I hope so." He nodded earnestly. "I've seen my mother struggle before she met Mr. Wilcox. And I've seen how women are treated as inferiors. There needs to be equality between us, not domination and oppression. And the women who are locked into lunatic asylums by husbands who want to be rid of them—it's unjust." He looked at her and color stained his cheeks. "Forgive me. I become rather passionate sometimes."

But Lavinia just smiled in return. "I like that you do. How is it you know such things?" She swallowed. "In regards to lunatic asylums."

"I've been studying under Mr. Brogan, a man who specializes in cases where women have been sent to asylums under manufactured pretenses. He has helped liberate well over a dozen women. What he does . . ." Mr. Wright broke off and searched the air in front of him before shaking his head. "He is an inspiration."

"And what if the admittance is not unwarranted?" Lavinia asked, her heart in her throat.

His eyes narrowed and he studied her as if she were entirely transparent, seeing more than she would like. "Very seldom is that the case. And I do not think a mad grandmother, or a penchant for writing poetry would constitute such extreme action."

He regarded her earnestly as he spoke her fears aloud, and she found herself completely captivated by this unusual man. They were approaching the wall where he'd found her, their turn about the room coming to an end far too quickly.

He slowed his pace, as though trying to capture additional time with her. "I enjoyed seeing you again."

"I enjoyed seeing you as well," she answered truthfully.

"Perhaps next time we can discuss what we are reading, seeing as small talk is the ultimate form of misery."

Her cheeks went hot as her own words were repeated back to her. "Perhaps I should not have been so blunt."

He took her gloved hand in his. "Please don't apologize for expressing your honest thoughts. I hope next time you might continue to be so forthright and possibly even share your poetry."

She sucked in her breath at the very idea. Her poetry was too fresh in its infancy, too vulnerable to allow anyone to read. But she found herself nodding anyway as he bestowed a kiss on the back of her hand and left her by the wall once more.

The smile did not leave her lips at his departure as she quietly reflected upon their conversation.

Mama collected Lavinia not half an hour later, citing a headache. But Lavinia knew the real reason: her father was at his club that evening with Lavinia's brother, and Mama was very nearly done with *Aurora Leigh*. There was nothing more glorious in all the world than a moment of silence in which to read those final satisfying pages of a good book.

Lavinia climbed into the carriage with her mother, their dresses a confection of puffed silk in sweet pastel shades that caught the light of the electric lamps outside.

"I saw you speaking to Mr. Wright again." Mama lifted her

chin in silent invitation for Lavinia to share about the gentle-man in question. "And you even took a turn about the room."

"It was preferable to dancing." Lavinia offered a mild shrug, revealing nothing of the frenzied emotions swirling through her. "What do you know of Mr. Wright?"

The carriage rolled forward, carting them home.

The streetlights flickered over Mama's face so the diamonds at her throat winked and shimmered like stars. "I did ask after him . . ."

"And?" Lavinia pressed.

"He's strange," Mama replied. "People say he's polite and kind enough, but that he's always wandering about with a book in his hands. He's fiercely protective over his mother and sisters, as I'm sure one can imagine with the untimely death of his fa-ther, poor thing. But they say he is a rather odd sort."

"A rather odd sort?" Lavinia repeated softly to herself.

Her mother nodded, her expression sympathetic.

But the report left Lavinia entirely elated.

"Did you enjoy the ball?" Mama asked, clearly trying to change the subject.

Lavinia let her thoughts trail languidly back to that brief turn about the room with Mr. Wright. The bits of gold in her dress glinted in the lights blinking by, setting her whole gown twinkling.

With an absolute sincerity, she replied. "It was magical."

CHAPTER TWENTY-THREE

Mrs. Rose Wharton

SOMETHING WAS AMISS WITH LADY DUXBURY.

Rose studied the countess, who fumbled her teacup, causing it to clatter on its saucer. Otis watched his mistress from his perch inside the glass vase, tail twitching.

An undercurrent of tension ran through the room, tightening small lines around Lady Duxbury's mouth despite her pleasant countenance. She had scarcely remembered to thank the young maid for their tea and refreshment upon delivery, remembering only as the girl was nearly halfway out of the room.

Worried expressions showed on Lady Lavinia's and Mrs. Clarke's faces, mirroring Rose's concern.

"Are you quite all right, Lady Duxbury?" Rose asked with the brash frankness Theodore so often chastised her for.

"Forgive me." Lady Duxbury put a hand to her brow. "I've had a letter which has upset me."

"Lady Meddleson," Mrs. Clarke murmured.

Something unspoken passed between her and Lady Duxbury.

"Was it the invitation?" Lady Lavinia asked with a frown. "I received one as well."

"But you don't want to go," Lady Duxbury deduced.

"Lady Meddleson makes me feel like an insect under a microscope." Lady Lavinia sighed and nudged at the honey-spice cake on her plate. "Mama says the soiree is to be the event of the season and everyone will be there."

"My husband says likewise," Mrs. Clarke replied.

"And you've received an invitation as well?" Rose asked, her stomach dipping. She knew the question before Mrs. Clarke answered. Which meant of the four women, Rose was the only one not to be invited.

"Unfortunately, I have," Mrs. Clarke answered spitefully.

There was an uncommon anger to her that day, something simmering just beneath the surface.

How very strange, especially when paired with how much the invitation had distressed Lady Duxbury. Though Lady Meddleson was entirely unpleasant, Rose had never noted any particular tension between herself and Mrs. Clarke before.

"Well, apparently I'm the only one who has not received an invitation." Rose lifted her teacup, desperate for something to wet the dryness of her mouth. "Much to the chagrin of my brother-in-law. He claims the reason is, of course, me." She sipped her tea, hoping the sweetness would clear the bitter disappointment from her expression.

"Lady Meddleson is a malicious woman whose opinion should not merit the weight Society affords it," Mrs. Clarke said.

Rose's brows lifted in surprise at Mrs. Clarke's blunt statement.

"Her opinion counts more because she says it does." Lady Lavinia sniffed haughtily and lifted her nose in the air in a perfect parody of Lady Meddleson.

Coming from the quiet and unassuming Lady Lavinia, the caricature was even more entertaining, and the women erupted into laughter.

When they caught their breath, Lady Duxbury addressed Lady Lavinia. "Let us speak of more agreeable topics than that wretched woman. Lady Lavinia, how has your poetry been progressing?"

Rose turned to Lady Lavinia expectantly. Because whatever the young woman had been doing, there was a marked difference in her—a confidence and an openness she'd never exhibited before.

"My poetry has been helpful, I believe." Lady Lavinia bit her lip, evidence that her shyness had not completely evaporated. "You were right when you said I had a passion inside me. Putting my thoughts on the page soothes the wildness in my soul. It's like I've spent my entire life suffocating and poetry has finally allowed me to breathe."

Rose's own chest seemed to lighten at the young woman's admission. Mrs. Clarke inhaled deeply beside Rose, as if feeling the same sense of liberation.

"Reading *Aurora Leigh*, and how she makes her own way in the world as a poetess, has been such an inspiration." Lady Lavinia's cheeks were flushed and her lovely green eyes shone bright, expressing more than effusive language could convey.

"Witnessing what an effect writing poetry has had on you is an absolute delight." Lady Duxbury clasped her hands in front of her heart.

"Thank you for guiding me in that direction," Lady Lavinia said earnestly. "I believe my life to be changed for the better."

Unbeknownst to Lady Duxbury, she had greatly improved Rose's life as well.

The herbs Rose took to quell her exhaustion were quite efficacious. The concoction was so successful that Rose also tried the recipe for a complexion paste, which worked better than an arsenic wafer.

But Rose could not admit as much without also sharing the news of her pregnancy, a secret she was not ready to divulge. Perhaps because she still had not figured out what to do.

Theodore had avoided her since their row about her reading.

She didn't know if that meant he'd given up on the restriction of her literature. Or if he'd given up on her.

Her brother-in-law visited frequently, his manner growing more and more unpleasant. On the last occasion, he'd faulted her for Theodore's missing invitation to Lady Meddleson's soiree—which was followed by that terrible threat . . .

As she recalled the incident, a chill descended her spine, the way a finger of icy air slips into the warmth of a housecoat on a frigid morning. Her brother-in-law had once been a commanding presence, but the cancer had consumed him, rendering his once strong, healthy figure to a diminutive shell—yet it had not lessened his acerbic manner. And though his fingers were spindly as an old man's, they still had managed to grip her forearm like a vise.

I will destroy you before you can drag this family into ruin. His breath had been sour with sickness, his eyes glinting with malintent.

Rose shivered.

"Before we adjourn to the library—" Lady Duxbury's gentle voice interrupted Rose's thoughts "—I have an invitation to present. I have an estate on the outskirts of London about an hour or so away by carriage, called Rosewood Cottage. It was a gift from the late Lord Duxbury." Her face remained blank as she spoke, offering no indication of her feelings for her former husband. "I thought an overnight excursion this Monday might be enjoyable. We can refer to the jaunt as a gardening expedition to placate spouses and fathers if they require convincing. I do hope you'll all be able to attend."

Theodore would have no qualms with Rose's attendance. Indeed, he would encourage her to go. The Countess of Duxbury was a respected member of Society. Rose's close acquaintance with her was highly regarded by both him and his brother.

Her friendship with Lady Duxbury and the other two women

was perhaps the only part of Society Rose had managed to get right.

"How lovely," she said. "Thank you for the invitation."

Lady Duxbury rose from her chair, once more composed. "Come, let us retire to the library."

The book of herbs was placed on the table along with a bit of stationery. Now that Rose understood the usefulness of the recipes, her interest was piqued at the remedies within those carefully written pages.

"And as far as Lady Meddleson is concerned," Lady Duxbury said, "Mrs. Clarke might know a way to assist you with an invitation, Mrs. Wharton."

The statement was followed by a pronounced look in Mrs. Clarke's direction. Once more, something passed between them and Mrs. Clarke stiffened.

"Whatever do you mean?" she asked.

But Lady Duxbury only smiled. "Keep reading." She patted Mrs. Clarke's hand. "Just keep reading."

And while the countess's words made entirely no sense to Rose, Mrs. Clarke gave a slow nod of understanding.

CHAPTER TWENTY-FOUR

Mrs. Eleanor Clarke

ANY LINGERING GUILT ELEANOR POSSESSED AT reading the diary was assuaged by Lady Duxbury's encouragement. The countess's expression as she told Eleanor to keep reading appeared genuine. As if seeking confirmation that, yes, Eleanor *was* reading her diary and would continue.

The invitation to Rosewood Cottage hovered in Eleanor's thoughts as they entered the library. What a relief to get away for even just one night, to escape Cecil's ill-tempered presence.

Lady Lavinia had so perfectly stated how Eleanor felt: like she was suffocating. This sojourn would provide an opportunity to breathe and help endure life until June, when Cecil's trip pulled him away for at least two months.

Now Eleanor simply needed to have him agree to allow her to go. But coming to weekly teas while Cecil worked was one thing. Leaving for an overnight trip was another matter entirely.

She would have to weigh his mood prior to her entreaty. Though unlikely, catching him in a rare genial disposition would be ideal.

Hopeful for the opportunity for that one precious night of freedom, Eleanor approached the bookshelf and extracted the hidden diary. She found her preferred chair, opened to the next entry and began to read, desperately curious to see what she might find on Lady Meddleson to sway her toward an invitation for Mrs. Wharton.

Eleanor only hoped she had read far enough . . .

CHAPTER TWENTY-FIVE

Lady Duxbury's Diary

January 1886

If my mother were still alive, she'd be immensely pleased to find I am no longer a viscountess, but a countess.

As a young widow, I wish I could say this second marriage was for love. I doubt I shall ever be so fortunate.

Rather, the decision was one of desperation, forced upon me by necessity.

Viscount Morset gambled, drank and caroused his estate into abject penury. There is little hope in this world for a penniless widow. Even less so for an heir with nothing to inherit but debt. My poor George.

I admit that upon the death of my former husband, I found myself venturing toward the little bookshop near Threadneedle Lane. Elias's shop.

Bedecked in widow's weeds with a black lace veil obstructing my face, I sought out the man to whom I'd once given my heart. The man whose son now was without a father.

Elias tended to his customers, oblivious to my presence. At his side was a comely blond, their shared smiles and joyous counte-

nance suggested a happy union, confirmed by the slim gold bands glinting on their ring fingers. I stayed there too long, staring in the window like a fool. A heartbroken, enamored fool. A little black-and-white cat nudged my shin, the peculiar white markings just under his nose looking curiously like a mustache, lending him a gentlemanly air.

He broke the spell that held me transfixed. I went to pet him in gratitude, but he whisked away into the shop. A place I had no intention of entering.

I was introduced to the Earl of Esterly sometime later, when my black weeds were cast off for the violet and purple hues of half-mourning. He found me beautiful, and I found him agreeable. In those days, he had been so thoughtful, so genuine. And certainly, his fortune held great appeal to an impoverished widow with a child to care for.

After some months of our acquaintance, he prevailed upon me with all his prepossessing confidence and seeming benevolence, expressing intent to make me his wife.

A destitute mother does not have the luxury of dithering when presented with such opportunity.

What started as an auspicious union, I'm afraid has been a considerable disappointment. My son confessed to me in the greatest confidence that my new husband, Silas, has been cruel.

I have seen the irritation flash in Silas's eyes when my darling George is about, and so I do not doubt my son's claims.

But when I conveyed my solicitude over George's well-being to Silas, he insinuated I was imagining such happenings. He went as far, in fact, as to suggest madness on my part.

Hysteria.

For every complaint of malice my son brought to my attention, Silas offered a ready excuse. A sharp comment had been directed at the dog, not my son. A raised voice had simply been the result of a hard day and was unintentional. A forgotten event for George had been due to an oversight on the footman's behalf, resulting in the poor man's reprimand. At the end of each conversation where I anticipated amends to be made, I somehow found myself offering my own apologies to Silas. Only when I departed did I become vexed to understand how craftily Silas managed to twist my words.

George's discontent grew. Again and again, I approached Silas with my concerns, yet he eluded all culpability and, again, expressed concerns for my sanity.

After a short time, I approached our discussions with great trepidation. He found ways to point out my every quirk and foible, angling them in a way to indicate my mind was not sound.

I haven't had a friend of significance since ~~Alice~~ Lady Meddleson. I do not trust other women. Not anymore. Not when I know how dear is the currency of secrets.

Perhaps I am mad, and this creeping sense of paranoia and distrust is breaking the first pivotal layer of my sanity.

It is a strange thing to confess, but Silas's constant implication that I am a lunatic has me questioning every aspect of my life, of my thoughts.

In the meantime, I endeavor to remain home as much as possible. I can conceive no other means to protect my son.

For when I'm in Silas's presence, he is magnanimous in his treatment of George, a caricature of a doting father. It is an act well performed. Were my husband not born into nobility, he might find renown on the stage as an actor.

I know my boy. I know his forthright and trustworthy nature. He is not a child given to mendacity.

I worry for the state of this marriage. For the taste in my mouth is bitter indeed.

CHAPTER TWENTY-SIX

Mrs. Rose Wharton

WHERE THE DEVIL WAS IT?

Rose opened and closed the drawers of Theodore's desk with enough force to send the contents within rattling. Pluto snuffled around the desk beside her, as though assisting her search.

She'd been reading *Aurora Leigh* after Lady Lavinia had finished the book. And what a terrifying shake-up such a concept must be for men—women wanting to assume a role as poet and "steal" the position from men. The fear that women might be better at conveying female protagonists rather than ones judged only on their appearances and pasts as men so often wrote.

Heaven forbid the heroine of a story be allowed a thought in her pretty head.

As these ridiculous injustices assaulted Rose, her search became more aggressive. She yanked open the middle drawer of Theodore's large desk, revealing a book.

But not one of hers.

Swell's Night Guide was scrawled in cartoonish letters amid a picture of men loitering around women whose bosoms were indecently exposed.

Rose sucked in a breath and the little life growing within

her belly fluttered like an anxious bird. Her poor unborn child, so affected by her nerves. Rose set a hand to her stomach to soothe the babe within.

While Rose was not privy to all of a man's goings-on in Society, she was not so ignorant as to what *Swell's Night Guide* offered: suggestions to the many nightly pleasures a man who intended to stray from his marital bed might enjoy.

Her knees were suddenly too weak to hold her upright and she sank back into Theodore's overstuffed chair. The leather creaked under her weight, though she scarcely heard it for the rushing pulse in her ears.

Fingers trembling, she turned the crisp pages of the book. There was an introduction to the debauchery contained within amid pictures of women partially clothed in provocative poses. There was even a list of words *en mode* for men to use when soliciting what delights they wanted for the right amount of coin.

The pages were stiff as she flipped through the book until she could not stand another moment of the bawdy images, the licentious text, the blatantly lewd insinuations.

And this vile book was in Theodore's possession, tucked unabashedly within his desk.

Most horrifying to her of all was the section on the women of Whitechapel, the very place she went daily with the Society for the Advancement of the Poor. She'd seen those women loitering outside the establishments, flicking their brightly colored skirts up to show their ankles as men passed, whispering offerings that made them stop with interest. She saw those very women later in her line, waiting to receive a free meal, babies propped on their hips, bruises shadowing their cheekbones and a hopeless glaze in their eyes.

Rose was helping those women, and Theodore . . .

She could not finish the thought. Bile rose in her throat.

She only just managed to grab for a crystal bowl with several of Theodore's favorite fountain pens before she was sick on all the fine writing instruments.

She wiped the back of her hand over her mouth, not a whit sorry.

Losing the contents of her stomach drained her, leaving her bones feeling too loose for her to do anything more than sit in her own misery. Pluto whimpered, and the warm weight of his head settled atop her slippers.

But Rose was not the type of woman to wallow.

She thought of those poor women in Whitechapel and everywhere else in London the sordid book had mapped out. And she thought of the books restricted from her. A raw fury kindled to life.

Energy jagged through her like hot, white lightning. She snatched the book from where it'd fallen to the floor, shoved up from the chair and stormed into the library, where she had last seen Theodore, Pluto scrabbling after her.

Sure enough, the top of Theodore's head showed over the high-backed leather chair beside the hearth.

The hard soles of her slippers slapped over the thick pile Persian rug that had been purchased last year with her father's money. Theodore's head swiveled back, craning to better see her and Pluto making their way to him like a rising tempest.

"Rose, what the—?"

She came around his chair and glared at him, baring her wrath in its full glory. "I find it interesting that you consider a benign novel some form of moral turpitude while you are violating the vows of our marriage."

Pluto barked one high-pitched yip.

Theodore had the gall to appear offended, his face reddening in the golden firelight. "I beg your pardon?"

She slammed the book on the table beside him, making the

furniture wobble and nearly upsetting his drink. "*Swell's*, Theodore, truly?" Her voice caught and she hated the audible crack of her pain.

Theodore stared at the book.

Pluto whimpered and edged against her, his warm body a comfort that just might break her.

"Is this what you're doing those nights when you say you are at the club?" Her words fed the fire of her furious indignation. "Or even the days when you claim to be spending so much time with your brother, learning to assume the earldom?" She balled her hands into fists. "Do you have any idea what those women endure? I see them day after day, after what is done to them. It sickens me to think you would be among those men."

Shaking his head, Theodore looked up at her, his eyes wide in the intentionally earnest way she was so familiar with. "It isn't what you think."

She folded her arms over her chest. "There aren't a lot of conclusions I can draw, given the evidence."

Theodore's lips flattened into a hard line. "It is mine."

The admission thrust a blade of betrayal into Rose's chest. She sucked in a gasp at its impact.

"Rose." Theodore leaped to his feet and reached for her.

She staggered back. Any words she might utter were caught in the snare of her tight throat. Ever loyal, Pluto put himself before her and growled.

Theodore stopped and ran a hand through his hair, leaving a piece jutting up at the side. A sigh dredged up from somewhere deep in his chest. "I didn't want the bloody thing."

Rose scoffed. "Didn't you?"

"I presume you noticed it was new." He glanced down at the book, contempt in his eyes.

Her thoughts brushed over the memory of how stiff the pages were, how they'd stuck crisply together.

A part of Rose yearned to believe him. Passionately wanted

to believe him. But another part, one that had suffered cut after cut of emotional wounds in the past six months of their spiraling marriage, remained skeptical.

"You said you didn't want the book," Rose said slowly. "Who gave it to you?"

Theodore hung his head. "Byron."

Rose shook her head, thoroughly vexed. How fitting that Theodore's brother had something to do with this.

Theodore lifted his gaze to her. "He says I'm too enamored with you, that I could never force you to be the woman you need to be because I am besotted. He believes that I should preoccupy myself with another romantic interest."

A torrent of emotions swept over Rose, stunning her into silence as she took stock of each feeling. Shock at her brother-in-law's temerity, offense that he should try to encourage her husband into another woman's bed, and a sense of hope so profound, she could almost breathe again.

Hope that Theodore truly did still love her.

"Do you want another romantic interest?" she asked, her voice small.

His gaze did not leave hers. "Never."

She choked out a sob. "Truly?"

With a growl, he flung the prurient thing into the hearth. Pluto snapped his focus to the book, as though he was as determined as Rose to see it burn. Greedy flames licked at the cover, crawling over the foul thing and curling the pages.

The contents might have crumbled into useless ash, but Rose didn't see. Theodore had pulled her into his arms where she fit perfectly snug against his hard chest. His mouth was on hers, his voice in her ear, whispering words of love. She devoured every one, realizing how in these past few months she had been helplessly desperate for his affection.

The tears came then. But they didn't pique his ire as they so often seemed to these days. Instead, he held her as she wept.

"I thought you had grown to hate me," she whispered against his shoulder, her words barely audible as they were absorbed into the soft wool of his dark jacket.

"Hate you?" Theodore pulled back. "Quite the opposite, my American rose." His endearment for her pulled a smile from her lips. "I love you. My brother's disapproval be damned. I love you, Rose Wharton."

He gazed down at her with blue eyes that so perfectly matched the summer sky in Manhattan, she'd stopped when she first saw him, compelled to remark on their color.

She'd been in love with him ever since.

And he was still in love with her.

Her hands folded against his, and she savored the prickle of the coarse hair at the back of his hands in contrast to the softness of his palm. As if this might all be a dream that would dissipate if she stopped reassuring herself that it was real.

"I've been so unhappy," Rose admitted.

Theodore winced. "I know. You have been unhappy, and Byron is unhappy and I am in the middle, unable to cure the misery on either side." He paused. "It has been difficult for me as well. In a way wholly different than you, of course. But I, too, have been unhappy."

She'd seen his suffering, in the shadows under his eyes from late nights at his desk poring over accounts and reports of the estates, in the defeated slump of his shoulders following visits from Byron and his onslaught of criticism, in the way Theodore so seldom smiled or laughed anymore.

"I know," she admitted. "My love for you is the reason I've been trying so very hard, yet nothing I do seems good enough." Rose tightened her hands around his, holding on out of fear that her admission might make him draw away.

But he didn't try to pull himself from her grip. "You have been stalwart in your endeavors to be a good countess. I must commend you more for what you've accomplished, especially with the Society for the Advancement of the Poor. Your work there has changed you. I see how much food goes from our kitchen to the society, how you consider children who beg and find ways to help them, even how you treat the staff as if they are friends rather than servants. Byron does not approve of the latter, but I do. I've always liked this kind, gentle part of you."

Rose's heart swelled under the compliment. Her work had become important to her. People had become important to her.

"And you've been accepted not only by Lady Duxbury," Theodore continued, "but also the ladies you take tea with, and even Mrs. Baskin and her wretched daughter."

Rose chuckled. "She truly is wretched."

"What if . . ." Theodore paused, thinking. "What if you are allowed to do as you please in the house when we are alone?" Theodore's fingertips glided over her hand now, following the dip of her knuckles with the pad of his forefinger. As if he, too, could not stop touching her. "You would have to behave differently when Byron is here, of course, to avoid censure on both our parts. But otherwise, you would do as you please, speak as you please and, of course, read as you please."

Pleasure spread through her like warm, golden honey. "I should like that very much."

"As would I." He smiled and she felt his joy in her soul, a balm to the wound inflicted earlier with her fears of his infidelity.

Their child within her womb fluttered and she wondered if the babe recognized its father's voice.

With their issues resolved, she ought to tell Theodore. Except he was pulling her toward him with a low murmur, a promise of intimacy she should like very much to see fulfilled.

Talk of the child could come later. When she was certain of the validity of his offer of freedom.

Because as much as she hated to admit it, even as they hastened eagerly to the privacy of her chamber, she was not the gullible girl she'd once been and no longer trusted so easily.

CHAPTER TWENTY-SEVEN

Mrs. Eleanor Clarke

NO.

As if Eleanor were not a grown woman, but a child asking permission to go to a fair or a friend's party.

She climbed the grand staircase, her muscles burning to race up them, to let the fury simmering inside her explode.

That, or scream.

She wanted to grip the rail hard enough to crack the marble, to face the open house and scream and scream and *scream* until she purged herself of all her rage.

If such a thing were possible.

She had been trapped in this marriage—in this life—for too long. A woman who had to be obedient despite being ill-used, a woman who had to be kind despite her husband's cruelty, a woman who had to be faithful despite her husband's blatant infidelity. Not that she truly minded the last fact, but the infraction was one more mass tossed onto the imbalanced scales between men and women.

There were so many of those discriminatory masses on the scales, all in the form of rules that never applied to men. Each one now stacked on Eleanor's shoulders with every step up the staircase.

A woman was a man's property when she was wed, and yet told she must want to be a wife. She must go to her bridal bed entirely innocent, but desirous, committing herself to a lifetime of never being able to say no. Her beauty was to be maintained, though she would be lambasted for the expense and denigrated for her vanity. Her duty included bearing a child, but her time with them was limited for fear of making the offspring soft.

Any joy she could grasp was stripped away by Cecil, who cavorted as he pleased.

No.

His one-word reply to her request for a single night at Lady Duxbury's Rosewood Cottage resonated in her mind. He hadn't even looked up from the document he'd been reading when she asked.

Her cheeks radiated heat as she made her way down the hall to her room, the skirt of her blue gown snapping about her ankles. There was no soothing effect to the pastel shade today.

She pushed into her bedchamber with such ferocity that her maid started with a little cry.

"I would like to wear the garnet silk gown for dinner," Eleanor said with finality.

Lady Lavinia had once discussed a book on Rome she'd read, how Spartan warriors wore red capes pinned to their armor before battle—the color of bravery.

And Eleanor wanted to be prepared for war.

This time, she would wear red, *not* magenta.

"I'm afraid . . ." Bennett's voice faltered, and she looked toward the bed.

Eleanor followed the maid's gaze, and her stomach clenched. A gown was already laid out on the velvet covers. She was there in two aggressive strides, staring down at the frock.

The delicate white silk was tissue-thin, and framed with a

nebulous, filmy tulle. No doubt Cecil had meant the garment to represent purity and devotion. But to Eleanor, the garment was a white flag cutting through the battlefield; it was capitulation.

A breath expelled from her. "I'll wear the red gown."

Her maid did not move, her expression fearful in understanding what Eleanor challenging Cecil would mean for her mistress. "But, my lady—"

"I'll wear the red," Eleanor said again, her voice firm.

Tonight was not for giving up. Tonight was for fighting back.

Cecil's eyes narrowed when Eleanor entered the dining room. "What happened to the white gown?"

"I haven't worn this one yet." She strode to her seat, back straight, shoulders strong in a show of unaccustomed confidence. A woman could change the world wearing a gown like this. "You had it made for me several months ago, if you recall."

The statement was a lie, but she was so often an afterthought in his life, he forgot what he'd said or done around her. She used that now to her advantage.

"Ah, yes." He nodded, his jowls quivering. "Took you bloody long enough to wear it."

"It is lovely," she said with sincerity. Of course the gown was lovely, she had been the one to commission its creation.

His gaze skimmed down her body in a way that usually made her want to shudder out of her skin. Tonight she lifted her head, a warrioress refusing to be cowed by her foe.

Cecil gave a grunt that might be approval or a show of irritation.

The servants stepped forward with asparagus soup, serving first Cecil and then Eleanor. She waited until he lifted a spoonful to his mouth before speaking. "I know you declined my request to attend Lady Duxbury's invitation to Rosewood Cot—"

Cecil's spoon clanked into the bowl and he scowled across

the table at her. "This matter has been addressed. Do not spoil my meal."

Everything in her wanted to shrink from his irritation, knowing how swiftly those embers could fan into the flames of fury. But not tonight. Not in this gown.

"There's a secret, you see." Eleanor carefully spooned a dainty mouthful of soup and let the words dangle in the air like a carrot for Cecil to snap at.

He slurped his soup, a large blunt finger tapping in contemplation on the crisp tablecloth.

The servants came forward and removed the soup bowls.

"A secret?" he said at last, taking her bait. "What type of secret?"

Eleanor brushed her fingers discreetly over the Spartan crimson silk. While she did not have a sword or a shield of polished bronze, she had knowledge. One must know their enemy to truly do battle, and there was no one in this world she knew better than Cecil. She armed herself with his vices and his hubris, all readily available to employ to her advantage.

"I'm not entirely sure," Eleanor said thoughtfully. "Lady Duxbury told us simply there was something of great import she wished to share when we were outside London. I presume whatever she wishes to divulge is best done away from whatever ears might be listening."

Cecil snorted. "If her servants are listening, she ought to sack the lot of them." Even as he said this, his gaze slid to the footman at his right. Loyalty was impossible to purchase, as every man and woman of means was well aware.

Except that Lady Duxbury's staff was truly loyal. For not only were they well paid, but they were also given something most were seldom afforded: consideration and respect.

A footman approached with a platter of roasted pork. Cecil took three hearty slices. Pork was his favorite.

Eleanor didn't press her case. She sat prettily as though she hadn't a thought in her head, a vapid countenance on her face like a doll's painted smile.

"A secret, eh . . . ?" Cecil shoved a forkful of meat into his mouth, masticating with wet smacking sounds. "I wonder if it's about those husbands of hers." He jabbed the air with his fork. "She killed them all, you mark my words. A veritable black widow, she is."

Eleanor cut into her meat. "I wouldn't presume."

He grunted again, teeth grinding into his meat. "She sent me a box of dates earlier, noting they were an apology for her intent to steal you away for a night. I wonder at her means of discovering my enjoyment of them."

The gift of the dates surprised Eleanor. She hadn't revealed her husband's affinity for dried dates to Lady Duxbury.

Cecil's tone suggested he suspected otherwise.

"That was generous of her," Eleanor replied noncommittally.

Cecil drained his wineglass and held it aloft to be refilled. "Just the one night?"

A footman rushed to fill his cup as Eleanor took a sip of wine, refraining from appearing too eager. "Yes," she answered after she'd swallowed. "The cook already has the list of what shall be served for the week. You won't even notice I'm gone."

He hummed to himself, falling upon his second piece of pork with zeal. "Very well," he conceded in a magnanimous tone. "You may go, but I shall like to hear about this secret as soon as you return."

"Of course." Eleanor smiled, and took a bite of her own meal, her appetite restored.

She had won.

CHAPTER TWENTY-EIGHT

Lady Lavinia Cavendish

LAVINIA'S CARRIAGE ROLLED TO A STOP IN FRONT of Rosewood Cottage, which was more of a manor than an actual cottage, as it was with most peers and their cottages in England. Lavinia's family included.

Rosewood Cottage was three stories tall, made of dusky red brickwork with pale stone accents artfully framing the doors and windows. Clematis climbed the walls, draping the building in verdant vines with occasional purple blooms.

The door opened and Lady Duxbury emerged with Mrs. Clarke and Mrs. Wharton following closely behind her as a footman helped Lavinia alight from the carriage onto the white pebbled path.

"Lady Lavinia, welcome." There was a relaxed air about Lady Duxbury in the softness of her smile and her lavender day dress.

Mrs. Wharton wore a lovely white muslin gown with a dark green sash around her slender waist, her rich chestnut hair pulled back into a simple bun, cheeks flushed with excitement. "We've decided to go by our Christian names while we're here," she said cheerfully by way of greeting. "Perhaps even afterward as well. Isn't that right, Eleanor?"

"Rose has decided it is ridiculous for us to continue to be so formal." Mrs. Clarke—Eleanor—threw a teasing grin at Rose.

"Leave it to the American to suggest such a thing," Rose jested in that self-deprecating way of hers. "But Eleanor agreed."

Eleanor nodded. "I did."

Lavinia grinned. "On that score, I'm just Lavinia." And she rather liked the sound of that.

They all looked to Lady Duxbury.

But while Lavinia had no qualms with casting aside formality with the other women, calling their illustrious leader anything other than Lady Duxbury seemed unsuitable. She was an iron force, always strong, always resolute, and entirely enigmatic, always knowing exactly the right thing to say. As if she could see into one's soul, helping wherever aid was needed—whether for an anxious young woman in need of poetry, or a boxer one hit away from death.

"Lady Duxbury?" Rose pressed coyly.

The countess tilted her chin, a smirk on her lips. "And ruin my mysterious air? Why, next you'll be asking if I killed my husbands."

Before they could express shock at her statement, she gave a delicate chuckle and waved a hand. "Come. Now that you've all arrived, let me show you to your rooms and introduce our special guests."

Lavinia faltered. Special guests? Were they not alone?

"No one you'll recognize from social circles in London, I assure you." Lady Duxbury led them into the house. "This excursion is not simply about friendship. I intend for our time together to be edifying as well. You'll understand soon."

A mysterious air indeed.

The interior of the cottage was just as grand as the clematis-draped exterior. The marble entryway had been polished to such a shine that Lavinia was instantly aware of her gravel-dusted shoes. A large staircase formed the centerpiece of the entryway, sweeping up halfway to a landing before splitting off toward the two wings, like a mermaid's tail. Together, they climbed the stairs behind Lady Duxbury, pausing partway up to examine a life-size painting of a woman with dark hair, her expression one of sorrow.

The woman's eyes seemed to connect with Lavinia's, as if peering into the darkest parts of her. Lavinia took an instinctive step back.

Eleanor stared up at the portrait, her head tilted to the side. "She looks so sad."

"I imagine she was." Lady Duxbury stood by Eleanor and regarded the art piece. "She was my late husband's mother and met a rather unhappy end."

Without further elaboration, Lady Duxbury led them upward to their individual bedchambers. Lavinia's room was decorated in a lovely burnt orange palette, showcasing polished oak furniture carved with delicately scrolling filigrees. A large desk sat before a window that consumed the length of the wall, overlooking a lake. The surface mirrored the clear sky above, absent the haze of factory smog shrouding London. Behind the lake was a forest, its trees crowded together, cloaking the depths in shadows.

Secrets.

There were many of them within this house. Their presence oozed from the walls and settled deep into the marrow of Lavinia's bones. There had been great sorrow here once.

Even as the thought came to her, words teemed in her mind, burning for escape. A journal sat atop the desk with a fountain pen at its side. A card with Lavinia's name was tented atop the plain black book.

A gift, the note indicated, for whatever Lavinia's heart wished to write.

She fell into the chair with such haste, she sat only on one hip as she opened the journal and began to write. A maid entered the room at some point, one Lady Duxbury graciously provided to see to her needs. Lavinia paused only long enough to politely acknowledge her presence and then was back to the notebook, recording every emotion that poured into her from the floorboards, the joists in the ancient wooden frames and even the discordantly cheerful paint trying to mask all that lay beneath.

When she laid down her pen, there was peace within her, a quiet that soothed the noise clamoring in her mind. She summoned the maid to assist her changing into a fresh day dress and wandered downstairs to find the others were already congregating in the drawing room with two curious new guests.

One woman swathed completely in thick black lace shifted about the room, pausing from time to time as her bare hand peeked out from beneath the dark garments to skim over various objects.

The other woman was just as intriguing in a pair of men's trousers and shirtsleeves. This masculine attire was paired with a wide straw hat weighed down with silk flowers and ribbons— she'd even gone so far as to perch a small yellow bird atop the floral mass. Her gaze went directly to Lavinia and she strode over, her gait broad and determined.

"You must be Lady Lavinia." The woman's accent was very much American, though her husky voice was far brasher and louder than Rose's. "You can call me Smith."

The confidence Smith exuded saturated the room, bathing it in her boldness so that everyone else appeared washed out by comparison, and the lone figure in widow's weeds all but faded into the shadows.

Just then, Lady Duxbury clapped her hands to collect their attention. "Now that we're all here, let us convene to the ballroom. Smith has something very special to show us."

Lavinia glanced at the woman in black. She did not acknowledge anyone else as she rested the flat of her palm against the wall, pausing as if she could sense the soft, rhythmic thud of its heartbeat. The woman did not follow them into the ballroom. Nor had any offer been given for her to do so.

How very strange.

Rose rushed ahead to speak to Smith as they followed Lady Duxbury, asking where the woman originated from in America. After so long being the only American, encountering a fellow countryman must have been refreshing for Rose. While Lavinia understood exactly how precious a like-minded friend could be, she worried that the American might draw Rose from their side.

The feeling was selfish, and Lavinia immediately chastised herself. But no sooner had she regretted that flash of jealousy than Rose fell back from Smith and rejoined Lavinia and Eleanor.

"She won't tell me what we're doing." Rose chuckled. "I tried to pull it out of her. She only winked and tipped the brim of her hat at me."

"It *is* a rather elaborate hat," Lavinia whispered. "Do you think it is a clue?"

No one had a chance to answer before they entered the ballroom to find a row of dress forms with pillows tied about them. A table had been laid out with various hats not unlike the one Smith wore.

The women looked at one another in silent question.

Lady Duxbury's eyes sparkled with amusement at their bewildered expressions. "For the first part of our house party, I give you . . . Smith." She held up her hand in introduction.

The American woman twirled on light feet before a dress form. As she did so, she swept the pin from her hat, sending the monstrosity of flowers and ribbons tumbling to the floor. Before it landed, Smith had jabbed her hatpin through the pillow with such force, the pointed end jutted from the other side of the dress form.

Smith spun once more, facing their stunned expressions, and bowed, bending at the waist in a way that suggested she was not wearing a corset.

Lavinia clapped along with Rose, but it was Eleanor who applauded the loudest, her mouth parted in astonished wonder.

"For too long, women have been known as the weaker sex." Smith put her hands on her hips, her feet spread wide. With such a stance she looked ready to battle anything thrown her way. "Today you're going to discover just how strong you really are. I'm going to teach you how to defend yourself with an item you always have on hand." She swept the hat from the ground, holding it aloft as she pulled the pin free from the wounded pillow. "Ladies, today, you will learn the art of hatpin fighting."

CHAPTER TWENTY-NINE

Mrs. Rose Wharton

ROSE HAD NEVER HEARD OF HATPIN FIGHTING, and she was discovering she wasn't especially good at it. Smith had made the task appear easy.

It was decidedly not.

"The first time isn't always a success," Smith said with assurance. "Try again."

Rose turned on her feet as instructed, preparing to face her "attacker." The hat was heavy on her head, ungainly where pinned to her generous bun. As she spun, she reached for her hatpin. Only her fingers grasped empty air. She groped blindly at the massive hat, catching a fistful of feathers.

"You'll get it on the next go," Lady Duxbury said from where she stood beside Smith.

"You've lost the element of surprise, I'm afraid, Mrs. Wharton." Smith hung her thumbs from the pockets of her trousers, her expression bemused. "Try again."

If Rose had expected any preferential treatment from her fellow countryman, she was mistaken.

In fact, her entire interaction with the woman was not what she had expected. She'd anticipated catching up on gossip about the Astors—there was always gossip about the Astors—and lamenting over missing coffee and sunshine. Except when she chatted with Smith, Rose instead found herself worried what she might miss with Eleanor and Lavinia.

They had only this one sojourn together and time was precious.

Finally, Rose had found a place to belong, with women who understood her and still accepted her regardless.

Beside Rose, Lavinia tried her hand at hatpin fighting. She spun about, pulling the pin free, but it slipped through her fingers. The thin bit of metal clattered to the wooden floor.

Lavinia frowned and twisted about, her hand on her abdomen. "This would be easier without a corset."

"It would," Smith agreed with a wink. "But I'm not here to tell you how to dress."

"So, these ungainly hats aren't your style?" Rose tilted her head toward Smith.

"Strength is my style, Mrs. Wharton," Smith replied. "Even if that means wearing a ridiculous hat."

"Ridiculous?" Lavinia asked in exaggerated offense. Hers was perhaps the worst of all, sprouting silk daisies with spindly stalks that wobbled when she moved.

"It's a statement, to be sure." Smith looked around them. "Nicely done, Mrs. Clarke."

Rose and Lavinia turned to find Eleanor with one petite hand curled around the decorative knob of the hatpin, its point buried deep into the heart of the pillow. Her cheeks were flushed, and perspiration shone on her brow.

"You've been hitting nearly every strike." Smith approached, nodding in approval. "Please demonstrate once more for the other two."

Eleanor pulled the hatpin from her wounded pillow and re-pinned her hat into place. "The trick is to remember where you've put the pin." Curls of ribbons spilled down her head like the tentacles of an elaborate octopus. She took a step away, putting her back to her pillow.

Quick as a sprite, she spun about, pulling the hatpin free, oblivious to the hat bouncing down her back as she delivered a mortal blow to the down stuffing.

Smith clapped and Rose and Lavinia joined her.

Eleanor started, as if she'd forgotten they were there. Then she beamed, putting a hand on her hip, much in the way Smith did, empowered with a glowing confidence.

"What's your secret?" Rose asked.

A shadow flickered over Eleanor's face. "I imagine needing to save my son."

"A woman will do anything to save her child." Lady Duxbury murmured the statement so quietly, Rose almost didn't hear.

Without thought, Rose's hand went to her stomach, where the swell of her own child was becoming harder to mask despite the draped front of her skirt shielding her abdomen.

Eventually, Rose's and Lavinia's clumsy efforts at the basic spin and attack were performed to Smith's satisfaction, which meant they moved on to more advanced methods. This included an aggressive step forward, paired with a jab, followed by a feint left to distract the attacker before jabbing a second time. In general, there were many jabs to be had in this particular sport.

By the time they were done, sweat dampened Rose's day dress, her face slick with perspiration, and she cursed whoever had invented the corset.

Smith congratulated their efforts upon completion of her training. "And now that you've performed each of these moves a dozen or so times . . ."

"At the very least," Rose added under her breath, earning her a snicker from Lavinia.

"Perhaps more than a dozen," Smith conceded. "But you'll know the action by rote should the need ever arise."

"Marvelous," Lady Duxbury said from her place beside Smith, applauding delicately. "You've all been simply marvelous."

Excitement tingled through Rose. She couldn't wait to see Theodore again, to regale him with her adventures in hatpin fighting.

He'd once been the person she longed to share everything with, no matter how large or small. Theodore was becoming that person again. Thus far, he had kept his promise, allowing her the freedoms she'd enjoyed before, his demeanor one of love and support.

She experienced a sudden pang of longing for her husband. To see him again, to share details of Rosewood Cottage, to show off her newfound skill. A smile touched her lips.

It was good to miss him.

"I've had a heartier luncheon than usual prepared on account of your exertions," Lady Duxbury said. "I've also allotted some time if you care to freshen up."

They chuckled, understanding *freshen up* being a polite way of insinuating they were indeed disheveled.

"I thought we all might enjoy a respite after we eat as well." Lady Duxbury's eyes twinkled mischievously. "Anticipate staying up late this evening for my next surprise."

Even as Lady Duxbury spoke, the figure in widow's weeds lurked in the background, floating almost preternaturally in the shadows.

If Rose's suspicions were correct, they would be attending a séance. Not that it would be anything new to her. She'd attended one before in Manhattan. Who hadn't?

The affair had been absurd, with an assistant who was absent any time music erupted, or curtains fluttered in a sudden breeze. The spiritualist cried out like a bad opera singer, shuddering as if possessed. Even such wailing wasn't enough to mask the gears grinding beneath the table as it spun in jerky spurts.

If nothing else, the séance ought to be amusing.

CHAPTER THIRTY

Mrs. Eleanor Clarke

ELEANOR'S MUSCLES WERE PLEASANTLY SORE as she made her way downstairs. The rest after luncheon had been restorative and she'd woken with an exhilarating energy.

Something had compelled her when packing to add a green velvet evening gown. The color didn't generally appeal to her. Now, however, it reminded her of the new growth of plants returning after a hard winter, those delicate shoots that broke through the unforgiving ground.

After her success at hatpin fighting, she felt invigorated to persevere as surely as those tender, seemingly fragile, buds.

"You're standing taller this evening," Rose said as she descended the other half of the stairs, her blush-pink gown whispering rhythmically with her steps.

"I feel stronger than I've been in a while," Eleanor admitted.

"If I could wield a hatpin like you, I'm sure I would, too." Rose glanced at the painting of the woman as they met at the landing and gave a little shudder. "Does it feel like she's staring at you?"

Eleanor looked up at the woman whose face was lifted just high enough for her imploring gaze to reach beyond the painting, her mouth soft with an unspoken sorrow, her hands over her heart, as though cradling a secret.

"Ah, here they are now," Lady Duxbury's voice called out before Eleanor could answer. "Ladies, please join us."

As they approached Lady Duxbury, the light from the lamps progressively dimmed until they were standing in the darkened drawing room. The thick velvet curtains had been drawn, blotting out even the moonlight.

The elegant mauve settee and other furniture had been pushed aside, making way for a round table framed with five chairs. The woman in widow's weeds stood nearby, shrouded in black lace that obscured face and figure.

"Ladies, allow me to introduce you to our spiritualist this evening, Mrs. Parish." Lady Duxbury's voice was a low, reverent whisper. The veil-covered hat tipped in silent greeting and the woman eased into a chair.

"Please join us." Lady Duxbury waved Eleanor and Rose toward the table where she and Lavinia now took their seats.

Eleanor took Mrs. Parish's left while Lady Duxbury flanked her right.

Mrs. Parish put her hands on the table, her long, tapered fingers facing upward. "Let us join hands." Her voice was papery soft, her age indiscernible.

"While I'm sure the history of the house can be easily discovered—" Lady Duxbury clasped hands with the medium "—I've told Mrs. Parish nothing about why I've asked her to come."

Eleanor let the spiritualist's dry, cool hand wrap around hers. On Eleanor's other side, Rose's hand was warm and supple.

There was a long moment of silence. The veil never once stirred, as though the woman did not breathe.

"There is much sadness in this house." Though she spoke abruptly, her delicate voice scarcely disturbed the quiet. "In some places sorrow lingers like candle smoke after its flame has been snuffed. In others, such as here, the sadness is oppressive. I feel as though I'm suffocating."

Eleanor couldn't stop herself from glancing around the room. The space that had been dappled with sunlight earlier was now bleak and empty.

"But none are quite as consuming as the nursery." The medium's hand tensed against Eleanor's, as though the admission caused her pain.

A profound sense of hopelessness flooded Eleanor. Beside her, Rose sucked in a quiet breath.

"Do you feel it as I do?" Mrs. Parish asked. "Such is the weight of her sorrow."

"How can I feel this so acutely?" Lavinia flicked an anxious glance around the table. "As if the light has been sucked from my soul?"

Eleanor closed her eyes, familiar with the burden of misery. She had learned a long time ago not to fight the sensation. Fighting only made the pain worse.

"Why the nursery?" Rose's hand tensed in Eleanor's. "Did a child die?"

"The child lived." The medium went quiet and leaned her head back. The mask of black lace swept toward her neck, obscuring any hint of flesh beneath. As if she were nothing more than an amorphous form of widow's weeds.

She remained thus for several moments before lowering her head. "The mother was the one who perished. By her own volition."

The skin around Lady Duxbury's eyes tightened, and she leaned the slightest bit closer, as if she did not want Mrs. Parish to sense how desperately she yearned to know more.

"What happened?" Rose asked beside Eleanor.

Mrs. Parish tilted her head, as if listening to words no one else could hear. "I'm having difficulty discerning. Shame extends beyond the veil of our world and creates a thick barrier. Do you have something of hers, as I asked?"

Lady Duxbury handed an item to the woman. Only when the medium turned the piece over in her hand did Eleanor recognize the jet hair comb as one she'd seen Lady Duxbury wear.

The medium scoffed and set the comb on the table with a hard clack. "You're testing me. There is sadness within that piece, yes. But not for the woman whose spirit I am to connect with." She held out her hand, fingers extending with impatience.

A smirk lifted the corner of Lady Duxbury's lips, and she passed a ring to the medium. The garnet at the center caught the light like a pomegranate aril. The ring landed in Mrs. Parish's outstretched palm, and she cried out, as though struck.

She withdrew her hand from Eleanor's and covered the ring, cradling the item within her palms. She exhaled a shaky breath and a tear dropped from the black lace, shattering on the back of her hand.

"She had a son." Emotion clogged the medium's thin voice. "One whom she loved with all her heart." She stroked the gold band of the ring the way Eleanor stroked her son's cheek. "But gloom ensnared her after the birth, dragging her into darkness with a madness she could not escape. Not even for the sake of her son."

Lavinia's eyes were wide in her narrow face. "What happened?"

"She tried." The medium's words caught. "Every day she tried. But the sadness was too intense, its effect all-consuming. On a beautiful spring day too lovely to bear, she kissed her sweet boy, opened the window . . ."

Abruptly, Mrs. Parish set the ring on the table in front of Lady Duxbury, as if the piece had burned her. "And the pain stopped."

If Mrs. Parish wept behind the thick widow's veil, she was

no longer alone. Eleanor touched a finger to her cheek, damp with her own tears.

"She wasn't mad." Eleanor's whisper was soft enough to fade into the air. Except the quiet was so great, she had the immediate attention of every woman in the room.

A flint struck within her, sparking hurt for the woman who had not been able to overcome that deep, confusing hopelessness.

"She wasn't mad," Eleanor repeated with vehemence, cracking the silence. "Something of a similar nature happened to me. When my son was born. He was beautiful, perfect in every way. I was equally healthy. In body, at least. In spirit, I was . . . bereft. Every day seemed bleak. Endless. Excruciating."

"Yes," the spiritualist breathed.

"When I feared I truly could not take any more, whatever darkness gripped me finally let go." She shook her head. "I do not know what caused my despondency but am grateful it finally ceased. This mother was not so fortunate."

"Did you worry you were mad?" Lavinia asked.

"What woman does not?" Rose asked with a brittle smirk. "When every deviation from a pleasant, empty smile is marked as hysteria."

"This is why we must be strong for one another." Lady Duxbury retrieved the ring and ran the pad of her forefinger gently over the smooth gold band. "Perhaps we can be strong as well for the former Lady Duxbury, mother to my late husband. Her story was buried with her, having only been divulged to my husband at his father's deathbed. My husband never understood why she did what she did. I think it's why he . . ." She faltered. "There were ways he struggled with the pain of such loss."

Lady Duxbury turned abruptly to Mrs. Parish. "Can you tell her that we understand her pain, that she is among friends? That together we have strength?"

Mrs. Parish folded her hand over Lady Duxbury's, the one which held the ring, clasping it between them.

A sense of lightness washed over Eleanor, as palpable as the grief had been earlier.

"She already knows." Mrs. Parish released Lady Duxbury's hand and slid black gloves onto her pale white hands. "You have set her at peace."

They all departed the room several minutes later in quiet contemplation, each lost in her own thoughts.

"I've never been to a séance like that before," Rose said in wonder as they began to climb the stairs. "That one almost felt . . . real."

It hadn't *almost* felt real. The authenticity of their connection to the former Lady Duxbury had touched the core of Eleanor's soul.

Rose grabbed her arm, stopping short as they came to the landing.

"What—?" The words died on Eleanor's lips as Rose gaped at the portrait.

Eleanor faced the painting and a preternatural chill prickled over her.

Whatever pain and sorrow had radiated from the portrait now seemed to glow with warmth and contentment. The woman's eyes sparkled, and the softness of her mouth appeared lifted at the corners. As though in a smile.

"She didn't look like that earlier," Rose whispered. "Did she?"

"I . . ." Eleanor's voice died away.

Because the painting hadn't changed. Not really. The woman's eyes still gazed down at them, her mouth still relaxed.

And yet, all that agony was gone, replaced with a quiet joy.

Was she smiling now?

But while Rose was left with an obvious sense of disquiet, Eleanor's was filled suddenly with hope. The power of women coming together could truly do marvelous things.

In her room once more, Eleanor sifted through the under-clothes she'd brought, and withdrew Lady Duxbury's diary. She wouldn't have dreamed of removing it from Lady Duxbury's library in London if she hadn't been tasked with unearthing information on Lady Meddleson, and clearly, she had not reached that particular diary entry yet.

Desperate to learn what was needed, Eleanor drew open the blue leather cover and settled in to read.

CHAPTER THIRTY-ONE

Lady Duxbury's Diary

February 1888

George is gravely ill.

    I write this from my son's bedside where I have kept vigil, the wheezing rattle from deep within his small chest the only evidence of life in my boy.

    Silas tells me I'm mad to remain so adamantly at my son's side. But I've ceased caring how anyone perceives me. They can haul me into an asylum if they must, but I refuse to leave until George is fully restored to pink-cheeked vitality.

    And Silas can burn in hell, him and his blasted inkwell, which prompted this tragedy.

    George had wandered into the study where Silas was working. Silas claims George became overly energetic, as boys are wont to do, and accidentally knocked the inkwell onto an important document. But George told a different tale, one where Silas became enraged at his presence and in a fit of vexation, Silas knocked the inkwell with his own hand.

    Regardless how fervently Silas places the blame at George's feet, and no matter how much Silas tries to twist my words, there is no doubt in my mind who is the culprit in this matter.

And who is the victim.

Oh, my boy. My sweet boy.

Silas locked him outside without even a coat despite the onset of a storm and bade him remain there. Then came the frigid rain.

The servants were too terrified of Silas's wrath to allow my son inside, and my poor George was too frightened of Silas's retribution to find a way in of his own accord. When I returned home from a luncheon Silas insisted I attend earlier that day, I found George still outside, thoroughly drenched, his lips blue with cold.

By that night, he blazed with fever.

The doctor's ministrations did nothing. My maid searched through her extensive book of curatives and brewed a tea from those brittle pages that finally reduced George's fever.

But for all the herbs within that arcane book, nothing has proved effective in ceasing the terrible rattle in his chest, or the unnatural stillness of his small body. The latter is what causes me the greatest worry.

I fear for the welfare of my son.

March 1888

My son is dead.

I am inconsolable. I am undone.

There is no palliative for this pain that echoes through my being. It consumes me, encompassing every sense, every thought, every agonizing breath.

Silas speaks words I do not hear. How can I when my ears are clogged with the splintering of my heart?

George was placed in a gleaming casket, generously procured at great cost to Silas. There is bitterness in that statement. It is thick enough to sour the sweetest attempts at contrition. Surely, the expense was not as great as Silas claims, for the casket was so terribly small. But then, my boy was so terribly small.

There were few people in attendance at his funeral. The scant acquaintances I once possessed have long since scattered into oblivion by Silas's jealous claims on my affection. And so there was no one other than the servants to weep over the ineffable loss.

The gash carved into the earth was a cold, dark thing meant to embrace my boy, to steal him from my arms, which long for nothing more than to cradle my child.

I sit in his empty room, absorbing the whole of my hurt in the hopes it will rob me of life. That I may join him.

Death is unforgiving. It deprived me of what I love best and then passed me over, abandoning me to my thoughts. They circle and circle and circle, sharp with the need for vengeance.

The hate comes smoother within me than grief, the edges less jagged. My rage is a tangible thing that leaves me with something to aspire to rather than this aching loss for which there is no recourse.

Come what may, I have nothing to lose.

I have already lost all.

CHAPTER THIRTY-TWO

Mrs. Rose Wharton

ROSE PAUSED AT THE PAINTING ON HER WAY down to breakfast the next morning, scrutinizing the artwork in the sunlight. But no, she was not mistaken. There was definitely something different about the portrait.

The contentment on the woman's face soothed whatever had been rough and unpolished within Rose upon their arrival to the cottage.

A quick glance around confirmed no one was nearby and she indulged her curiosity, gently running her fingertips over the woman's face. The sweep of oil paint was hard to the touch. There had been no alteration or the paint would have been wet for days.

And yet, Rose would swear on her life that the portrait was different. A shiver rattled down her spine.

Whatever Mrs. Parish had done the evening before, she had turned around Rose's skepticism. She might even go so far as to claim herself a believer.

And whether she was or not, she smiled warmly up at the painting and touched her hands over her heart, mirroring the portrait to convey a silent camaraderie.

Tea was set out at breakfast along with several pastries and cold meats and cheeses. A familiar roasted aroma caught her attention.

Rose tipped her nose into the air and gave a discreet sniff. Why, yes, that was—

"Coffee, ma'am?" Lady Duxbury's young maid held up a porcelain pot.

"By all means, thank you." Rose settled into a chair and the maid poured the dark liquid into a teacup.

"Your husband said you preferred coffee," Lady Duxbury said from the head of the table. "My maid procured some prior to our departure."

"That was kind of you." Rose took a comforting sip. The coffee was rich, perfectly brewed to the point of full flavor without becoming bitter.

The courtesy was considerate, especially when so many English found the aroma of coffee offensive. Rose's brother-in-law refused to allow it at the country estate when she was visiting. Not that his lack of accommodation was surprising.

Eleanor sat across from Rose with a lemon pastry on her plate. "Thank you for coordinating such fascinating entertainments. I had anticipated enjoying my time here, but this has been truly exceptional."

"I'm grateful to all of you as well," Lady Duxbury said. "For the lightness you've brought to Rosewood Cottage."

Rose pressed her lips together and considered bringing up the painting again when Lavinia spoke up. "I can't believe we'll be returning home this morning."

"Not this morning." Lady Duxbury smiled and took a sip of tea. "We'll depart after luncheon. This morning, I have one more surprise."

Eleanor sat forward in anticipation.

There was a glow about her since the lessons in hatpin fighting, an incandescent confidence that left her cheeks rosy and her eyes bright. Rose's heart swelled, knowing precisely what this newfound self-assuredness meant to her friend.

"Can we have a hint as to what the surprise is?" Lavinia asked.

"I have a garden I'd like to show you." Lady Duxbury gave a suggestive lift of a brow. "While unusual, its contents can be quite efficacious. But before we proceed, I want to offer something."

She set her teacup down, its clink loud in the suddenly silent room as they listened with rapt attention. "I want you to feel comfortable in this home, as if it's yours. Rosewood Cottage is available to any of you at any time should you have need. The servants here are most discreet."

An offer of freedom. Made especially to women who had precious little as of late.

A month ago, Rose would have planned how she might best use such a gift, back when she was considering the possibility of leaving Theodore.

Now, with the opportunity spread before her, the idea of abandoning him shifted uneasily into something disagreeable. More than disagreeable. The idea of life without him hollowed her out and left a vast emptiness in its wake.

Eleanor, however, looked very much like a skittish horse about to bolt from where she sat across the table. The muscles of her neck tensed, her breath quickening.

"Even if I am not here." Lady Duxbury looked around at each of them. "For an evening away. A year away. For refuge. For somewhere no one might ever think to look for you. I have informed the servants to always have Rosewood Cottage at the ready to receive you without question."

Her gaze came to rest on Eleanor just as the woman tugged at her sleeves in that anxious habit of hers. But before the fitted pink silk could be yanked back into place, Rose saw what she had been hiding all this time.

A smattering of dark bruises encircled her wrist, mottled

shades of brown and yellow and black and purple, jarring against the fairness of her porcelain skin.

All at once, the pieces clicked together. Eleanor's quiet, demure reserve, the way she never offered information on herself at social events despite knowing everything about everyone else. The ferocity of her efforts at hatpin fighting.

I imagine needing to save my son.

Her abused wrist was so thin, so delicate, it was a wonder Mr. Clarke hadn't snapped it like a twig.

Rose dragged her gaze up from where the slim sleeve now covered those wretched bruises and found her friend looking directly at her.

"Eleanor," Rose breathed.

Spots of color showed on Eleanor's cheeks and she cleared her throat, looking pointedly at Lady Duxbury. "That is terribly generous of you, Lady Duxbury."

"My offer is given in full sincerity." Lady Duxbury put a hand to her chest, her fingers finding the glossy surface of her hair brooch.

The curiosity of that brooch nipped at the back of Rose's mind. Like Eleanor, Lady Duxbury was adept at prevaricating, understanding much about others without giving away anything about herself. What in her past had left her so skilled in that regard?

"With that settled, shall we adjourn to the gardens?" Lady Duxbury rose, and they all joined her.

The air in the garden was fragrant with the promise of summer, of sun-warmed grass and sweet-smelling blossoms; the perfume of a carefree lifestyle outside London.

"It's lovely," Lavinia breathed. "I could see the garden from my room, but up close, it's exquisite."

"This isn't even what I wanted you to see." Lady Duxbury waved over her maid, who carried a basket of gloves and leather aprons. "I should like you to put these on."

Rose eyed the heavy adornments with a frown, her palm wandering to the bulge of her belly that now had the roundness of a small orange. "Is there something dangerous where we're going?"

"Forgive me, but you may wish to remain in the garden here." Lady Duxbury spoke softly, her words meant only for Rose's ears, her expression one of knowing.

The life within Rose flicked against her womb. What had started as barely perceptible flutters were now insistent bumps, impossible to ignore. She left her hand lying over her child and spoke loud enough for the others to hear. "I'm in a delicate way and think I shall stay here, safely among the carnations."

Eleanor gasped. "Oh, Rose, that is delightful news."

Rose grinned at her friend's enthusiasm.

"Your husband must be overjoyed," Lavinia added.

The happiness leeched out of Rose. She could brush off the comment with a benign affirmation. But these were the women she'd come to trust. "I . . . I haven't told him yet."

"Won't his brother be delighted at the prospect of an heir for the family name?" Lavinia asked.

"Yes, but . . ." Rose bit her lip. "I didn't know if I planned to stay in England or not . . . with Theodore or not. A terrible thing to say, I know."

"Some men aren't worth staying for if you have a way out." Eleanor flashed a quick smile after her desolate words and looked up at the sky. "Goodness, the day is going by far too quickly. Shall we proceed to the garden?"

As they pulled on their thick gloves and were helped into their heavy aprons, Rose waved them off and wandered past a cluster of daisies. Resolute in her newly made decision.

The time had come to tell Theodore.

CHAPTER THIRTY-THREE

Mrs. Eleanor Clarke

ELEANOR FOLLOWED LADY DUXBURY AS SHE led them toward their last surprise.

While Lavinia kept pace with the countess, Eleanor lagged behind, weighed down by her thoughts. She glanced over her shoulder, where Rose wandered among the flower beds, her hand settled lovingly over her stomach.

Eleanor recalled those early days of pregnancy, the hope that a baby might mend whatever was broken in Cecil, soften his harshness. But having William only added another layer of vulnerability to Eleanor that Cecil exploited.

Rose was brave in admitting she'd considered leaving her husband. Even when she was with child.

Eleanor could never leave.

Or could she?

Her heart fluttered like a trapped moth against her ribs.

What if she *did* leave? What if she fled to Rosewood Cottage while she worked out where to go next?

But she couldn't abandon William, not with *him*. And Cecil would scour the ends of the earth in search of her if she took their son.

Was remaining hidden from a man with such power and influence even possible?

The prospect rippled through Eleanor like a cool breeze on a hot day.

Hope.

Possibility.

Lavinia's voice carried back from where she walked ahead, her tone bright as she fired off a round of questions about Rosewood Cottage. The young woman's poetry seemed to have unlocked a passion for all things, allowing her to cast off her shyness and find her voice.

Lady Duxbury answered each question with her usual patience, her responses careful, never revealing much of anything about herself. As a result, Lavinia and Rose likely knew little about Lady Duxbury's life beyond threads of gossip.

And while Eleanor still was no wiser as to whether that gossip was true, she had been privy to Lady Duxbury's history in a way no one else had.

Reading the entry with her son's death had been a blow to Eleanor, as surely as if she'd known little George. And perhaps she did, through the pages of the diary, and through filling in gaps of her knowledge of George with thoughts of her own sweet son.

Lady Duxbury stopped in front of an old wooden fence at the back of the property, the slats sagging with age, presumably abandoned years ago. But what could it contain so far from the cottage?

Lady Duxbury withdrew a key from her pocket, and unlocked the ancient mechanism.

Inside, the garden was anything but abandoned. Manicured plant beds stretched out in a sea of green, filled with the most unusual vines and blooms. Some Eleanor even recognized. The somber purple of belladonna flowers, the vivid coral hues of foxglove.

Eleanor's hands were damp within the thick leather gloves. She pulled at the base of one to allow a trickle of air to seep in.

"Keep your gloves on," Lady Duxbury cautioned. "Everything in here is poisonous."

"Poisonous?" Lavinia echoed as she approached a small plot bristling with frothy sprigs of what appeared to be Queen Anne's lace.

"That's hemlock," Lady Duxbury cautioned.

Lavinia immediately stopped walking, but still studied the plant from afar. "It looks just like Queen Anne's lace."

A little smile curled at Lady Duxbury's lips. "Some can be deceptive."

"Why do you grow them if they're harmful?" Eleanor asked.

"One has uses for these plants from time to time," Lady Duxbury said in a nonchalant tone. "And they can be helpful. Bruised foxglove leaves produce a juice that is beneficial in healing ulcers and strengthening a weak heart. And belladonna . . ."

"Can have a calming effect and ease colic," Eleanor finished. "As well as soothe painful skin ailments."

Lady Duxbury regarded Eleanor with quiet pride. "Precisely. And so much more. I see you've been studying the book of herbal remedies."

"I find the use of herbs and flowers fascinating."

"It is." Lady Duxbury nodded. "In small doses, many poisons can actually heal."

Eleanor could not stop her next question. "And in large doses?"

"They're fatal." Lady Duxbury strode onward, offering no more explanation.

Lavinia straightened from where she studied a stalk of purple flowers. "Why the secrecy of the garden?"

Lady Duxbury smirked. "You've heard the rumors, I'm sure. I certainly do not need more fodder for gossip." She paused to indicate the lovely cluster of purple flowers. "That is monkshood, also known as wolfsbane or aconite. It can bring down a fever or ease sore joints. It is also incredibly lethal and can kill within hours."

"And you learned all this from the book of herbs," Lavinia concluded. "But how did you obtain such a book?"

"It was gifted to me," Lady Duxbury answered. "I had a very dear maid when I was married to my second husband, the Earl of Esterly. She seemed to have a cure for everything." A shadow crossed her face. "Almost everything." She cleared her throat. "My maid shared her knowledge with me and, after Lord Esterly's passing, I continued to employ her. She helped me considerably through the years."

"That's her book," Lavinia said. "The one you encouraged us to look through."

Lady Duxbury gave a solemn nod. "Yes. With no children of her own, she gifted the book to me on her deathbed. I have cherished the knowledge ever since."

The countess languidly strode back toward the partially open gate of her clandestine poison garden. "My housekeeper at Rosewood Cottage has the only other key to this gate. As with the house, you may use the garden at any time, should you have need of the plants within."

Her gaze landed pointedly on Eleanor as she said this.

All at once, Eleanor understood the purpose of this sojourn, the reason for Lady Duxbury's diary, the availability of the cottage, the access to such powerful herbs.

Lady Duxbury was offering Eleanor a chance to escape.

But was she brave enough to try?

Oblivious to the thoughts roaring through Eleanor's mind, Lavinia regarded the floral white trumpets of a plant and mused, "I think my mother has this growing in her garden."

"Datura," Lady Duxbury said without hesitating. "Many women have several of these plants in their gardens without even realizing what they are." Lady Duxbury smiled to herself. "So many innocent poisons."

They exited the garden and she locked the gate behind them, sealing her secret within the unassuming fence once more.

Lavinia increased her pace with girlish delight as they approached the house. "I'm going to tell Rose about the garden."

When she was out of earshot, Lady Duxbury turned to Eleanor. "Have you found what you need on Lady Meddleson yet?"

"Not yet," Eleanor offered apologetically. "Your son . . . I could not go on."

Lady Duxbury closed her eyes, yielding to pain the way one does in the wake of powerful loss. Her fingertips grazed the brooch and she blinked her eyes open. "Please do continue to read. Lady Meddleson's help will improve Rose's chances in Society and her brother-in-law's approval. If you've read about. . . my son, you're close to finding what you need." Lady Duxbury pulled off her thick gloves and Eleanor followed suit, appreciating the cool air against her damp palms. "I wish I could simply speak of such things, but . . ."

Lady Duxbury drew a labored inhale.

"I understand." Eleanor touched Lady Duxbury's forearm in quiet support. "If I'm close as you say, I'll read more before we depart. May I perhaps borrow your carriage a while longer to call on Lady Meddleson before I'm returned home?"

Cecil claimed to have need of his carriage during Eleanor's return. She suspected the excuse was contrived, creating a complication to make accepting Lady Duxbury's invitation difficult despite his approval.

Lady Duxbury had been all too happy to provide her carriage to enable Eleanor's attendance. Now having the countess's carriage worked in Eleanor's favor.

"Of course you may." Concern showed in Lady Duxbury's eyes. "I hope this trip does not cost you too dearly."

Eleanor focused on fitting the gloves together rather than meeting the other woman's eye. There was always a price to pay with Cecil. "I'm grateful to have come regardless."

They joined the others, and their candid conversation fell away to amicable silence.

As soon as they returned to the house to prepare for their departure, Eleanor made good on her promise. Not that she minded. Returning to the diary was a worthy distraction from what she would face with Cecil when she finally returned home.

CHAPTER THIRTY-FOUR

Lady Duxbury's Diary

April 1889

I am to be married.

I am not a blushing, fresh-faced bride by any means. Indeed, I believe it is impossible for my cheeks to flush any longer.

No, I am a desperate woman who is thoroughly and irreparably broken.

Silas is dead, perishing not long after my son. He was found cold and stiff one morning. His was a smoother passing than that of my son, whose lungs rasped with death for an agonizing fortnight.

I was left a widow, generous in wealth and worldly goods and bereft in all else.

My thoughts turned to Elias, as they had after the passing of my first husband.

Ensconced in widow's weeds, I went to the bookshop on Threadneedle Lane, finding a golden-haired little girl alongside Elias's blond wife, with eyes as large and velvety brown as those of my George.

The reminder of my own boy was like a knife plunged deep in my heart. I nearly tripped on their little white mustached cat in my haste to flee.

This caused me to run headlong into Lady Meddleson, of all wretched souls. I rushed away without so much as a greeting, wrapped tight in my black shawl and my misery.

For I truly had no one.

I have never held affection for my own family—nor they for me—and did not bother to turn to them. My father and brother are engrossed in the running of the estate, having made favorable investments, my sister busy with her bevy of healthy children, possessing no concept of the pain of loss.

I fully intended to live alone, subsisting on my fortune until death came for me and I could fall into the embrace of the unfeeling earth alongside my son.

And then came the Earl of Duxbury.

Edgar is greatly advanced in age, old enough to be my grandfather with spotted hands and a shock of white hair. Age has bowed him and he requires the aid of a cane. Upon our introduction at a picnic, he requested I sit at his right. I offered no complaint as I was simply biding my time until I could return home where heavy curtains blotted out the overbright sun and curious, "well-meaning" acquaintances could be turned away.

After all, I only agreed to attend the picnic to keep a toe dipped in Society. A woman with two dead husbands in the prime of their lives sets tongues wagging. Especially if she becomes a recluse.

At every social outing that followed, Edgar was there, apologizing for his inability to take me on the dance floor at balls, and with me seated to his right at dinner parties. His attentiveness drew me, his interest in hearing about my life, and the sympathy he offered at my loss.

In time, I considered him to be a dear friend. Perhaps that is why his offer of marriage came as a surprise. But his ebullient praise of my person and agreeable friendship were not what swayed me to acquiesce.

What led me to say yes were those spotted hands, and the frailty of that slim frame held aloft with the aid of a glossy, silver-tipped cane.

A man in such decrepitude cannot hurt me.

That is one reason.

The other is entirely selfish.

I was forced into my two prior marriages—first by my parents who cared little for me, and then by desperate circumstances. This time I chose Edgar because he loves me and vows to offer me protection, an insulation from the world, which has caused so much harm.

It does not matter to him that I may not return his affection. He wants only to have me at his side.

I do not anticipate that happiness is within my grasp, but perhaps I might finally feel protected by someone who genuinely cares for me. It is my hope that this will be a pleasant union of respect and appreciation. And given my suffering over George's loss, I am desperate for any respite from my pain.

January 1893

I have been captive for seventeen days.

It is not the longest I have endured imprisonment at the seemingly feeble hands of my husband. Nor, as you will recall, is it the first time I have been forced into compliance by such means.

Lady Meddleson is determined to eradicate any whisper of contentment I might ever possess. Shortly after my marriage to Edgar, she sought an audience with him, informing him of my visit to look in on Elias. What's more, she shared what she knew of Elias having been my son's father.

This challenged my husband's sensibilities, rendering him anxious that his young wife might be lured from his side by a man of her own age. His mother died when he was a babe, and he's been fearful of being left alone ever since, or so he says. No matter how much I beseech Edgar, his worries are greater than my promise of fealty.

I am well acquainted with loneliness and so I might be considerate of his concerns had he not gone to such measures. As it is, I fail to comprehend how he justifies keeping me immured in the confines of my room.

My bedchamber is grand, yes, gilded with delicate gold leaf, sumptuous with velvets, the high silk walls ornamented with art. I know every square inch of my opulent cage, from which I am only released to make appearances in Society, and when my husband is home to offer him the companionship he so desperately craves.

He gifts me books in return for my compliance, ostensibly to mollify my displeasure. Nothing can right the wrong of this imprisonment, but I confess the companionship of those books I have yearned for has brought me some small measure of comfort.

Despite his favors, I am little more than a doll to be taken out, played with and quietly tucked away.

But I am a vengeful doll, whose thoughts burn with the need to denounce Lady Meddleson.

Though I am relegated to my room, my servants are free to come and go—biddable to any number of tasks for a bit of coin, and my maid has always been fiercely loyal after having followed me since my second marriage. It took her scarcely a fortnight to shake free a dirty secret from the pedestal that Lady Meddleson placed herself upon.

There was a child, a by-blow from a passionate tryst with a footman, a son who now resides in a village on the outskirts of London. Meanwhile, Lord and Lady Meddleson remain barren.

Lady Meddleson has wealth, power and influence. But all she ever wanted was love and happiness—of which she has neither. Perhaps that is why she hurts me so, out of jealousy for any modicum of joy I might possess. Any scrap of love.

I clutch the pearl of knowledge about her little boy, unsure how I shall spend this fortune. For unlike Lady Meddleson, I cannot implicate a child. I know too well what suffering might be visited upon the offspring from the mother's sin.

Until then I wait in my beautiful prison and wonder how best to seek my revenge.

And how many more days I can stand this captivity.

CHAPTER THIRTY-FIVE

Lady Lavinia Cavendish

LIGHT AND CONTENTMENT FILLED THE CABIN AS Lavinia's carriage bounced over country roads and then clattered onto the paved streets of London. A new poem was burgeoning in her mind, the words unfurling like a blossoming flower.

Empowered by the hatpin fighting, awed by the séance, intrigued by the poison garden and filled with joy from the loving embrace of friendship, every one of those experiences played in Lavinia's imagination like sunlight dancing over water.

Though she had only spent one night away from home, she had come away a changed woman. Given how Rose now openly cradled her stomach with her palm and the confidence in Eleanor's stride, Lavinia was not the only one. Each woman was finding her strength. Even Lady Duxbury seemed to have a new sense of peace about her.

The carriage rolled to a stop in front of Lavinia's townhouse, and she alighted onto the stone path, rushing into her home lest she lose the first fledgling words of her poem. She repeated the opening to herself again and again, as if doing so might score the stanza into her mind. The rest of the poem clung to that one line, the bonding to weave what followed.

In the deadly shadows of nightshade . . .

Ada, the lady's maid Lavinia and her sister shared, was a sour-faced woman with a penchant for reporting every transgression to Papa. She blocked Lavinia's path to the stairs as if she'd been lying in wait for Lavinia's arrival.

Ada gave a satisfied smirk. "Lord Eversville requests your presence in his study."

Lavinia shifted around the woman and ascended the stairs, her fingers aching to clasp a pen, her soul desperate for the scratch of a nib on paper, to bleed out her emotions onto the page.

In the deadly shadows of nightshade . . .

The maid blocked Lavinia's path a second time. "He instructed me to have you join him immediately upon your arrival."

Lavinia drew back affronted. "A moment, please, Ada."

"Now." The woman did not move. "I'll not be sacked because you didn't heed your father's orders."

"You'll never be sacked, not with all the secrets you report," Lavinia retorted, her words dripping with spite. With that, she spun on her heel and marched down to see her father.

Being called to Papa's study was never favorable.

In the deadly shadows of nightshade . . .

She pushed open the door and found her father sitting at his desk, fingertips steepled together as he stared at the rug. His gaze shot to her when she entered the room, his expression stern. Her mother was at his side, her eyes red-rimmed.

It was then Lavinia realized her father's elbows were braced on either side of a short pile of books.

No, not books.

Journals.

Her journals.

Her poetry.

Those three slim books, unprotected, at risk of being pulled open and baring her soul.

Nausea swirled in the pit of her stomach. Ice and fire churning with bile and the tang of fear.

"Please don't—" she began.

"Sit." Her father bit out the order, that mark creasing his brow.

That mark, just below his hairline, had first appeared when Lavinia tried to decline a coming out ball, voicing her intention to eschew marriage and spend her days at the country manor reading instead. The mark deepened when she rejected the only offer of marriage ever bestowed upon her. The mark became permanently etched the night she'd punched her brother like a proper pugilist.

Papa no longer needed to furrow his brow for the mark to show.

Lavinia let the door slip from her fingertips and bang shut behind her. She made her way to the wooden chair in front of her father's desk and slid into the seat.

"What is the meaning of this?" Color rose in her father's face.

"Those are my journals," Lavinia offered feebly.

"I know they're your journals," he replied. "I've read them."

Her heart pounded so hard, spots blossomed in her vision. "It's poetry."

"Poetry?" Her father's heavy brows lifted, crinkling his forehead. "Poetry?" he repeated, bellowing the word so loudly, Lavinia started.

He lifted a book from the stack and snapped it open to a page in the middle. "The emotions rage inside me like a conflagration and sometimes I wish they would burn me whole." His voice was hard, making her words obscene, shameful.

Licking his thumb, he flicked through several pages and read again. "Sorrow rips from my breast, so that I am gaping, mortally wounded." He threw the book aside. It landed on the floor like a broken bird, pages bent and askew.

He reached for another, opening to a random page. "The sky has no limits and nor does my delight. I rise like Icarus on wax wings, soaring through the day and on into the night." And then another still. "The ground does not judge. Its demeanor cold and uncaring. How I crave its embrace, to tumble over me, clogging my ears, my eyes, my mouth, so my screams are silenced and I, too, am as cold and uncaring."

Her mother hiccupped a sob and pressed a wadded handkerchief to her eyes.

He slapped the book closed and glared at Lavinia, his nostrils flaring. "We thought you to be much improved. We hoped that you truly had overcome your hysteria, that the teas you've been attending with Lady Duxbury had facilitated your comfort in Society." He sighed. "Ada informs me you've been reading again."

Lavinia scowled at the maid's name and Mama looked away from where she sat beside Papa, her heartbroken gaze fixed on a bouquet of vibrant red gladiolus thrusting up from a gilded vase.

"I confess I have known about this reading of yours for some time," he continued. "I did not intervene in light of your pleasant countenance and your ready acceptance of social invitations." He scoffed. "I thought you fully prepared for Delilah's coming out ball."

"I am," Lavinia protested. "It is why I've been attending dinner parties and balls in preparation, and why—"

"These writings suggest otherwise." His flung his hand at the journals.

"I put my feelings on the page so I can release them," Lavinia cried, unable to help the desperate pitch to her voice. "This is not madness. This is passion."

But Lady Duxbury's words that had sounded beautiful and

inspiring now sounded pathetic and small coming from Lavinia. Self-loathing filled her, dulling her spirit, her fight.

"This is *madness*." Her father pounded his fist into one of the
books with a force that cracked its spine. He stood so abruptly,
his heavy chair toppled over. "Your writing reveals your hysteria." He slapped the heel of his palm on the table. "What you
feel, Lavinia . . . it is not normal."

It is not normal.

She *was not normal.*

She had pretended for a while, slipping on a mask and feign-
ing in a world where she could never truly belong.

"Harold," her mother said plaintively, reaching for him.

He shook her off, his face scarlet. "Don't Harold me. Delilah's coming out is next week. We cannot have Lavinia behav-
ing in such a way that someone might notice. We must protect
our good name."

Lavinia's mother stiffened. "What do you mean to do?"
There was a tenor to her query that left Lavinia chilled.

"We've tried our best with her, Helen." Her father scrubbed
a hand over his head, so his gray hair stood in spikes.

Anger coiled within Lavinia, begging for release, to lash against
Papa for what he threatened.

"What do you intend to do with me?" Lavinia asked, her
throat tight.

The high color in her father's face washed away. With dis-
quieting calm, he righted his chair and sank into it. A man
defeated. "I think it is time, Helen."

"No." Her mother shook her head, eyes welling with tears.
"Please no. Not like my mother."

Not like my mother.

The lunatic asylum.

Lavinia's heartbeat thundered loud enough to drown out her
mother's sobs.

The lunatic asylum.

Lavinia had not lashed out. She had not sobbed or begged. She had not been hysterical. For all that had been thrown her way, she had maintained composure better than her own father.

And still she had failed.

She couldn't stay in this room where her beautiful words were twisted into something ugly. Where the very thing that once gave her freedom now ensnared her.

She understood that the wings of her poetry were made of wax. And she had flown too close to the sun.

There was naught left but to plunge to the earth.

Without a word, she leaped from her chair and rushed from the room, nearly toppling Ada, who crouched by the door listening to words not meant for her.

Lavinia did not stop until she reached her bedchamber and had the door shut and locked behind her. Only then did she fling herself onto the bed, her face buried in the pillow as she released the maelstrom of her tears.

In the back of her mind, the beginning of a poem teased at her memory.

In the shadows of deadly nightshade . . .

No. That wasn't it.

Like a loose thread pulled on a delicate bit of lace, the forgotten words slipped away, stitch by stitch, irreparable. The *feel* of words was no longer inside her, only a lingering ghost of a stanza that should have been.

But the ruined poem didn't matter.

None of it did.

Not anymore.

For like her broken poem, she, too, was now little more than a bit of unraveled thread, damaged and readily discarded.

Exactly like her grandmother.

CHAPTER THIRTY-SIX

Mrs. Rose Wharton

ROSE PRACTICALLY SKIPPED UP THE THREE stairs leading to the townhouse she shared with Theodore, light as a cloud with excitement.

Confessing her pregnancy to her friends had been far easier than she'd expected, melting away her lingering trepidation. Whether through their support, or the realization of how much she had missed Theodore while at Rosewood Cottage, the time had finally come to tell him he was going to be a father.

Their butler welcomed her into the foyer, taking her gloves and hat. "Lord Amsel is in the study with Mr. Wharton, ma'am."

Rose's joy crashed to an abrupt halt.

"How wonderful," she murmured with more heart than she felt. "Will he be staying for dinner?"

Please don't let him be staying for dinner.

"He will, ma'am. I've notified the cook."

Rose thanked him and retreated up to her bedchamber to fortify herself to deal with Byron. She emerged sometime later in a pale pink silk gown her brother-in-law had once complimented, her hair swept up in the latest fashion and adorned with silk roses.

Not that the effort mattered. Byron still scowled at her when she joined him and Theodore in the drawing room, both men getting to their feet out of courtesy.

The room was a sunny yellow, a way to compensate for the weak sunlight trying to push through the windows. Her father's money was evident in the glossy silk walls, gleaming mahogany furniture and the thick canary-and-burnt-umber Turkish carpet absorbing most of the English chill from the hardwood floor.

"I trust you enjoyed your time away?" Though Byron's low, raspy voice was a byproduct of his illness, the quiet lent him an intimidating tone. As if each word were a whispered threat.

"I did, thank you." Rose ran her hand over the back of the settee, following the arch at the top, reminiscent of a violin's curve.

From behind Byron, Theodore grimaced, his mouth drawn as he gave a slight shake of his head.

Byron was disappointed.

With her.

"You should have been with your husband rather than gallivanting off with friends." Byron swirled his drink, the amber liquid catching light like stars against the cut-crystal glass. "Lady Meddleson attended Lady Stepton's ball last night. You might have made yourself indispensable to the countess to secure an invitation to her soiree."

A tide of frustration swelled within Rose. "Not everyone has been invited to the soiree."

He scoffed, the sound derogatory. "I have."

Rose squared her shoulders. "You shouldn't go."

"Shouldn't I?" The illness had eaten away at his body, leaving his once youthful face haggard. But his eyes remained clear and sharp, and he pinioned her with his glare.

"Rose is concerned for your health," Theodore said gently. "We don't want you exhausting yourself. Save your strength."

"For what?" Byron snapped. "If I don't attend, the Whartons won't make an appearance at the soiree at all."

His claim was preposterous. Rose knew he would still attend even if she and Theodore *were* invited.

Byron clung with a white-knuckled grip to the memory of the man he had been. A man of importance, who excelled at every sport, who stayed out until dawn reveling with friends and charming women. A man dubbed the most eligible bachelor consecutively for four seasons until his diagnosis.

His life had been squandered by hubris and the assumption he was invincible. There was an element of sadness to how much he had lost, and despite Rose's dislike of the man, his decline pulled at her sympathy.

He wobbled on his feet, a young man trapped in the cage of a frail body. "You should be finding every way possible to appeal to Lady Meddleson." A horrible wheeze sounded in his chest as he gasped out his next sentence. "Despite your vulgar American ways and that hideous accent."

His desperate breath made Rose's lungs hungry for air, and she pulled in a deep inhale.

"Now, see here." Theodore stepped between Byron and Rose, his hand out defensively, as if he could physically repel the words from landing like blows. "You will not speak to my wife in such a manner."

"You deserve better than her." Byron turned the point of his glare on his younger brother. "You have disappointed me in many ways, Theodore, but none so great as in your choice of a wife."

Whatever control Rose held on herself snapped. It was one thing to attack her, whose very presence would always be deplorable to Byron. It was another thing entirely to denigrate Theodore, who fought so hard for his brother's approval.

"How dare you?" Rose demanded fiercely. "I'm well aware you find me wanting, but how dare you think so poorly of your brother? His every waking moment is spent in pursuit of pleasing you."

"Rose . . ."

Theodore's protest was a verbal fly she batted away, too caught in the throes of her anger to pay him mind.

"Do you realize how often he worries he's letting you down?" she demanded. "And you stand here, criticizing him, who responsibly married while you squandered your youth."

Byron's face colored from red to aubergine as he sputtered, "I dare say—"

"I am not done." She lifted her chin in a haughty fashion her mother employed when approaching the Astors. "You may be sick, but it does not mean I will hold my tongue in speaking the truth. No matter how much you find him wanting, Theodore is a better man than you have ever been."

"Rose." There was a sharpness to Theodore's voice that finally caught her attention.

The life within her womb startled with an anxious bump.

"That is enough." Theodore's eyes were hard with displeasure. "Perhaps dining in your room this evening would be for the best."

He was dismissing her?

Heat stung her eyes, but she wouldn't give Byron the satisfaction of seeing her tears. As if on cue, the dinner bell rang.

"Good evening, husband." She inclined her head toward Byron, ensuring her gaze did not meet his lest he see the emotion threatening to spill over. "Good evening, Lord Amsel."

With that, she strode from the drawing room with measured steps, holding together a confidence that splintered apart the moment she was alone in her room.

When a tray was brought up, laden with the food she had ordered to please her husband, she did not touch a morsel. How could she when her heart ached so dreadfully?

Whatever hope she'd embraced upon her return home that

afternoon had been dashed. Meanwhile, Theodore's child wriggled and squirmed within her.

She put a hand on her stomach, filled anew with dread for her baby.

The door to her room began to open and she pushed to her feet, fully expecting Theodore.

But Theodore was not the person to step over the threshold. It was Byron.

In the privacy of her bedchamber.

Rose drew back, pulling her wrapper more snuggly around her body. "Remove yourself from—"

He closed the door behind him and faced her.

"I am here to issue a warning." His thready voice filled the room, forcing her to listen. "You will be an obedient wife, a woman worthy of the Wharton name. If you do anything to threaten this family, I will ensure you disappear."

She opened her mouth to protest, but he stepped closer, bringing with him the stink of sickness, a distinct malodor tinged with death that had gathered around him in the last month.

"Women disappear all the time." His eyes were hard chips of ice, unblinking, unfeeling. "Hysteria is an easy diagnosis. Your outburst down there alone would qualify."

A warning prickled down her spine. "What do you mean?" The strength she intended to infuse in her voice failed her.

She was aware of the answer.

Everyone knew how easily women were placed in asylums. Problems easily tucked away.

Byron watched her with his unyielding gaze. "Oh, you understand very well what I mean. And with your father's money, I can afford a donation to the facility significant enough to ensure no one will ever find you. Not even my wayward brother."

Rose shook her head, wanting to protest, but found she could not speak around the sudden dryness of her mouth.

"Inquiries have already been quietly made." With a lift of

his brow, Byron turned and was gone, as silently and swiftly as he'd come. A specter leaving the air crowded with his stench and his threats.

Rose sank onto the edge of her bed, unable to stand on legs that trembled. Her wealth that had salvaged the Wharton name might now be used to tighten a noose around her own neck.

Theodore didn't return to his bedchamber until late that night. The clock reflected the time just after two in the morning.

She pulled herself from bed, her feet chilling as she padded to the door separating their rooms. A click of the handle proved it was locked.

Her heart sank at the metallic catch barring her from entry.

In her bid to defend Theodore, she'd laid his vulnerability to the person he most longed to impress. Whenever she had a chance to speak with Theodore again, she would defend herself and plead with him to protect her against Byron's wrath.

She knocked on the door, every part of her aching for her husband's warm embrace, for the show of love and support. Her request went unanswered. As solid as the locked door separating them.

Would he believe her if she told him what Byron said? And even if he did, if he was put between the Wharton legacy or his wife, which would he choose?

Her heart was sure of the answer as she backed away and returned to her cold bed alone.

CHAPTER THIRTY-SEVEN

Mrs. Eleanor Clarke

ELEANOR WAITED IN LADY DUXBURY'S CARRIAGE for her calling card to be received by Lady Meddleson. Generally speaking, the wife of a merchant did not visit a countess without an invitation.

Under normal circumstance, Eleanor's calling card would have been thrown out and Eleanor and Cecil conveniently removed from the upcoming soiree. Except Eleanor had written a note on the card's back, one Lady Meddleson would not be able to ignore.

I am in possession of a rumor which must be confirmed.

Eleanor spent a lifetime dealing with powerful people awed by their own sense of worth and knew best how to handle them. Implying Lady Meddleson was an expert on rumors would flatter her into inviting Eleanor inside.

As anticipated, she was shown into Lady Meddleson's drawing room. Several gilt-edged mirrors lined the far wall, reflecting Eleanor's image as she entered, a trick to expand a small room. But Eleanor was learning to see past tricks these days.

Multiple reflections of Lady Meddleson greeted Eleanor, bidding her to take the seat nearest her. Of all the chairs, the one Lady Meddleson indicated was the least adorned, plain wood with a worn brown cotton seat. The insult was intentional, a reminder of Eleanor's rank.

She hesitated only a moment before settling gracefully onto the blue silk settee opposite Lady Meddleson. Eleanor's pulse raced at her bold move.

But she'd come here armed with a message, to garner a payment for the heavy toll the woman had exacted on Lady Duxbury's life.

"I see you've made yourself comfortable," Lady Meddleson said in her flowery voice.

"I have, thank you." Eleanor swept her hand over the lush fabric of the seat reserved for duchesses and countesses. Yet, here she sat, a viscount's daughter married to a man who made his fortune in excrement, a man whose wealth could buy a dozen homes with drawing rooms so large not even one gilt-edged mirror was needed to expand its size.

The sweet smile gracing Lady Meddleson's thin lips soured. "What can I do for you? Something about a rumor?"

"Indeed. I recently heard about a footman's son living in the country despite his mother being barren in her marriage." Eleanor reached for her teacup and took a sip as the color drained from beneath Lady Meddleson's overly powdered face.

"I beg your pardon?" She gaped in quite an unladylike fashion.

"I'm referring to a footman you may be acquainted—"

"Enough." The delicate feminine voice Lady Meddleson had cultivated fractured with a disagreeable screech. "How dare you come into my home with such accusations?" She scowled, her lips bracketed between the parenthetical lines on either side of her mouth.

"I didn't accuse you." Eleanor set aside her teacup. "But since the topic of conversation has been raised, yes, I know. Far more than you'd like me to, and enough for Society to easily unearth the truth for themselves."

The blood that had drained from Lady Meddleson's face now poured back in, staining her cheeks in brilliant strawberry-colored blotches. "I assume you're here with this unpleasantness because you want something. What is it?"

"I want you to invite Mrs. Wharton to your soiree."

Lady Meddleson scoffed, her graceful nature as easily discarded as the soft femininity of her voice. "That crass American woman?"

"I do not share your disapprobation of Mrs. Wharton, and if more people were to become acquainted with her, they would find her most agreeable."

"She doesn't belong here." Lady Meddleson curled her lip. "She's nothing more than a vulgar fool."

"You underestimate her." Eleanor added a bit of sugar into her tea to offset the bitterness of the other woman. "Invite her to your soiree or your secrets will grace the opening lines of every scandal sheet in London."

Lady Meddleson lifted her chin, squaring her gaze at Eleanor. "I've certainly underestimated *you*."

Eleanor had never been considered a worthy adversary. Power radiated through her now, leaving her spine straight and her chin tipped a notch higher.

"So, you will be inviting Mrs. Wharton," Eleanor confirmed.

Lady Meddleson's nostrils flared. "The invitation will go out this afternoon."

"I look forward to seeing her there." Eleanor offered her most gracious smile, the one tirelessly perfected an age ago when she was presented to a stream of would-be mothers-in-law at her coming out.

"Will that be all?" Lady Meddleson's lips pursed in irritation.

"One more thing . . ."

Eleanor stood, towering above the countess, whose body tensed like a cornered rat.

There was no better way for the message to be delivered than this. "Lady Duxbury sends her regards."

With that, Eleanor turned to leave, her confidence reflected back to her from multiple mirrors as she strode from the room composed in self-assuredness.

Lady Duxbury's carriage had been parked at the rear of the house, a convenience to avoid the worst of the heavier afternoon traffic. Or so said the butler. More likely a way for Lady Meddleson to keep tongues from wagging.

Unease caught at Eleanor's nerves as she went out back to the mews. The carriage stood unattended.

Where was Lady Duxbury's footman?

Eleanor stepped into the alley and found the man collapsed on the ground. Before she could go to him, a strong arm grabbed her from behind.

Without thought, Eleanor spun around and tugged her hatpin free. Her bonnet tumbled into the mud. She didn't waste time seeing where it fell. Instead, she lunged forward, thrusting the point into the ruffian's shoulder.

The sharp end slid effortlessly through his filthy jacket, into the area just below his collarbone. The man's eyes went wide over his grizzled beard, looking first to the injury at his shoulder and then following the slender stem of the hatpin to where she still held the jeweled end in the ball of her fist.

With a start, she released her weapon.

She had *stabbed* someone.

Not a pillow full of down strapped to a mannequin. Something living.

A man.

He staggered back, the hatpin jutting from his shoulder as though he were a macabre pincushion.

That was when Eleanor screamed, a terrified shriek that sent the man running and brought the servants from the nearby houses. Lady Meddleson's butler was among those to answer her cries, apologizing profusely for the placement of the carriage, which had put Eleanor at such risk.

Though several men searched the surrounding area, Eleanor's attacker was not located. Her bloodied hatpin, however, was discovered in a neighboring property. Eleanor pulled her handkerchief from her reticule and slicked it over the makeshift weapon, wiping away the blood.

The butler's eyes bulged at the action. "I only sought to expedite your return home," he stammered in apology. "The main road becomes so congested this time of day."

In the absence of her bonnet, which was now ruined, Eleanor thrust the hatpin through her loose bun.

The butler's gaze followed the hatpin and he swallowed, the knob in his throat bobbing. "Please do forgive me, ma'am."

The circumstances were far too coincidental to, in fact, be a coincidence. Especially considering Lady Meddleson's failure to see to her guest's welfare following the attack.

Lady Duxbury's footman was brought round and, once they confirmed he was well, the carriage was prepared. This time left waiting for her at the front of the townhouse. Traffic was indeed congested and there was a sense of nakedness to being outdoors bareheaded, but the ordeal had passed.

Mud drenched her once-fine bonnet, leaving the flowers sodden and the brim sagging inward.

Still, the attack could have been worse.

So much worse.

Whatever the man had wanted with her, he'd assaulted the strong footman to get it.

Her reticule perhaps?

Her?

A chill raked over her skin as a cluster of what-if scenarios crowded in her mind. The many ways she might have been wounded. Perhaps killed.

What would become of her son if she were dead?

She climbed into the carriage on shaky legs, hands trembling when they touched the proffered palm of the footman. "Are you certain you're well, ma'am?" he asked.

"You're the one still bleeding." She frowned at the cut just over his brow. "If my handkerchief wasn't soiled with blood already, I'd offer it to you."

He helped her to the carriage seat and hesitated before closing the door. "If I may be so bold, ma'am, that was right brave of you." He smiled, the grin breaking through the monochrome veneer all footmen wore, revealing how very young he was.

Likely another of Lady Duxbury's rescues.

Once the door clicked shut and Eleanor was entirely alone, she drooped back against the padded seat, the bones in her body liquid with exhaustion.

Her dress was muddied at the hem, her hat was ruined and her handkerchief streaked with blood and dirt. She examined the reticule, knowing the stains against the light-colored satin would never come out. The clasp that had never seemed to work quite right hung open, revealing Lady Duxbury's journal within.

There were several more entries, and with the heavy traffic this time of day, Eleanor might have time to read them all. Certainly, she could use the distraction from the endless stream of thoughts reminding her of the fate she narrowly avoided.

She plucked the diary from her reticule, thumbed to her last location and began to read.

CHAPTER THIRTY-EIGHT

Lady Duxbury's Diary

November 1893

I was wrong in my previous entry. It appears I am still capable of blushing.

I am widowed once more, liberated from my prison by the weak heart of my ailing captor. Angina pectoris. *My savior.*

After finding myself a widow thrice over, I have vowed not to wed again. Never will I fall prey to the lies of men, their empty vows of protection and care.

And yet, I could never vow not to love again, for there was always Elias . . .

Donning my widow's weeds once more, I ventured to the bookshop near Threadneedle Lane and found the doors and windows shuttered. Fear gripped my heart then, not only for my love, but for the little girl with golden hair and velvety brown eyes so like my George.

I asked a man on the street and discovered cholera had ravaged the area two years prior, sweeping away many lives, including Elias's wife and daughter. In his misery, he could not keep the business running, especially as he became ill with consumption.

"And he is dead?" I asked in horror.

"He's up there." The man jerked his head to the filthy dark window above the shop. "Though won't be for much longer. Rent's due and he don't have it."

After the man confirmed he was indeed the landlord, I dug a note from my reticule and purchased the building outright. The man scarcely knew what to say as he held the note, mouth gaping like a fish.

I didn't wait for a response. Instead, I rang at the door like the madwoman Silas once claimed I was. My desperation was such that I would have broken the door down with my bare fists if the landlord hadn't handed me a rusty key. It stuck in the lock before finally giving way.

The building smelled of dust and disuse and I climbed the rickety stairs with my heart in my throat, certain I was too late.

Consumption has left many graves carved into the English landscape. Especially so in London.

When finally, a weak voice answered my calls, I nearly wept with relief.

Elias, my Elias, was alive.

I pushed into the room from where his frail voice emanated and found him lying on a bed of rags. The air was thick with the odor of illness as well as another scent I'd come to know well—the whisper of impending death.

Elias lay in bed, too weak to rise, the little mustached cat thin as a rail where it curled up at his side. I ran to him despite his warning of contagion. I pulled the veil from my face, and he wept, asking if I were an angel come to take him to his family. My heart broke, knowing well that longing to be reunited with a loved one, even in the afterlife. I assured him I was real, that I was his Clara come to see him to good health.

Elias stroked my face with clammy hands, unable to believe

I was real, asking if I was the widow who visited his shop from time to time. When I confessed that yes, I was, he, too, admitted that he had never stopped loving me.

I tended to him, caring not that the illness might catch me in its grasp and carry me to an untimely grave.

I wanted to ask after his precipitous marriage. Why he had abandoned me when I was a girl locked away with his child growing in my womb. I wanted to know why he never sought me out as I did him.

But now was not for questions. Those would come after a doctor had seen to Elias and his accommodations were made habitable.

Now was for the joy of a reunion long considered an impossibility. Now was for igniting a fledging flame of hope and for basking in its glow. Now was for the truest, warmest of blushes.

So you see, I can blush again. And might finally have a chance at true happiness.

January 1894

Never have I known such joy as the love of my Elias.

After his improvement under the care of a doctor, I moved him and his now-plump cat to my country estate in Northumberland. Despite my disregard for the possibility that people might realize we were lovers, he was most adamant that we maintain the facade of friendship to protect my reputation.

There was illness deep in his chest when he coughed, but I ignored the persistent evidence despite knowing well its fatal sound. That death rattle had taken our boy as surely as it meant to take Elias.

We lived lavishly, ate grandly and relished every blissful moment together. There was much to reclaim in what we lost in our years of separation. A separation that might never have occurred if Lady Meddleson had not intervened so maliciously.

I learned the message I gave her to pass to Elias all those years ago was never delivered. Elias was as ignorant of my captivity at the hands of my parents as he was of our child. But Lady Meddleson did still pass on a message.

She informed him I was no maid of the manor at all, but its mistress, and that I was in love with Viscount Morset, who could give me the life I deserved. There was no mention of Elias's child, or how desperately I awaited his rescue.

Elias wept when he learned of this, and I wept with him when I shared how our son died.

Assuming himself jilted after what he thought was my rejection, Elias licked his wounds for several years before finally finding a woman he could love. He had a happy life; I will always take comfort in that. But the loss of his family hollowed him out as surely as the loss of our George devastated me.

I cannot help but imagine what might have become of our lives if Lady Meddleson had never thrust her insidious lies between us.

We might have had a life of joy together. Our George might still be alive.

We celebrated Christmas in one another's company and had a cypress tree cut and brought indoors. We lit it with the merry golden glow of a dozen candles that left the ornaments sparkling, and laughed when the little cat tried to bat the glass bulbs to the floor. We sang carols, Elias in a whisper-thin voice, mine strong enough for us both.

And there were presents. For him, a photograph of George just after he'd turned five, those large brown eyes gazing up at the camera with all his innocence and love. A gift that moved us both to tears. For me, a lovely brooch with a wave of Elias's rich, dark hair swept into a lovely pattern and topped with a crystal cap to keep the design safe.

As 1893 gave way to 1894, Elias took his last breaths. That rattle that had carried away our son did likewise for his father.

Those last moments of 1893 were painful, for Elias as his

coughs produced flecks of blood, and for me as he begged for relief from his agony.

And then he was gone, my love erased from this world for all eternity. Reunited with our son in Heaven.

And I was once more alone.

I placed the picture of George in the small locket housed within the brooch Elias had gifted me. Both loves of my life tucked safe against my heart.

Both lost to me in this mortal existence.

In our many conversations, Elias entreated upon me to find purpose in life. Not wedded bliss, as he knew I harbor no desire to love beyond him. Rather, he bade me to use my wealth and influence to better the world. Perhaps to help those abandoned and left to their suffering, as so often happened with me.

This pursuit is one which I have given great consideration. Perhaps I will put the idea into action when I emerge from the pain of my immeasurable loss.

For now, I mourn. For my love, for my son, for everything that has been taken from me.

CHAPTER THIRTY-NINE

Mrs. Eleanor Clarke

ELEANOR PRESSED THE KNUCKLE OF HER FORE-finger under each eye to blot her tears as she closed Lady Duxbury's journal. No longer was the countess mysterious. She was a woman who had been hurt and misused, a woman who understood others who bore similar hardship in their lives.

The carriage stopped in front of Eleanor's townhouse and an icy ball of dread congealed in her stomach. Squaring her shoulders, she entered her home.

After all, it was ridiculous to feel suddenly cowed after what she'd been through. For heaven's sake, she had fended off a would-be assailant with her hatpin. She ought to be brimming with self-assurance.

However, in her absence, she had no foundation by which to gauge Cecil's mood. There was no morning of a whistled jaunty tune to predict a fortuitous day, or more likely, the threat of his bilious mood by his berating of his poor valet for transgressions that were likely never committed. There was no map of Cecil's facial expressions that would guide Eleanor in navigating his temperament.

"Your son wailed for the entirety of your stay at Rosewood Cottage." Cecil's bored drawl echoed through the entryway and prickled a warning at the back of her neck.

She spun round to find him standing by the entrance of his study, a glass with several fingers of amber liquid glinting within.

Given the slur of his words, the glass was not his first despite the early hour. Not that the appropriate hour for drinking mattered to Cecil. His wealth made him king of his own world.

"Is William ill?" Eleanor asked tentatively.

"That's what I thought, but apparently his fool of a nurse informed him of your absence, and he did not cease his sniveling." Cecil lifted the glass to his lips, draining half the liquid in one unflinching gulp.

A thread of pain tugged at Eleanor's heart for her son's distress.

"Mama," William's small voice cried out, the sound emanating from the study behind Cecil.

"William?" Eleanor rushed forward, fear of her husband's wrath replaced with anxiety that their son had been left alone with Cecil.

He rolled his eyes. "He'll be glad now that his *mama* has returned. No care for his father or the grand estate I've assembled for him to inherit someday." His words blurred where they joined, loosely strung together.

William ran to Eleanor, his arms extended, his wide gaze locked on hers with desperation as she pulled him into her protective embrace. He clutched at her the way he'd done when he was a babe and she'd insisted on helping the nurse bathe him. Back in those precious days when she'd been allowed to see her son daily.

The water frightened him and rather than go in, he would curl his body around her like a small monkey, arms and legs locked into place.

It was the only other time she'd ever seen him so terrified.

Eleanor ran a soothing hand over his silky hair, as if she might absorb his fear and spare him the discomfort of its grip. "Where is his nurse?"

"Sacked her." Cecil slurped at his drink. Scotch, by the sharp scent.

He was always worse with Scotch.

"When?" Eleanor asked with alarm.

Had William been with Cecil all day? Her heart seized.

She clung to their son, wishing she could wrap herself around him like a barrier.

"Last night, when she couldn't do her bloody job in quieting the lad." Cecil stepped forward.

All night, too?

"You were gone." Cecil sneered. "Not being a mother."

That Cecil had given her leave to go scarcely mattered. Her priority now was William and ensuring his safety.

"Let me put him back in his nursery and have my maid see to him," Eleanor cajoled. "Then we can talk."

No matter what Cecil brought her way, she wanted William to be somewhere else. Somewhere safe.

And that meant away from his father, especially with that malevolent glint in his eyes.

Oh, how she hated Scotch . . .

Cecil glowered at her. "You're a terrible mother abandoning your son as you have. It's why I've canceled my trip to Peru."

"But you were going in June." Just days away. Eleanor blinked, her brain refusing to accept the words he threw at her. "But why . . . ?"

"I'm staying here. To keep an eye on you." His glare sliced into her, a threat more malicious than Eleanor had ever seen before.

"Please." Eleanor swallowed. "Please let me take William to his room. It is time for his nap."

"Take him." As Cecil slung his arm toward the stairs, liquor sloshed over the rim of his glass and splashed across the clean floor. "I'll meet you in your room." The intent in his growl left the hair on her arms prickling.

Eleanor climbed the stairs on legs she could not feel. All of her was numb save for the punch of her heart against her ribs.

Cecil would not be leaving in June.

From what he'd implied, the cage she lived in would shrink even smaller. There would be no freedom, no quiet extra moments with William.

Tears swam in her eyes, blurring the stairs as she approached the landing to the nursery.

Bennett was already waiting for her, likely informed by the butler to be ready to help with William. Eleanor tried to smile at her maid, but the attempt wobbled on her lips.

The whole world wobbled, thrown off its axis by Cecil's declaration that he would not be leaving for Peru.

"Come now, love." Eleanor forced strength into her voice as she whispered to her son. "It's time to rest."

She hugged William against her to keep him from seeing her tears.

Bennett hovered over Eleanor like an anxious hen, her nervousness palpable. For while no one witnessed Cecil's brutal treatment of Eleanor, her maid saw the effects. Bennett's careful hands were the ones that placed cool cloths on hot bruises and shushed away her tears. Just as it was she who concealed the books Eleanor secreted home from Lady Duxbury's library.

William fell asleep quickly, lulled by the steady sway every mother acquires upon the birth of their child, an innate rocking side to side of shared body heat while pressed heart to heart. She settled him in his small bed and turned to her maid, who watched her with a pinched expression.

"He is more important than I am, Bennett," Eleanor said by way of soothing her oldest friend.

"I've never seen Mr. Clarke this angry." The maid's eyes flicked anxiously to the door as if she expected Cecil to burst through.

"He's not going to go to Peru." Eleanor's words caught in her throat. "He canceled the trip because of me. Because I left for one night."

Bennett's eyes went wide.

Eleanor lowered her voice to barely a whisper. "Lady Duxbury can help me escape."

The words were out of her mouth before she could draw them back. But she didn't want to draw them back.

She could not live like this anymore.

Bennett put her hands over her heart, eyes damp as she whispered, "Bless that woman."

"There is not much time," Eleanor continued quietly. "Once we've hired a new nursemaid, sneaking William away will be impossible, and I will not leave him."

The sacking of William's nurse had opened a door that Eleanor fully intended to walk through before it could slam in her face.

"I'll prepare everything," Bennett said. "I'll be discreet, gather your jewelry to sell, pack clothing that will not be noticed."

Eleanor embraced her maid with a force that conveyed everything she did not trust herself to say.

"I'll see to you later," the maid said softly, wiping her eyes as Eleanor let her go.

Eleanor gave a grateful nod and slipped from the room.

Soon.

Soon, she would be free, as would William. Yes, they would have to look over their shoulders for years. Yes, they would live in fear of discovery. But they would be free.

And now, she must face Cecil.

She proceeded on a death march toward her bedchamber, reminding herself what she had accomplished in only two short days.

She had put Lady Meddleson in her place and by doing so, hopefully aided Rose's acceptance in Society. She had helped to alter a woman's life from beyond the veil of the dead in the séance that eased her suffering. She had employed her hatpin to defend herself from an attacker.

As she paused before her door, she recounted these achievements, reminding herself that she was not the woman she'd been only weeks before.

With a steadying breath, she walked in, back straight, head lifted, eyes meeting Cecil's to show him that no matter what he did to her, she could take it.

Because she was strong.

She was a mother willing to do anything to protect her son.

CHAPTER FORTY

Lady Lavinia Cavendish

HOW FITTING THAT THE SKY APPEARED BRUISED
the day of Lavinia's last meeting with the Secret Book Society.
Those beleaguered clouds loosed their grief in great, freezing
drops until the world drooped in mutual misery.

Lavinia took in everything as she entered Lady Duxbury's
beautiful home, savoring each minute detail—the fragrant cleanliness of carbolic at the entryway that guaranteed a germ-free
home, the sprawling array of plants that gave Lady Duxbury's
drawing room a tropical ambience, the welcoming comfort that
washed over Lavinia like a balm.

Here she had been free. She had been loved for who she was.

As she passed the library, she gazed longingly at the rows and
rows and rows of books, the adventures she would no longer
have at her fingertips, characters she would never meet. Worlds
were lost in that realization. Lives she would never live snapped
closed to her exploration.

There would be no books in the madhouse. No comforts of
any kind for that matter.

She had not spent her existence under the threat of a lunatic's asylum without researching its evils. And there were many.

There was no pleasure to be had in those stark places of torment and hell.

In addition to a lack of books, there would be no friends.

The last thought choked her with a sob, self-pitying and woeful. Certainly, she had cried enough tears over her impending demise, but such acknowledgment did not stem the tide of her sorrow.

"Lavinia?" Lady Duxbury emerged from the drawing room. "What is it?"

"Papa found my poetry." She hiccupped on the last word. "He thinks it's proof of my madness. I'm allowed only this one last visit to bid my farewells."

Lady Duxbury's brows shot up in alarm. "To bid your farewells?"

"He means to . . . to send me . . . to the asylum," Lavinia gasped out through her tears.

A great and terrible despondency washed over her, drowning all sense of hope.

Lady Duxbury put an arm around her and gently led her into the drawing room. Lavinia sank into her usual chair nearest the door, and recalled the many secrets she'd shared and witnessed from this location. There was a familiar warmth to the pale green walls and the little birds adorning the silky surface, as though they flitted and soared about on a sage-green sky.

Another voice echoed into the drawing room behind them.

"I have an invitation." Rose entered with an envelope held aloft, a prize on prominent display. Her lovely rose-vined boots fell soft against the carpet as she approached. "Lady Meddleson appears to have had a change of—" she caught sight of Lavinia and her words died away "—heart." She rushed over and knelt on the floor, her expression filled first with concern, then hardened into anger. "What's happened? Is it Mr. Wright? Has he done something untoward?"

"Nothing like that." Lavinia accepted a handkerchief from Lady Duxbury and wiped at her eyes. "Though I'll never see him again, either." The admission made her tears come harder.

Lady Duxbury rubbed soothing circles against the back of Lavinia's day dress as she told Rose in a quiet voice what had happened. In the course of her explanation, Lavinia's tears lost their force and her breath resumed its steady rhythm. There was nothing to be done about her face, which was likely splotchy with emotion.

Alas, she had never been a pretty crier. Not like her younger sister, who managed dainty little tears. No scrunched nose, swollen eyes or ruddy complexion for her.

Delilah.

Lavinia would be missing Delilah's debut that evening, the very thing she'd tried so hard to prepare herself for.

Lavinia had let her down.

"How ridiculous that your father should think you mad because of your poetry," Rose declared loudly. "Has he never read Edgar Allan Poe? Just because he wrote about killing the man with one eye didn't make him a murderer. Or what about Samuel Taylor Coleridge and that dead albatross he wore around his neck after he shot it? It's creative expression, nothing more."

"You're correct, Rose, it's all symbolism and creative expression." Lady Duxbury's eyes narrowed in thought. "I suspect your father has not read much poetry, Lavinia?"

Lavinia considered the question, recalling the miserably dry books stagnating in her father's library. "I'm not certain, but I don't believe so."

"As I suspected." Lady Duxbury held up a finger. "A moment." Then she swept from the room.

Lavinia nodded to the envelope Rose had laid unceremoniously on the floor. "Is that an invitation to Lady Meddleson's soiree?"

Rose nodded, her dark brown eyes liquid with worry.

"I'm so pleased you finally received one." Lavinia smiled at her friend, the pull of her lips feeling almost foreign after so much grief.

For her freedom. For her life. For her poetry.

"Though I don't think you should go," Lavinia said.

Rose blinked. "Why ever not?"

"You're too good for the likes of her."

Rose smiled then too, a tender smile that brought light to the dark place in Lavinia's heart.

"Here." Lady Duxbury returned with a pile of books. "Several works by Samuel Taylor Coleridge and William Blake. There are more examples in the library, but these should be sufficient."

Rose shifted out of the way, taking her seat as Lavinia accepted the stack, their heft in her lap more symbolic than she cared to admit. "These are for my father?"

"Your mother," Lady Duxbury corrected. "You've been sharing your books with her, have you not?"

Heat crept over Lavinia's cheeks. "How did you know?"

"You are a fast reader and yet you often need extra time for books, even when they aren't long." Lady Duxbury gracefully took her seat. "I can only imagine you have been sharing with your mother as I have shared with you. Perhaps she's even found the power of independence and self-assuredness as you have."

Lavinia cherished what her time with the Secret Book Society had added in her life, in how they had helped her find her voice, and to embrace her passion as something beautiful.

Even now, knowing what her poetry had cost her, Lavinia would do it all again.

"Have your mother give those books to your father," Lady Duxbury instructed. "Ask her to have him read these twisted minds of men who have been touted for their brilliance and acumen. I believe what he reads will make him understand you."

Lavinia wrapped her fingers around the worn corners of the well-loved books. "Do you truly think these will change his mind?"

"I should hope so." Lady Duxbury took her seat, the conviction of her affirmation lending strength to Lavinia. "What's more, I hope that in reading those highly acclaimed works, your father realizes that his daughter is a genius."

Lavinia's spirits lifted with such praise.

"If he does not, he's a fool." Rose inclined her head at Lavinia. "I hope you'll forgive me for saying as much."

Lavinia laughed in spite of herself, grateful for Rose's bluntness in such a fitting moment. Setting the stack of books on a table beside her, Lavinia considered her mother, the way she scarcely stood up to Papa. "Do you think my mother will actually give these to my father?"

"Of that I am certain." Lady Duxbury's expression became earnest. "She knows you are in danger. A mother will do anything to protect her child." She sipped her tea. "And you need only say the word and my carriage and Rosewood Cottage are at your disposal."

Lavinia eased back in her chair, buoyed with confidence once more.

What a transformation since her arrival at Lady Duxbury's townhouse, when she'd intended to offer her final tearful farewells. Now her downtrodden spirits were elevated with hope and the loving support of genuine friendship.

The maid entered with a tea tray, the movements of her hands dexterous despite the knotting of scars.

Lady Duxbury cast a quick glance at the large clock, its brass pendulum reflecting the room back to them with each swing. She frowned to herself. "Has there been word from Mrs. Clarke?"

The young maid paused after setting a teacup before each woman. "No, my lady, but I did see a carriage pull up."

The tension on Lady Duxbury's face eased somewhat. "Ah, she must be arriving now. Thank you, Mary."

The young woman bobbed a quick curtsy and left the room. Lady Duxbury's gaze followed her so anxiously that Lavinia found herself turning toward the open doorway to watch for Eleanor.

"It is my duty to assist, ma'am." The butler's voice echoed from the entryway. Lavinia strained in her seat, pushing toward the sound.

The butler entered the room with Eleanor leaning against his arm, his bear paw of a hand covering her petite one. "That wasn't necessary, Davies, but thank you for the kindness."

She had to turn her head to speak to him, revealing a livid red-and-black bruise on her cheekbone.

"I'm not always a kind man." The butler's usually crisp voice was practically a growl. "You need only say the word, Mrs. Clarke."

She patted his giant arm, revealing the flash of a new ring with multicolored stones on her right hand. "That won't be necessary, but thank you."

The butler released her with obvious hesitation and remained standing in the doorway until she took her seat, his hulking frame filling the entryway as though prepared to take on the world to keep the women from harm.

"That will be all, Davies," Lady Duxbury said in a gentle voice. "Thank you."

His square jaw flexed and he turned away, though he would likely remain nearby.

But Lavinia was no longer looking after him—none of them were. Not when Eleanor sat before them with her face swollen and bruised.

"You said you would help us leave if we needed to escape," Eleanor said quietly, glancing down at her hands. "I humbly request your assistance in doing so now."

"Did your husband do this?" Rose asked, aghast.

"He did," Eleanor replied tightly. When she lifted her head, her eyes glinted with determination. "I'm going to leave my husband. And I want to do it tonight."

CHAPTER FORTY-ONE

Mrs. Eleanor Clarke

ELEANOR'S BREATH HITCHED FOLLOWING HER declaration to leave Cecil. It was bold. Decisive. Everything she had never been. And everything she was learning quickly to become.

"Whatever you need of us, we'll do it," Lady Duxbury vowed. "I can send word for Rosewood Cottage to be prepared—" She shook her head resolutely. "No, I have another estate in Northumberland. I haven't been since . . ." Her fingertip skimmed the cap of her brooch. "The location is more remote. You and your son will be safe there while we form a plan."

Eleanor breathed easier knowing that Lady Duxbury anticipated that William would be coming as well.

"I have a hired carriage with a discreet driver that can collect you at any time of day," Lady Duxbury continued. "That way no witnesses can link your disappearance back to me."

Eleanor nodded at this wise forethought. Every privately owned carriage was unique, associating the conveyance to its owner. If Cecil knew Lady Duxbury had secreted Eleanor away, he could easily discover every property she owned and begin his search.

An icy chill prickled over Eleanor's arms, at the knowledge that she would be hunted the moment she was free.

"You'll wear my widow's weeds to obscure your appearance while you travel." Lady Duxbury nodded to herself as she spoke. "You need only stay in Northumberland for a day or two while I secure another location that is not attached to my name." The countess recounted the plan as if it had been drafted weeks ago. "Davies will accompany you and ensure you remain safe."

"I wouldn't want to deprive you of your butler," Eleanor protested.

"I would have it no other way, and I assure you, neither would he."

"You can go to America," Rose said abruptly.

Eleanor hesitated. America . . . It was so far away . . . A world she'd scarcely ever considered for travel, let alone to live. Certainly, another continent would be safer than remaining in England. The idea slowly took root in her mind.

Rose sat straighter. "I can send a telegraph to my father immediately. He *will* help."

"What of your son?" Lavinia's eyes were red-rimmed, her face flushed. As though she'd been crying. "How will you remove him from the house?"

"My husband dismissed his nurse while I was at Rosewood Cottage," Eleanor replied. "In doing so, he unwittingly created an opportunity for me to take William without having anyone notice." She hesitated. "Lavinia, are you well?"

"Is your son safe until then?" Lavinia asked, prevaricating around what she clearly did not want to say.

"He is safe for now, but I fear for him regardless." Eleanor's hand went to the bruise at her cheekbone. Even the brush of her fingertips made the tender skin ache. She thought once more of how William had clung to her, his little muscles shaking with terror. "My husband knows William is my greatest weakness. I want to protect my son and ensure he does not grow up to be like Cecil."

"Does your husband know you are here today?" Lady Duxbury asked.

"He insisted upon my attendance."

"To let me see what the trip cost you." Lady Duxbury gave a heavy sigh.

Eleanor clasped her hands in her lap, ashamed.

Ashamed of how Cecil had treated her, how he wanted her on display to her friends, to make them hurt in kind. Ashamed of how he treated every noblewoman with disdain, as though punishing them would punish the young duchess who once rejected him in his youth, freeing him of the memory of that scornful humiliation.

The new ring—a lavish gift to excuse his brutish behavior— sparkled on Eleanor's right hand, the glitter of gems set in a wavy line, crowding in six round stones.

The burnished warm glow of citrine, the brilliant blue lapis, a rich purple amethyst, a blood-red ruby, the marbled indigo of kyanite and a deep green emerald.

The stones sat heavy on her finger. Heavier still on her heart. She hated that he forced her to wear the hideous thing to this gathering.

She was familiar with the acrostic jewelry that had been popular in her youth, the careful alphabet of gemstones. How young she'd been then, eager for a gentleman to gift her with a bauble that spelled out his love.

But this was not love.

Citrine.

Lapis.

Amethyst.

Ruby.

Kyanite.

Emerald.

CLARKE.

No, this was not love. Nor was this an apology. This was ownership.

Another way to claim her.

She jerked the ring off her finger and set it on the table where the heavy band clanked against the varnished surface.

"Clarke." Rose read the stones aloud from where she sat beside Eleanor.

"I do not know why he wants others to know I am his when he so clearly reviles me." Eleanor stared at the abysmal ring.

"Because you are a doll to him, something pretty he owns," Lady Duxbury answered, her voice soft with musing.

Eleanor knew exactly where the countess's thoughts were, traversing the pain of a miserable past where she, too, had been ill-used.

"Not anymore," Eleanor said with vehemence. "I cannot stay another moment with him."

"That ring will help you get far." Rose grinned. "I'm sure we can sell it for a princely sum."

Eleanor let her gaze linger on the ring, seeing the object in a new light. Because she would need money. Funds to live on, to afford housing and clothing and food, as well as the means to escape should they be found.

And Cecil would find her. Of that she was certain. She would need an alternative location for every home she established, somewhere to escape. If she was able to escape in time.

"Let us speak of other things," Eleanor said quickly. "Rose, perhaps you might tell us about how you informed your husband that he would be a father? If it is not too intimate, of course."

But even as Eleanor qualified her question for fear of impropriety, Lavinia offered a smile. "Yes, do tell us."

"I . . ." Rose looked around at all of them.

It was not often their American friend was rendered speechless. Something was clearly amiss.

CHAPTER FORTY-TWO

Mrs. Rose Wharton

"I DIDN'T TELL MY HUSBAND ABOUT THE BABY."
The confession whooshed out of Rose. "I was going to, but
when I arrived home, my brother-in-law was there."

She relayed the story, including how she had shamed her
husband in front of his brother, and how Byron had threatened
to have her sent to the asylum. Even as she did so, she bore in
mind Lavinia's plight, how very near the young woman was to
being committed herself.

Rose concluded with how Theodore had disappeared that
morning without bothering to let her know he was leaving.

"How cruel that women are so easily threatened with asylums," Eleanor said in quiet sympathy. "If men were at risk of
being placed within them on a whim, the world would rage."

"That was one of the aspects of *Sense and Sensibility* I appreciated," Lavinia said. "That a woman like Marianne, who feels
so passionately, never once was called *hysterical* nor was *asylum*
mentioned."

"Because the author was a woman." Lady Duxbury gave a
mirthless laugh and poured more tea into their cups.

"But your brother-in-law wouldn't dare do such a thing now." Lavinia gave Rose a sly smile.

"I should hope not." Rose withdrew the invitation from Lady Meddleson from her reticule and showed it to Eleanor. "I've received an invitation for Lady Meddleson's soiree."

"Oh, have you?" Eleanor regarded Rose with feigned innocence.

Rose looked between Eleanor and Lady Duxbury, who shared a conspiratorial look. "I'm sure there was a scheme afoot to achieve this miracle."

"I may have visited her." Eleanor lifted her shoulders in a nonchalant shrug.

Rose winced, unable to pull her gaze from the bruises mottling Eleanor's lovely face.

Oblivious to Rose's observation, Eleanor grinned. "And I may have employed some of my hatpin fighting skills while there."

"On Lady Meddleson?" Lavinia giggled. "I should have liked to see that."

"Outside." Eleanor explained how she had been accosted by the vagabond and saved herself from ill intent. "But fighting back was more than just defending myself. In that moment, I understood I could be brave. I could do the things that terrify me."

"You absolutely can." Lady Duxbury's chest expanded with a proud inhale.

Rose understood that pride. She'd felt exactly that bravery, that *strength*, when she stood up to Byron.

"And if I can defend myself against a would-be assailant with my hatpin . . ." Eleanor nodded resolutely. "I can leave Cecil." Whether consciously or unconsciously, she touched a hand to the vicious bruise on her face. "My wrongdoings stacked in his mind while I was away. Leaving for Rosewood Cottage, yes." She averted her gaze from Lady Duxbury's. "But also my delay in coming home, that I left William home to cry in my absence, how my hat was ruined during my attack . . ." Her voice trailed off, but they all already knew the truth.

"No, I can't live like this anymore." Eleanor took a deep breath, her shoulders lowering on the exhale. A woman preparing herself for something she feared. "My maid has already begun packing for us."

"I can have someone collect the items later today," Rose offered. "A donation for the Society for the Advancement of the Poor." She winked. "I've been seeking aid for weeks, so a 'donation' won't seem extraordinary if he asks around."

Truthfully, most of the items collected by the Society for the Advancement of the Poor had been purchased by her brand-new. Dresses and trousers to replace ones that had been outgrown, and shoes for the many bare feet she saw every day. Even a new cap for Sam, the boy with the missing front tooth who dreamed of a better life and worked like a man to make it come true.

Rose gave Eleanor a confident smile. "Once your effects are collected, I'll ensure they are sent to Lady Duxbury to deposit into the hired carriage."

"Well done, Rose." Lady Duxbury nodded. "A clever use of the charitable society you've dedicated your efforts to."

Rose sat back, grateful to be of assistance.

"Oh, Eleanor, your shoes," Lavinia exclaimed.

They all looked at Eleanor's feet. The blue slippers had become wet in the rain, the delicate silk splitting at the seams like an overripe berry.

The color drained from Eleanor's face, ebbing the glow of bravery and replacing it with a look of unmistakable fear.

"I would offer my own footwear for you to borrow, but they may be too large." Lady Duxbury slid a foot forward, revealing a surprisingly big lavender slipper. With how petite Eleanor was, they would likely slide right off. "We can summon a footman to fetch a pair from the shops."

Eleanor bit her lip, her brows clenching together. "Cecil is expecting me home soon. There is no time."

"Take mine." Lavinia hastened to pull off her black slippers.

"Mine might be a better fit," Rose offered, pointing to her rose-embroidered boots.

"Oh, not your lovely boots, Rose," Eleanor protested. "Really, this isn't necessary."

But they all knew it *was* necessary. Especially after her ruined hat and how angry her husband already was.

How violent.

"And what will you do when you return home with damaged shoes?" Rose asked. "You need to avoid any kind of attention from your husband in preparation for tonight."

Lavinia handed her slippers to Eleanor. "Please, take them."

Except that Lavinia's father was already threatening her with an asylum. How might he feel when she returned home in ruined shoes that were not hers? Or worse—barefoot.

"No, take mine." Rose abruptly undid the stiff lacing on her boots, her fingers working down the trail of embroidered roses. She pulled them off and handed them to Eleanor, who sat for a moment, holding them in her hands.

Eleanor bit her lip. "I'm so grateful for this gesture. For all of you." She blinked and sniffed delicately. "You have given me so much more than I ever expected. My heart aches to know this might well be the last time I see you."

Tears came to Rose's eyes and she rushed forward to embrace her friend. "We shall miss you terribly. I'll come visit you in America."

Eleanor laughed through her tears. "I should like that very much."

Rose leaned back. "Now, put the boots on. You have much to prepare for this evening."

Eleanor smiled, first at Rose, then Lady Duxbury, then Lavinia. After another heartfelt thanks, she slid her feet into the boots and laced them up.

"They fit," she declared, tilting one on its heel to admire the embroidery.

The women left that afternoon in a sorry state with tear-stained faces and heavy hearts, with Rose in stockinged feet as she scuttled three doors down to her own townhouse. And with Eleanor wearing the black kidskin leather boots with the delicate rose embroidery running alongside the laces.

CHAPTER FORTY-THREE

Mrs. Eleanor Clarke

THE HEELS OF THE ROSE-EMBROIDERED BOOTS clacked over the marble entryway and echoed off the expanse of Eleanor's home. After tonight, she would never cross this threshold again.

Rather than the cold, impersonal chill of a great town-house, she would find something too small to ever feel cold, where voices didn't echo and tears were not muffled behind closed doors. She didn't want servants and elaborate parties and sprawling manicured gardens. A two-bedroom cottage in the country, quaint and quiet with lily of the valley planted out front with their delicate white bells and lovely floral perfume.

She could smell them now. Her eyes closed where she stood, letting her senses tip into the fantasy. In her mind, she could make out her little home in the distance with gray-blue shutters and a slate roof, where a gentle breeze stirred laundry hanging on a line and whispered against her skin, breathing one powerful word in her ear.

Freedom.

"Eleanor." Cecil hissed her name like a parent snapping at a naughty child.

She jumped and slowly turned to where he stood in the doorway of his study. This would be the last day of her life with him.

Yet, rather than relief, paranoia gripped her, as though he might hear her thoughts, know her plans.

Ridiculous. There was nothing for him to find. Not unless he was a mind reader.

Nothing except . . .

"What is this?" He widened his study door, revealing Eleanor's travel trunk, still as new as it had been when they returned from their short honeymoon to France several years earlier.

Eleanor's pulse leaped. "A donation for the Society for the Advancement of the Poor." Her vision swam with lightheadedness. Somehow, she kept her voice firm, as if she was not about to faint. "Mrs. Wharton will be sending a footman by later to collect those. She's such a supporter of the society, always attending—"

Cecil's face grew redder as she spoke, going from pink irritation to scarlet outrage. "I'm sure they're grateful for all the jewels you're sending them."

"Jewels?" Eleanor's stomach dropped down to Rose's boots. "There must be a mistake."

"In that case, we have a thief in our midst." He widened the door farther, revealing Eleanor's maid, her head lowered. But despite Bennett's averted face, Eleanor caught sight of the woman's bruised jawline.

Bennett's arms were wrapped protectively around herself.

Fury lashed through Eleanor. In that moment, she didn't think of her plan to leave or her fear of stoking Cecil's wrath. She thought only of her poor, innocent maid, who had always sought to help Eleanor.

"How dare you?" Eleanor demanded of Cecil. "What have you done to Bennett?"

"I was getting answers in my own home," he growled. "She

stole your jewelry." He spit on the floor at Bennett's feet. "The thief."

She flinched. "I'm sorry, sir."

"The constable will deal with the likes of you." He sneered. "No doubt he'll string you up by your worthless neck."

Just as vividly as Eleanor had seen her future away from Cecil moments before, she now saw the future laid out for Bennett. Debtor's prison if she was lucky, death if she wasn't. A short end to a hard life.

A fate worse than Eleanor's by far.

"Stop," Eleanor cried. "She didn't steal those."

Cecil turned to Eleanor, his expression suddenly placid. "I beg your pardon, Mrs. Clarke? Pray tell what other reason there might be for your jewelry being in a trunk containing clothes belonging to yourself and our son." The last two words were bitten out with a vehemence that left ice prickling in Eleanor's veins.

He knew.

Bennett lifted her head, revealing a blackened eye that had already swelled shut. "You don't need to lie for me, ma'am. I took those gems to sell. I planned to run off with them."

Eleanor shook her head, but before she could speak, Cecil's fist landed in Bennett's gut, doubling her over.

A scream wrenched from Eleanor's throat. "Stop. It was me."

Cecil turned to Eleanor, the breath huffing from his thick torso. He lifted a single brow. "You?"

Her heart thudded in her chest. "I was going to leave."

"Leave? To go where?"

Eleanor closed her eyes, wishing to recall the vision of that lovely cottage once more. But she only saw the way Cecil's fist had driven into poor Bennett's slim body. "Away from here."

"With my son?" Cecil roared, closing in on her.

Eleanor's eyes flew open and her body tensed. There was

no denying the truth any longer. Her chance to run was gone. Now there was only the opportunity to fight. "Yes, with our son. To get us both away from you."

"Bennett, leave." Cecil looked pointedly at the maid. "I'd like to speak to my wife."

Bennett straightened, her hands balling into fists at her sides. "I won't leave you alone with her, sir."

Cecil stepped toward her, drawing his hand back. Despite Bennett's courage, she cringed.

Eleanor rushed forward, putting herself between her husband and her maid. "Please leave us, Bennett."

Still, Eleanor's oldest friend did not go.

Eleanor turned to Bennett, regarding the woman who had seen Eleanor at her worst, who had kept her secrets and quietly helped her heal, who now risked everything in a final bid to help.

"That is an order, Bennett," Eleanor said softly, her eyes pleading. "Please."

Her maid hesitated before grudgingly walking away, her gaze fixed on Eleanor until she was out the door.

A wildness came into Cecil's eyes that chilled Eleanor to the marrow of her bones. "You think you can leave me? That you can humiliate me? I'm Cecil Clarke." He thumped himself on the chest.

Everything in her demanded she run. But she held her ground, refusing to back away. He jerked a fist at her, his body tense as if he meant to strike but held back at the last moment.

Despite herself, she flinched.

His lip curled up. "You're pathetic. I don't know how I never saw it. Likely I was too blinded by your family's noble blood to see your true weakness." He stared down at her with contempt. "I'll do better than you the second time around."

The hair on her arms rose, the skin beneath prickling with gooseflesh. "What do you mean?"

Perhaps he meant divorce. Such a thing was rare, but not impossible. Especially with Cecil's wealth.

Yet, even the brightest parts within her could not summon a whisper of hope for such an outcome.

He towered over her, his nostrils flaring. As if he could nourish his rage with the smell of her fear.

"I mean no one is ever going to see you again," he answered levelly. "Not your family, not your friends, nor your precious Lady Duxbury. Not even our son."

His last statement coiled around her neck and squeezed, choking the air from her lungs. "William . . ."

A knock sounded at the door.

Cecil smiled coldly down at Eleanor as he called out for the person to enter.

Dr. Gimbal opened the door and crossed into the study, the physician Eleanor had seen for the past five years. He did not turn in her direction as he approached Cecil and handed him a letter.

Her husband accepted the document and skimmed its contents. "This is the intake form for Leavenhall Lunatic Asylum, signed by yourself and another physician?"

Eleanor stiffened with shock. "Lunatic asylum? I'm not mad."

Cecil regarded the doctor with bored disinterest, as if Eleanor had not spoken. "It is signed?"

Eleanor stared at Dr. Gimbal.

Under his care, she had received counsel and gentle advice in that first frustrating year of marriage when she had failed to conceive. Later, he'd counseled her through a difficult pregnancy and an even more difficult delivery when she suffered a fever following William's birth. And it had been Dr. Gimbal who helped lift the dark veil that had fallen over her world once William was born, encouraging her back into her role as a mother.

In Dr. Gimbal's dealings with Eleanor, he had spoken of his

own wife and her struggles, not only with conception but post-partum melancholy as well. He had shared with Eleanor the names of his children and how his youngest had an affinity for collecting paper flowers, scattering them all over her room, so they resembled a field of wildflowers.

Eleanor had gifted him several paper flowers later that year, commissioned from a vendor in Paris, for the express purpose of his daughter's joy.

And now Dr. Gimbal stood before Eleanor, unable to meet her gaze as he presented Cecil with the means to seal her away from the world forever.

As if reading her thoughts, Dr. Gimbal swallowed and fixed his focus on the tips of his brown leather shoes. Flecks of mud dotted the polished surface. "Yes," he confirmed in a thin voice. "It has been signed by both myself and a colleague."

Cecil returned his attention to the form. "Extreme despondency following the delivery of a healthy son," he murmured as if he found the line of great interest. "Likely a danger to herself and others." His head bobbed in an approving nod that made his jowls quiver.

Those words were a blade thrusting directly into Eleanor's heart.

Cecil would know that, of course.

No doubt he intended to have her be witness to Dr. Gimbal's betrayal. This man who had shown her kindness, who had been at her side in her most intimate moments of desperation and pain, who had carried her through them all with compassion and understanding and respect; this man was now being employed to see her condemned.

"You may go." Cecil folded the letter in half. "Notify the butler that we are ready for the carriage. And notify the constable I should like to see him as well. It appears I have a thief in my employ."

"No," Eleanor exclaimed. "You can't do this. I confessed.

Bennett has done nothing wrong. Please. Don't send me away. I'll stay. I'll do what you ask of me. I'll—"

Cecil cut a sharp look in her direction. "Don't make a scene, Eleanor."

"Dr. Gimbal, please," she gasped. "You know my melancholy was only for a brief spell, as your own wife's was. And I've recovered fully."

The doctor met her eyes before flicking his gaze away, as if doing so scalded him. But not so fast that Eleanor did not witness the emotion there. Those many years of warm benevolence now blazed with shame.

"William." Eleanor choked on his name. "I'll never see my son again."

The desperation rose in her like a violent wave. She lunged for the doctor, grabbing at his sleeve to beseech his help.

A grip of iron clasped around her arm, hauling her back.

"At least save my maid," Eleanor begged. "She's done nothing wrong. Neither of us has. We're innocent."

"Go now." Cecil's order hissed next to Eleanor's ear.

The doctor did not look back as he fled the room.

Abandoning her to a fate sealed with his own signature.

Cecil spun Eleanor around and the crack of his hand against her jaw sent her reeling. "If you make a scene, you will only be proving my claims correct."

Stars flickered in her eyes, impeding her vision as she blinked at him, her brain rocking in its skull from the blow.

"You're to be led to the back of the house," he continued, his voice alarmingly calm. "I suggest you enter the carriage without incident, or you truly never will see William again."

Did he mean there was a chance to still see William somehow?

Before she could ask, she was being forced through the house. A footman joined Cecil, nudging her past the averted gazes that hid a household of betrayal. She was thus escorted through the rear of the house. The rain had abated, leaving the afternoon discordantly sunny. From there, she was shoved into a waiting carriage where the doors were locked behind her from the outside.

She snapped the window latch and pushed the glass outward as far as it could go. There was barely enough room to squeeze an arm through, let alone her entire body.

Hopelessness swelled around her, blending with the landscape of her desperation until the entire portrait of her future was too bleak to behold. The carriage lurched and rattled off down the road.

A boy caught her attention in the distance, a child unattended, his dingy attire marking him an outsider in a well-to-do neighborhood as he walked about with a small tub, bellowing, "Get your boots blacked 'ere!"

An idea hit her suddenly, an opportunity she might not have again. The notion was reckless, but worth the risk.

She fetched a guinea from her pocket, the one Cecil always insisted she carry because one never knew when money might be needed. Because to him, money solved all of life's problems.

In this case, that just might be true.

She held the guinea out the window. "Boy," she said, "I have an errand for you."

He turned, drawn by the glint of coin in the afternoon light.

She would have to speak fast. There wasn't much time before the driver noticed.

"Go to 27 Grosvenor Square and ask to see Lady Duxbury. Inform her I'm being taken to the Leavenhall Lunatic Asylum."

He squinted at the carriage, using the flat of his hand to shield the sun from his eyes. Eleanor threw the coin to the road, where it clinked once and then disappeared into the boy's hand.

"How will they believe me?" His skepticism was a millstone, threatening to crush her fledgling hope.

Eleanor's thoughts were wild, blurred by her race against time. What could she offer as proof?

All at once, she set to the laces of the rose-embroidered boots, her fingers flying until she could loosen one enough to yank off. She had already passed the boy, but fitted the hard sole and slack leg of the boot through the window. She turned in her seat, face pressed to cold glass to watch the footwear splatter into the mud.

The carriage turned the corner then, before she could see if the boy went for the boot, or took her guinea and ran.

Regardless of what happened, her only hope lay in that one discarded boot.

CHAPTER FORTY-FOUR

Lady Lavinia Cavendish

LAVINIA HELD THE STACK OF BOOKS, A COL-
lection of prose penned by masters of poetry. Men whose emotions produced equal parts beauty and torment. A potential
pathway to her own freedom.

Mama met Lavinia in the doorway, her gaze immediately
falling on the books. She sighed. "Lavinia . . ."

"It isn't what you think," Lavinia rushed. "These aren't books
for me to read. This is poetry, written by men with passion.
Men who were famous and acclaimed in their lives."

Mama peered at one of the books. "Is that William Blake?"
A whimsical expression lifted her concern.

"Do you know his work?" Lavinia asked.

"'To see a world in a grain of sand and a heaven in a wild
flower, hold infinity in the palm of your hand and eternity in
an hour.'" The poem poured from Mama without a stumble or
hesitation.

Lavinia hugged the books to her chest. "That's beautiful."

"There was another line I loved . . ." Mama tilted her head
in thought. "'No bird soars too high if he soars with his own
wings.'"

"I think I like that better than Icarus and his wax wings."

"Icarus." Mama scoffed. "I always thought it was unfair that he was given wax wings. What is the point of wings . . ."

". . . if you are limited where you can fly?" Lavinia finished with a grin.

Mama looked down at the books, the ghost of a smile still gracing her lips.

"You understand me more than you realize," Lavinia said softly. "Will you use your passion for poetry now to save me from your mother's fate?"

Mama's gaze searched Lavinia's face. "I would do anything for you." Resolute, she accepted the books and strode down the hall, toward Papa's study.

Lavinia pretended to be preoccupied with a bit of lace on her sleeve, but as soon as the door to the study was closed, she rushed over and pressed her ear to the keyhole.

"What is that?" Papa asked from behind the door.

My salvation.

My hope.

"Books." Mama must have stepped forward because the familiar spot near his desk creaked with the flex of a cranky floorboard. "Poetry. Not Lavinia's," she added hurriedly.

Such assurance pulled at the fresh wound in Lavinia's chest.

Papa grunted.

"Such disinterest, Harold?" Mama's tone was playful. "From the man who wooed me with Tennyson."

He chuckled. "It took me months to memorize *Marriage Morning* for you."

"And it was terribly romantic."

Lavinia wrinkled her nose at the image of her father as a romantic.

"I loved poetry when I was younger," Mama continued. "Much like Lavinia."

"That is a different kind of poetry." The gruffness was back in Papa's voice.

Lavinia shifted to alleviate the pressure in her knees where she knelt by the keyhole.

"A different kind of poetry?" Mama asked. "Surely, you've heard of Samuel Taylor Coleridge?"

"Perhaps."

"Perhaps." Mama laughed. "There isn't a literate person who hasn't heard his name. His poetry is compelling. It is passionate . . . and, yes, sometimes macabre. Perhaps give these a read."

"What is the meaning of this, Helen? There is so much to do for Delilah's coming out this evening without revisiting—"

"Read them," Mama implored. "Read them and think of our Lavinia and what she has written."

A long pause stretched out, straining at Lavinia's taut nerves.

"This is important to me," her mother added. "And even more important to our daughter. If these men can twist poetry as Lavinia does and be lauded for their genius, how could we condemn our daughter to an asylum for a similar talent? Surely, not simply because she's a woman."

There was a note of mirth in Mama's tone.

Papa hated to be laughed at.

"Of course not," he objected sharply.

"We don't want a future for her like my mother had." Mama's voice was gentler now.

"I know." The tension to Papa's response spoke of that mark creasing deeper at his brow.

"At least just read one," Mama insisted. "Perhaps before this evening so that Lavinia might attend Delilah's coming out."

The leather of Papa's old chair creaked and he sighed. "Very well. One. But I'm not saying she can attend."

Lavinia leaned back with relief and caught the maid watching her with narrowed eyes. Likely jealous Lavinia occupied her favorite eavesdropping spot.

But even the maid's presence could not dull Lavinia's spirit.

Poetry had a voice that was impossible not to hear, one that absorbed into the soul. If her father truly did read at least one book, she was certain he could not remain immune to its allure. He would have to see, to understand, to feel. And that might prove her salvation.

She returned to her bedchamber and paced the small space, restless with built-up energy. She had not taken a book from Lady Duxbury's library, knowing she might never be able to return it. But now the absence of something to read pained her, overshadowed only by the loss of her own poetry.

A knock at her door sent her scrambling. Her mother's maid, a woman far sweeter in disposition than Ada, stood there with a letter in her hand. "For you," she whispered discreetly.

Lavinia accepted the correspondence and waited until the woman's footsteps trailed down the hall before slipping her finger under the green seal and unfolding the note. Immediately, the slant of Lady Duxbury's elegant penmanship was recognizable.

Lavinia,
Forgive the insistence, but you must come at once. The matter is
of great importance.

With appreciation,
Lady Duxbury

Worry edged into Lavinia's thoughts. No doubt the countess's request had to do with Eleanor's plans to leave her husband that night. But Lavinia was not to leave the house, bound by her father's orders.

Of course, she could sneak down the servants' stairs and out the back door.

But no, it was far too risky, and she would be a fool to do so on her own.

She would have to enlist her mother's help once more.

CHAPTER FORTY-FIVE

Mrs. Rose Wharton

UPON ROSE'S ARRIVAL HOME, SHE SOUGHT THE immediate assistance of a footman to acquire Eleanor's effects. This would, of course, be done under the guise of a donation to the Society for the Advancement of the Poor.

Theodore had not yet returned. Nor had he done so by the time the footman was dispatched to Eleanor's home.

Rose sighed and pulled Pluto into her lap, idly stroking his velvety ears.

The day felt heavy with waiting.

Waiting to ensure Eleanor's parcels were safely collected.

Waiting for Theodore to return.

Waiting to discover the reason for his absence.

Waiting for the inevitable arrival of her brother-in-law so that she might nobly inform him of the prized invitation to Lady Meddleson's soiree.

The child within her was made restless by Rose's disquiet, the kicks fraught with anxiety, the spins agitated and aggressive.

Rose lounged in bed with sweets her churning stomach could not tolerate and a book she could not read. Not that the story was not engrossing. She'd specifically taken Charles Dickens's

Oliver Twist from Lady Duxbury's to better understand the lives she sought to improve with her charity work. But her roiling thoughts kept her focus from remaining on the small print.

She was still trying to read without success when Theodore finally came home, announced by a knock at the adjoining door between their rooms.

Her heart caught in the snare of her affection at the sight of her handsome husband. The way it always did when she gazed at him.

A fraction of a heartbeat later, she recalled the way she'd humiliated him in front of his brother, resulting in the locked door between them.

"I'm sorry for what I said," Rose began.

Her words were spoken at the precise moment Theodore started, "I shouldn't have acted so precipitously."

They both stopped, smiled at each other in that shared way couples did when they knew one another to the roots of their souls. Rose slid off the bed and went to her husband, allowing herself to be drawn into the lean strength of his embrace.

"I missed you last night," Rose whispered against the warm pulse at his neck. "I didn't mean to say what I did in front of Byron."

He nodded, the rasp of his unshaven chin catching at her hair. "You've endured a lot with my brother. And with me," he added in a regretful tone. "I'm grateful you have your weekly tea, and for the friends you've made there. As far as Lady Meddleson is concerned, I don't give a whit if she accepts you or not." He leaned away and angled his head down to gaze at her. "I will always accept you and that is all that matters."

"That's unfortunate that you no longer care about Lady Meddleson's regard." Rose sighed.

Theodore's brows knit together.

"Because she invited us to her soiree." Rose grinned up at him.

He laughed and the skin at his eyes crinkled in a way that hinted at how attractive he would be in his older years. "When did this happen?"

"Just this morning. I have been desperate to tell you but you'd run off." She pouted playfully up at him.

"Ah, well, I had good reason." He released her and dipped back into his bedchamber, returning a second later with a paper-wrapped parcel. "I have something for you."

She accepted the rectangular-shaped gift. "What is this?"

"Something that took a fair bit of effort to acquire and whose delivery has been so delayed, I fetched it myself from the shop in Bath."

"Now I'm exceedingly curious."

He nodded, his blue eyes sparkling. "Open it."

Eleanor carried the gift to her vanity and unspooled the bow with a delicate tug, peeling back the wrap to reveal a book.

A rather odd-looking book with *The Stories of America's Women* written in hand-printed lettering on the front.

"What is this?" she asked around a smile.

"I deprived you of books for too long." Theodore opened the cover to reveal various newspaper clippings compiled into a book. "I commissioned one of your father's agents to collect stories being published in American newspapers, particularly by women. Not only for the joy of reading, but for a taste of home."

"Theodore." She breathed his name, savoring the whimsical feel of it on her tongue. "This is exquisite."

"*You* are exquisite." He pulled her into the warmth of his arms.

She leaned forward, prepared to fall head over heels into the kiss, eyes closing, mouth parting.

A knock sounded at the door.

They shared a breathy laugh and Theodore leaned his forehead against hers.

"Forgive me, ma'am," her maid said from the other side of the door. "There is an urgent message for you."

Theodore pulled Rose closer regardless, but she held him off with the lift of her forefinger. "Actually, this is good timing. I have something very important to tell you."

His brow rose in that debonair way of his.

The time had come.

Rose threw him a secretive smile and ran her hand over her lower stomach as she called for her maid to enter.

The young woman stopped short when she saw Theodore in Rose's room. "Forgive me, ma'am." She set a small white envelope on the vanity, offered a quick curtsy and fled the room, letting the door close behind her.

"What do you have to tell me?" Theodore asked, his tone teasing and playful in a way that made her recall those sunny days in Manhattan, the way they had flirted on sun-dappled walks through the park and resumed their banter again in elaborate ballrooms in the sparkle of gilded nights.

Rather than speak, she took one of his hands in hers and guided the flat of his palm to her stomach. His eyes lit with wonder.

"Rose, are you . . ." He pressed the fullness of his hand over the round bump, large fingers gentle where they embraced their child. "Does this mean you're . . ."

"Yes." She laughed and tears sprang to her eyes, brought on by relief, excitement and joy—pure, loving joy.

Theodore blinked at her, his eyes glossy with tears.

And just like that, there he was again. That tender, sensitive soul who had captured her heart. The man who compelled her to bravely cast aside her mother's aspirations for a match of greater nobility.

This was the man who had won Rose over with his compassion and goodness, a match that transcended wealth and title to win the highest prize of all: love.

He gazed down at her stomach, his delight quieting to contemplation. "Are you so advanced that the child has already quickened?" When he looked up again, a glimmer of pain showed in his expression. "Rose, why did you not tell me?"

"We have been so unhappy . . . and your brother . . ."

He frowned. "My brother, what?"

"He threatened me, saying he could get rid of me so that I might stop being an embarrassment to your family."

Theodore's jaw tensed. "I beg your pardon?" A flush crept up his cheeks and danger flashed in his eyes. "I give you my word that nothing will happen to you." He pulled her into his arms, all comfort and protection. So reminiscent of how he used to be.

Rose melted against his chest. "I'm sorry I did not tell you. I was so worried . . ." She meant to say more, to confess that she had considered leaving, but the words caught in her throat.

"I'm sorry for how fraught our lives have been." He leaned back to look at her. "Let us put the pain in the past and move forward, celebrating this gift we can share."

Rose sniffed and wiped at her eyes, nodding.

"By God, Rose." He laughed, his eyes dancing with gladness. "We're going to be parents."

They embraced again, remaining like that for a long moment, savoring the shared warmth of one another's bodies, and the quiet, precious happiness of the child growing in Rose's womb.

Theodore released Rose with a kiss and raised his brow. "What was this business I heard of your boots missing when you returned home from Lady Duxbury's today?"

She opened her mouth to answer when another knock sounded at the door.

Theodore's head dropped back in exasperation.

"Ma'am, it's terribly urgent."

Rose gave Theodore a playfully chastising look. "Come in."

Her maid entered, hands twisting in front of her. "The footman has returned empty-handed. He was informed Mrs. Clarke was indisposed."

Alarm shot through Rose. "Indisposed?"

Her maid nodded. "There was disquiet in the household from what he said, ma'am."

Rose frowned. "Disquiet in what regard?"

"There was a great amount of activity, ma'am. The servants seemed out of sorts." The maid gave a helpless shrug. "Perhaps Lady Duxbury's note might indicate what has transpired."

The note! The missive had been all but forgotten on the vanity.

Rose spun around, snatching up the envelope, breaking the green wax seal embossed with Queen Anne's lace, and tearing the letter open. Her gaze skimmed the careful script.

Rose,
Forgive the insistence, but you must come at once. The matter is of great importance.

With appreciation,
Lady Duxbury

A cold sensation prickled down Rose's spine. Something had gone terribly wrong.

CHAPTER FORTY-SIX

Lady Lavinia Cavendish

LAVINIA'S MOTHER GRUDGINGLY AGREED TO help her sneak out of the house, given the urgency of Lady Duxbury's missive. Mama told Papa they were going to the modiste for a last-minute fitting before the ball.

The excuse was a flimsy one, especially since Lavinia would likely not be going to her younger sister's coming out that evening. But Papa had been too busy to question them.

Lavinia arrived to find Lady Duxbury in an agitated state, pacing up and down the drawing room.

Her focus snapped to Lavinia and her mother as they entered. "Eleanor has been sent to the Leavenhall Lunatic Asylum. There must be a way to free her."

"Is there a solicitor perhaps?" a voice behind Lavinia asked.

She turned to find Rose entering the room, red-faced and breathless. "Forgive me. I was delayed in opening your message."

"I think I know a solicitor," Lavinia said hesitantly.

Everyone looked at her, including Mama.

"Mr. Wright," Lavinia said slowly. "Law fascinates him and he's been studying for several years, much to his stepfather's chagrin."

"Is he a solicitor?" Lady Duxbury pressed.

"He is not to the caliber of a solicitor who can aid Eleanor," Lavinia replied hesitantly and did not look at her mother as she went on. "But the man who he has apprenticed with is and specializes in helping women wrongfully admitted to lunatic asylums. I can't recall his name, but I will ask after him."

"Yes." Lady Duxbury nodded. "That is our best option. Please reach out to your Mr. Wright. I will seek out my solicitor as well."

"What can I do?" Rose wrung her hands, looking uncustomarily helpless.

"Make sure no one finds out about Eleanor, lest she be ruined in Society," Lady Duxbury said firmly. She looked to Lavinia's mother, as if in confirmation, and Mama nodded.

The tension eased somewhat from Lady Duxbury's shoulders. "Spread a rumor about Eleanor being ill, but do not allow the idea of her being sent to a lunatic's asylum to be suspected."

"No one will find out," Rose said firmly.

Lavinia left their meeting more anxious than when it began. She waited until she and her mother were in the carriage to begin her entreaty. "I must go to Delilah's debut tonight."

Mama sighed. "Lavinia, you know your father worries—"

"I do not know how I might appropriately speak with Mr. Wright otherwise." Lavinia took a deep breath to quell the rise of desperation threatening to ripple her composure. "I have worked so hard to see Delilah come out and I know Mr. Wright will be there. Aside from the poetry I've written, I have comported myself with propriety and good grace."

"I've done all I can." Mama reached forward and put her hand on Lavinia's. "You are the one who will need to convince your father now."

Once they returned home, Lavinia found herself outside the study door for a second time that day, her heart jumping like a scared rabbit as she knocked.

"Enter," came her father's distracted reply.

The door creaked open, but he scarcely looked up. His focus was fixed on a black leather book spread open before him.

"Papa."

His head lifted a fraction of a second before his eyes followed. He blinked, as if surprised to see her standing there. "Lavinia."

Her request hovered on the edge of her tongue, on the inhale of a slight breath.

But he spoke before she could. "This book is highly disturbing."

Whatever flame of hope flickered within her snuffed out at his words.

"Yet compelling in the most fascinating manner." Papa looked up at her, his brows rising. "Grotesquely so."

Lavinia put her hands behind her back, cautiously examining the book from her vantage point. Was that truly the collected works of Samuel Taylor Coleridge? "What are you reading?" she asked innocently.

"A book your mother gave me," he murmured as he thumbed through the pages. "One of several, in fact. Poetry."

"I see." Lavinia watched him uncertainly, unable to identify his expression.

"I read several others as well," Papa continued. "Then I read the verses you had written."

Lavinia could scarcely breathe for the pounding of her heart. "Oh?"

"Your mother asked me to." His tone softened. "I don't want to send you away, either, Livi."

Lavinia let silence fill the space between them, tensing for what might come next.

"It is very much my desire that you have an agreeable life, but I have your siblings to protect, as well as our family's reputation." Papa gave her his full attention.

Lavinia's mouth was suddenly dry. "What did you think? About my poetry after . . . after having read the others?"

"This poem by Coleridge about a man wearing a dead albatross around his neck . . . Well, it's rather strange."

"Coleridge was not mad." Lavinia hated the tremble in her voice. "And I am not, either."

"I think . . . you have great passion." He spoke slowly, choosing his words with care. "I think penning these thoughts contains that excessive emotion. And I think so long as they are not acted upon, writing poetry is a suitable pursuit for you to continue given your social obligations do not suffer."

"I beg your pardon?" Lavinia asked again, no longer trusting her ears.

"Your mother reminded me that men with such passions can exist on the page with no adverse effect on their everyday life." Papa frowned. "As a father, I read words of your pain and suffering and feared you might bring yourself harm."

"I do not want to harm myself." Lavinia spoke around the knot in her throat. "Harnessing that emotion into poetry allows me to free it from my heart. So that I can be the daughter you wish me to be. So that. . . So that you might love me again."

The tension on her father's face cleared. "What do you mean?"

"I know I'm difficult to love, that I bring you shame." The knot became a ball, a hard and solid ache lodged in the back of her throat.

"I have never stopped loving you, Livi." He pushed up from his chair and came around the desk. "I worried for you because I love you."

Papa's arms opened and she ran into them, letting the strength of his arms curl her into an embrace that carried the familiar sandalwood and spice of the shaving soap he'd used for as long as memory served her.

He pressed a kiss to the crown of her head, the way he used

to do before she had strained the bonds of their relationship, before the onset of a temperament that was too wild to tame. Before that mark ever creased his brow.

She leaned into that embrace, cherishing not only his affection, of which she had been too long starved, but also his acceptance. Hard-won and seemingly impossible to reclaim.

He released her. "Now, pray tell what brought you into my study?"

As the vise-like grip of concern abated, a giddy lightheadedness took its place and Lavinia beamed up at her father. "I wish desperately to attend Delilah's ball tonight. I promise to be on my absolute best behavior."

Papa nodded, his expression affectionate and indulgent. "Yes, you may attend and I know Delilah will be equally as pleased by your presence at her debut. She was here earlier pleading your cause. In fact, even Robert sought me out to ask that you might be given a bit more time."

Lavinia's brows shot up. Her brother had entreated their father for *her*?

Papa cleared his throat. "Now, go on. I imagine you and Delilah will need all the time between now and the ball to prepare."

Lavinia smiled victoriously. Not only was she able to attend Delilah's ball, but she could continue to write poetry as well. In her haste, she rushed from the room, nearly toppling the maid, who was crouched by the keyhole.

There was a ball to prepare for.

A girl's debut was extraordinarily special, and judging by the smile on Delilah's face, this night would be locked in her heart forever. For a girl who had been born on the cusp of death and managed to live against the odds, she was the purest, kindest soul ever put on the earth. If anyone deserved a night such as this, it was their Delilah.

The ball was equally as special to Lavinia, for the opportunity to witness her sister's delight, but also for the genuine confidence Lavinia exuded that evening.

The crowds were still too close, too warm, too loud. But without the prospect of madness squeezing in on her, with her poetry being accepted by her father, her discomfort among the crush of people was simply an inconvenience rather than overpowering.

Her mother had commissioned the gown well over three months ago for Lavinia. It was a costly and brilliant emerald-green watered silk gown with delicate creamy *crepe de soie* that wrapped over her bare shoulders and flounced into delicate rows of white across the full skirt, like a flower just beginning to bloom.

The frock was feminine, and the colors complemented her pale skin and made her green eyes shine in an otherworldly shade.

For the first time in her life, Lavinia felt beautiful.

She strode through the room with her shoulders back, her head lifted. And then she saw him.

Mr. Wright.

As if sensing her attention, he made his way toward her, the crowds parting from his path.

"Lady Lavinia." He bent low and kissed her hand, letting his lips linger a moment too long. Just enough for her to sense the heat of his mouth beneath her thin lace gloves. "You look . . . beautiful . . . beyond beautiful . . . beyond words that I am clearly at a loss of in this moment."

She laughed as he straightened and met her mirth with a shy grin.

"I'll take that as the most flattering compliment I've ever received."

His grin widened. "I've been anticipating this ball all week to see you again."

"I hoped you would be here." She did not pull her gaze from

his as she spoke. Never had she stared so deeply into someone's eyes. "I need to ask you something."

"Of course." He offered her his arm. "Would you care to take a turn around the room?"

"Actually . . . I should like to dance."

His brows shot up in surprise. "Lady Lavinia dancing at a ball. What a lucky chap I am. And perhaps if I am luckier still, you might regale me with details about your poetry."

She took his arm and he led her toward the dance floor. People watched as they passed, the reserved daughter of Lord Eversville heading to the dance floor. With each step, she caught their whispers as if they were physical things ensnared in the delicate *crepe de soie* of her dress.

Beautiful.

Never noticed her before.

Graceful.

Exquisite.

Surely, they were not speaking of her. And yet, the direction of their heads following her indicated that, yes, they were indeed.

Mr. Wright joined a group of dancers on the floor, making up the fourth couple in the quadrille. "Before I share details of my poetry," she said quietly. "I'm afraid I must request your assistance."

"It is always at your disposal." He bowed to her and she curtsied as the opening notes of the orchestra unspooled across the dance floor.

The couples to their right and left jauntily danced into the center of the circle. "I have a friend in need," Lavinia said, grateful for the din of the music to keep her words private in so public a setting.

"A gentleman?"

She gave him a sly look. "Jealous?"

His brow quirked. "Need I be?"

"My friend is a woman." The playfulness fell from her tone as she quickly explained Eleanor's situation, making sure to withhold her name in case of any eavesdroppers.

The couples to their right and left completed their part of the dance, leaving Lavinia and Mr. Wright to bound forward and take the place of the couple opposite them, before trading spots once more.

His hand was firm on hers, strong as he guided her through the steps. When they returned to their place, Lavinia's breath came faster, and the quickening of her pulse was only partly due to the exertion.

"I'll speak to my mentor at once," Mr. Wright said. "This is precisely what Mr. Brogan specializes in." He hesitated. "But I must confess something first."

Her stomach tightened with the many things this confession might entail.

News of his leaving for a grand tour.

The admission of an engagement.

Before her mind could weave a tapestry of heartbreaking scenarios, he spoke, regarding her earnestly. "I wish to court you. I intended to speak with you before approaching your father to confirm your interest as I should not like a lady to feel forced into my company." His lips pressed together in contemplation. "I feel a bit of a cad asking this on the heels of your request. It is important to me that you understand your decision will in no way impact my inclination to assist your friend."

The two couples beside them bounded into their places, signaling it was once more time for Lavinia and Mr. Wright to dance.

"Will you allow me to court you?" Mr. Wright asked as the music swept them into a vigorous quadrille.

Lavinia answered exuberantly despite being somewhat out of breath. "Yes."

Pleasure showed on his face and for a moment, he missed a

step in the dance, causing Lavinia to give a good-natured laugh, yielding to her giddiness.

"Now," he said as they resumed their places, chests rising and falling while they caught their breath, "I'd like to know what sort of things you write about."

She told him everything, holding nothing back—not her poetry's vibrance nor its explosive passion or how she'd struggled with controlling her emotion before discovering the power of expression.

When she was done, he did not pull away, nor summon excuses to depart her side. His mouth hitched up in a lopsided smile. "Incredible. Lavinia, you are incredible."

And likewise, she found him extraordinary in all the most wonderful ways.

The rest of the night passed in a dizzying rush with Delilah the absolute belle of the ball, all lovely smiles and a full dance card that kept her gracefully sailing across the dance floor. Throughout the magic of the evening, Lavinia couldn't help anticipating the moment she would be allowed to court Mr. Wright.

The only blemish on the evening was the ever-pressing fear for Eleanor. Yes, Mr. Brogan would offer his assistance, but would it be enough?

Could Eleanor be saved?

CHAPTER FORTY-SEVEN

Mrs. Eleanor Clarke

"WAKE UP."

Before Eleanor could acknowledge the gruff voice, it had already moved down to the next cell, barking out the same command. One that was to be repeated on and on and on down the row.

She sat up, eager to be off the straw-filled mattress where the shafts of sharp hay stabbed at her, pricking her awake until any hope of sleep was abandoned. Those long hours throughout the night had been interminable, plagued with memories from the day before. The rough hands divesting her of her jewelry, the humiliation of being checked over for the possibility of anything she might be smuggling on her person.

She'd been stripped of her fine gown and put in a plain dress of coarse fabric that chafed against her skin. The women who handled her were cruel, mocking her modesty with crude remarks and laughter.

Even now her insides shriveled to recall such degradation.

Yet, she had endured their treatment without fighting back—for William.

Everything was for William.

If she was good, she might be released eventually, to find him. To let him know she loved him and that she'd never wanted to leave.

Dr. Gimbal had been there the entire time, his betrayal extending beyond the letter he signed as he accompanied her to ensure she was locked away. There had been bluster on his part, his insistence that she have her own cell, that she had been given a sufficient blanket, that the clothes she received were free of stains and louse, that she be allowed to choose the task of her assigned labor. As if he intended to make her feel safe.

There was no safety in this place. One was kept in a cell where the screams of the damned echoed off the chipped gray walls all night long.

Away from her son.

The blanket had not been sufficient. Not when the building welcomed no more heat than it did light. She'd been locked inside her cell after Dr. Gimbal's departure, the only light coming from a small window too high to reach. As the sun went down, her world slowly plunged into darkness.

That was when the screams began, when tortured souls cried and shrieked and raged.

She had lain in that hell for the entire night, wondering how many more she could bear. How long it might take to be released and see William again.

If she would.

Cecil was not one to forgive.

Panic consumed her, clawing within the confines of her chest.

What if she was there for weeks? Months? Years?

The last thought left a metallic taste in the back of her throat. She stretched out her legs and her feet touched the wall opposite her bed.

Who could live in a cell scarcely bigger than a coffin for *years*?

And if this was what she endured in a lunatic's asylum, what was poor Bennett suffering through? Likely in prison. The very thought of Eleanor's maid, of how bravely she'd stood up to Cecil to try to protect Eleanor, was more than her wounded heart could bear. Tears pricked her eyes.

A woman entered Eleanor's small cell, without knocking, without request. Eleanor ducked her head to hide her tears.

"This is no fine establishment, ma'am." The last word was said in a mocking tone. "No one bringing you a pitcher of water for your morning ablutions. Go on, see to cleaning yourself, unless you think it beyond the likes of you."

Eleanor got to her feet, her back protesting the movement. The lumps in the bed had made lying flat impossible and left her hips tilted at an awkward angle. Her skin was still raw from the scratchy blanket and vicious bits of hay.

Still, she was eager to clean herself, to wash away the filth of the place.

The hall was chaos. Women going this way and that, voices rising in cries and shouts. They jostled her as she tried to move to where most were congregating.

There she found a long sink that resembled a horse's trough, adorned with jutting spigots every few feet. She made her way to one, eager to wash her face.

The water had a tinny odor, one she did not care to savor. She cupped it in her hands and splashed her face before she could think, sucking in her breath at the freezing temperature.

"Cold, isn't it?" The woman beside her gave an apologetic smile. She was just slightly taller than Eleanor, her dark hair pulled up into a fashionable bun. Her accent was one of fine upbringing.

An ally.

"I shouldn't be here." Eleanor could not keep the quiver from her voice. "My husband is trying to punish me by having me here. I just want to see my son." The impact of the longing she'd tried so hard to push away all night now returned with a force that threatened to break her composure. "I wasn't even permitted to say goodbye. I just want to see my son."

"You and many others here." The woman nodded to the end of the trough where another woman was dunking her head under the icy jet of water pulsing from the spigot. "Her husband did likewise ten years ago."

Eleanor's mouth worked mutely before she could utter the single, horrifying word. "Ten?"

No.

She couldn't survive ten years here.

This place was too loud, too filthy, too cold. She couldn't stay another week, let alone ten years.

"Is that what happened to you?" Eleanor asked. "Did your husband send you here?"

The corner of the woman's mouth lifted and she melted into the bustle of the crowd.

A cake of soap lay in an opaque gray puddle, slimy when Eleanor took hold of it. It did not lather and left a slick, greasy residue behind. She rubbed at her face and nearly gagged on the odor of tallow and ash, the stink clinging to her skin even when she tried to scrub it away.

Her eyes were still watering from the assault of the soap when a nurse came at her, armed with a brush and determination as she jerked the pins from Eleanor's wilting coif. The woman aggressively combed Eleanor's hair in jerking, angry swipes, before binding it back in a simple braid. This was followed by further mortification as the woman conducted a thorough check of her person for fleas.

They were shuffled to a long table where thick gruel was slapped into tin bowls dented with age and wear, the metallic taste bleeding into the food.

The woman next to Eleanor didn't bother to eat, instead opting to spin her spoon between her long fingers, scarred in a way that reminded Eleanor of Lady Duxbury's maid. "I saw ye talkin' to Miss Bea earlier. The one in the blue skirt."

Eleanor nodded.

"I wouldn't do that 'twere I ye."

While the woman known as Miss Bea was refined and respectable, this woman seemed sharp-eyed and weasel-like. "Why shouldn't I speak with her?"

The woman shrugged. "She killed twelve people."

Eleanor stiffened, her gaze immediately finding Miss Bea across the room only to discover the woman's eyes were fixed on Eleanor, boring into her with interest.

A chill gripped her, exacerbated by the coolness of the rooms encased in heavy stone, the cold paste of the gruel and the terror of what she was facing.

Years.

It couldn't be years.

A shiver rattled through her again and again, leaving her trembling.

The boot.

She'd tried not to think on it too intently, that one whisper of hope she might have.

There were too many variables that might see her plan fail.

If the boy pocketed the money and did not do as she asked.

If Davies kicked the boy out without waiting to hear his message.

If Lady Duxbury could not find a way to extract Eleanor from this hell.

The odds stacked against success were too great. She could not allow herself to hope.

Yelling filled the corridor of cells, echoing off the walls as the women were herded to what Eleanor learned was called the airing court, a sad cage of brick and stone with only a square of blue sky above to hint at the world beyond. The world to which they had once belonged.

Their shoes clattered over the cobblestones, filling the oppressive silence.

The boot Eleanor had been given upon arrival to replace the missing one was too small and pinched her toes.

Miss Bea approached and the stern expression she wore flicked up into a smile. But now that Eleanor looked more closely, that smile did not warm the cool, blue depths of the woman's eyes.

The smile was a mask, something worn over the face of a monster.

Eleanor staggered back and bumped into one of the nurses.

"Leave off." Strong arms shoved her back into the crowd of women.

Miss Bea reached for Eleanor, but she pivoted, avoiding the woman's grip. Eleanor's ill-fitting shoe slipped over the wet stone, and she thumped into someone. They mistook the impact for a shove and threw a punch at a prisoner beside Eleanor in retaliation.

Miss Bea watched the exchange with a bemused grin as blood spurted from the prisoner's face. The spatter left a hot, coppery odor in the air, charging the small square with a frenetic energy that erupted into anarchy.

Shrill whistles pierced the air, unheeded by women who punched and kicked and bit and scratched. Eleanor backed away, pressing herself against a wall that left damp grit on her palms.

Several more nurses arrived and order was established through brutish arms ripping apart the more aggressive of the women amid threats of something called paraldehyde. It was the latter that finally quieted the melee.

A woman in a white smock put her hands on her generous hips with an air of authority that suggested she was in charge. "Who is responsible for this?"

Miss Bea pointed at Eleanor.

No.

Eleanor had to be on her best behavior. To be released. To see William.

"It wasn't me," Eleanor protested. "I was pushed. It was . . ."

But hands were already grabbing her, dragging her back down the hall, beyond the rows of cells being tidied by an exhausted group of prisoners. Beyond even a massive open room with straw scattered on the floor and wooden buckets in corners. A room that likely was not meant for animals, but for humans.

Perhaps Dr. Gimbal's insistence on having a private cell had been more generous than Eleanor realized.

"Please, I assure you, the altercation was not entirely my fault," she insisted, trying to keep her voice steady lest it crack with her desperation.

"Not entirely my fault," mocked one of the nurses in a high-pitched, exaggerated aristocratic accent.

"New ones are always a bother." The other nurse scowled at Eleanor as they entered a tiled room where chains hung from the wall.

Horror washed over Eleanor.

She pulled back, but the nurses' grips were like iron, as strong and merciless as Cecil's. Eleanor's feet stumbled as she was dragged over the tile, her body held aloft between the two female staff members.

"No," Eleanor choked.

But even as she protested, her arm was jerked back and a manacle clasped around her wrist.

The taller of the two tsked, shaking her head as she locked Eleanor's other arm. "You'll learn." Her voice was flat, her clear gray eyes absent even a shred of empathy.

The nurses disappeared and the pipes juddered overhead. Eleanor looked up as water burst from the nozzle, blasting her with a force that needled her skin, the icy temperature a shock to the entirety of her system.

Everything in her screamed to run, to lurch away, but as she did, the manacles caught at her wrists, holding her in place. She continued to pull, yanking her arms to no avail.

Water gushed from the spout, the pressure stinging her skin and rushing against her mouth no matter what way she turned. She tried to scream but choked, coughing and sputtering.

Freeing herself from the onslaught of freezing water was impossible. Finally, she collapsed to the ground, her arms held aloft by the chain, and bent her head forward to protect her face as the water pummeled at her back.

"Twelve more minutes." The nurse's voice was barely audible against the rush of water.

Twelve minutes, Eleanor learned that day, could last a lifetime.

When she was finally pulled up from where she knelt on the floor, her legs could not support the weight of her sodden gown and an uncontrollable shiver racked her body, making her teeth clack.

The nurse lifted a needle, the affixed glass tube filled with liquid.

"What . . . what is . . . that?" Eleanor managed to get out through her chattering.

"Paraldehyde." The thick needle punctured the crook of her elbow with a painful pinch that swelled with pressure in her veins as whatever had so terrified the rowdy group into submission earlier was now plunged into Eleanor's body.

The effect was immediate. A blackening at the edge of her vision. An exhaustion she could not fight. An oblivion she readily crawled to.

And as a darkness consumed her, she had only one thought.

The boot.

The boot was her only hope.

CHAPTER FORTY-EIGHT

Mrs. Rose Wharton

ROSE FELT IT UNCONSCIONABLE TO ATTEND Lady Meddleson's soiree without Eleanor. Especially when Eleanor had been integral in obtaining the invitation. And yet, Rose knew her attendance was imperative. If nothing else, to stem the tide of gossip at Eleanor's absence. Already three days had passed since she was placed in the asylum.

Theodore had the capital idea not to tell his brother about Rose's invitation. The shock on Byron's face when she and Theodore entered Lady Meddleson's drawing room had almost been worth the misery he'd put them through over the whole foolish event.

Almost.

As they waited for the dinner gong, Theodore was swept away by Byron's long reach, leaving Rose to approach Lavinia, who practically glowed where she stood by her parents.

"The success of your sister's debut was noted in all the gossip columns this morning," Rose said by way of greeting. "As was how beautiful you looked, especially dancing with Mr. Wright. Twice."

Lavinia's face flushed, not with embarrassment, but with the delicate pink of love's first touch. "What's more, he's offered his assistance," Lavinia said in a hushed tone.

His assistance with Eleanor. The words were unsaid, but Rose understood all the same and the familiar tension of worry pulled at her.

Here they were, wearing their finest clothes in anticipation of eating an abundance of delicacies created by a French chef in the event of the season, while Eleanor was locked away in an asylum to be forgotten.

But Rose would never forget. Neither would Lavinia. Or Lady Duxbury.

And they would ensure no one else forgot, either.

"Mr. Wright's mentor can help," Lavinia replied. "He sent me a note with the solicitor's information, which I immediately had delivered to Lady Duxbury."

"What did your father say when you received correspondence from Mr. Wright?" Rose asked, knowing Lavinia's maid loved to inform Lord Eversville of all the goings-on in his household, especially regarding his wayward daughter.

"My maid wasn't given leave to read the note as it came attached to a bouquet of orchids." Lavinia stood a little taller. "And my mother gave my father the poetry books to read. I know I was skeptical, but Lady Duxbury was correct."

"In what way was I correct?"

They spun around to find Lady Duxbury standing directly behind them, her slender body swathed in a low-cut pale lilac silk and silver brocade that lent her eyes a purplish hue. Her black glossy hair was pinned up with amethyst-studded combs that matched a lovely gold amethyst necklace and earbobs. At her breast, she still wore the hair brooch, embedded in an artful ripple of silk.

Conversations stopped around them as people stared, in awe of the countess's appearance. Lady Duxbury ignored every one of them.

"My father read the books you gave me," Lavinia replied. "I'm allowed to stay and I can continue to write poetry." There was such relief in her voice that Rose longed to hug her, to celebrate that precious thing Lavinia anticipated she never would have from her father.

True acceptance.

"Your father has a reputation for being an intelligent man." Lady Duxbury patted Lavinia's forearm. "And one who loves his daughters."

Lady Meddleson entered the room like a queen and swept a regal gaze over her subjects. Her eye caught on Lady Duxbury and there was a momentary lapse in her delicate smile, like a cloud moving over the sun. It was back in a flash, so quick one might have missed the look of shocked displeasure if they were not paying attention.

"Lady Meddleson doesn't appear pleased that you're here," Rose said under her breath.

"There is history between us." Lady Duxbury's gaze narrowed.

The countess didn't elaborate, but Rose suspected that history had something to do with her invitation to the soiree.

Lady Meddleson approached and nodded to each of them in turn. "Lady Lavinia, Mrs. Wharton." A flinty hardness showed in her eyes despite her docile expression. "Lady Duxbury. I didn't think you'd come."

"And miss the event of the season?" Lady Duxbury lifted her brow, elegant and naturally beautiful compared to the artful appearance that must have taken Lady Meddleson hours to accomplish. "I received your bouquet. The assortment was . . ."

"Beautiful?" Lady Meddleson bit out a smile.

"Strange." Lady Duxbury was slightly taller than her adversary and stared down at her for a long moment before stating, "I hope you have all you've ever wanted. You've destroyed much to get it."

The air practically vibrated with tension and for a moment, Lady Meddleson seemed ready to shatter the pleasant shell she worked so hard to construct.

"If you'll excuse me," she hissed. "I must see to my other guests."

Lady Duxbury watched her go with a pleasant enough countenance, but her eyes burned with hate.

"Oh, Mrs. Wharton." Mrs. Baskin stopped in front of Rose. Thankfully, her miserable daughter Miss Jane did not join her. "Have you seen Mrs. Clarke? I know she was to be here, and I require her advice on a charity event I mean to put on."

"She mentioned feeling rather unwell when I saw her last," Lady Duxbury supplied.

Mrs. Baskin started. "Lady Duxbury, I didn't even see you there! What a joy to have you in attendance. Lady Meddleson is such an incredible hostess. She can lure even you from your home."

Mrs. Baskin laughed heartily, finding mirth in her own humor. Lady Duxbury's smile was so tight, Rose wondered if tiny hairline cracks might splinter around her mouth.

But Rose understood immediately what Lady Duxbury was on about. "I hear there has been a fever going around," Rose added.

Lavinia, being the clever girl she was, nodded her head, her expression grave. "Yes, I heard as much as well. Perhaps Mrs. Clarke is afflicted. Some people are abed for at least a fortnight."

"Oh, how dreadful." Mrs. Baskin put a hand to her chest, the diamonds affixed to her wrists and fingers sparkling in the light of the oil lamps. "I've heard the very same thing about that fever," she said of the illness that did not exist. But then, Mrs. Baskin loved to be in the know with the latest gossip. "A fortnight! Who has time for such illness?"

Eleanor's husband entered the crowded drawing room, appearing not at all concerned that he did not have his wife on his arm. He greeted the gentleman nearest him with a jovial exclamation.

Rose tensed.

They had not expected him to show at Lady Meddleson's soiree without Eleanor. After all, Eleanor's role in Society was what precipitated their invitation, not Mr. Clarke's wealth.

Rose shot a worried look at Lady Duxbury, who offered a subtle shake of her head. "He'll comply if he knows what's good for him," she murmured.

"Mr. Clarke," Mrs. Baskin exclaimed. "I heard of Mrs. Clarke's illness and hope she will be recovered soon. You know when I was ill with fever, my maid . . ."

Rose turned away from the conversation, the tension in her shoulders releasing. Thank goodness for Mrs. Baskin's officious ways.

Lavinia smothered a giggle behind her hand.

"It appears our work will be done for us," Lady Duxbury said with a pleased smirk.

"That was excellent thinking to imply such a long recovery," Lady Duxbury said under her breath. "Though hopefully, we will not need a fortnight."

The dinner gong sounded.

Lady Duxbury hung back with Lavinia and Rose as the crowd pressed forward toward the dining room. "We are walking into a viper's nest, my girls. Even with Mrs. Baskin's unintentional aid, we must administer the antidote before the poison can enter the gossip stream."

Theodore left his brother to approach Rose, offering his arm to escort her into dinner.

She only hoped Mr. Clarke's own sense of societal preservation would outweigh his self-importance. After all, it would do him no good for the world to know his wife had been sent to an asylum.

The soiree was an immense success for Rose and Theodore, with Lady Meddleson even addressing Rose on several occasions throughout the night. The meal passed in course after course of *consommé*, fried sole, croquettes of fowl with piquant sauce and a decadent cheese course followed by a lovely pudding adorned with marzipan flowers.

Rose continued to eat, despite being full, although her bites were becoming smaller and she found herself wishing she'd loosened her corset a little more, and not just for the baby.

The true crowning moment of the evening, however, was at the end when Byron approached her before they all relocated to the ballroom. Exhaustion was evident in the slope of his shoulders and the absence of color in his face. The event was clearly taking its toll on his failing body.

Rose indicated a chair for him to sit, but he waved her off.

"I don't know how you managed to secure an invitation this evening, but I'm glad you did." The grudging praise appeared to pain him as he spoke, but still Rose's chest filled with pride.

"I'll never approve of your boldness," he continued. "But there is a temerity to you that I don't find grating."

"Such flattery," Rose teased, accepting the spiked compliment. He scoffed.

"I want a woman who will fight for this family," he said. "I may not agree with your methods, but I know you'll protect the Wharton family and the Amsel estate. If for nothing else, then for Theodore."

"No one cares more for this family than Theodore," she said gently, careful to keep from overstepping as she had before. "He wants only to be a good earl."

Byron nodded, his expression softening. "I'm aware."

With that, he turned toward the entryway, likely eager for the comfort of his bed.

"Dare I ask what was said in that conversation?"

Rose found her husband had joined her. "I think he's finally accepted me. Reluctantly, of course, and I believe doing so aggrieved him, but I'll take what I can."

"He knows you are willing to do anything for me." Theodore gazed down at her, his eyes twinkling as he leaned close and whispered, "Even befriend Lady Meddleson."

Rose covered her mouth with her hands to keep from laughing aloud.

He gave that lopsided grin that made her heartbeat skip. "You're so bold, my American rose, and I love that about you."

She quirked a skeptical brow. "Do you?"

"I always have." He glanced around to ensure no one was nearby and pressed a quick kiss to her lips. "I always will."

Then he embraced her, his hand gently touching her lower stomach before offering his arm to lead her to the ballroom.

Soon, they would be a happy family, a complete family. And the Amsel estate would have its heir.

Even through this triumph, worry for Eleanor nipped at the back of Rose's mind. She hoped Lady Duxbury was right, that a fortnight would not be required to rescue her.

Eleanor was strong, of that Rose was certain. And Eleanor would likely require every bit of that strength until she could be freed.

CHAPTER FORTY-NINE

Lady Lavinia Cavendish

LAVINIA'S PULSE TICKED ERRATICALLY AS THE carriage passed under the wrought-iron sign for Leavenhall Lunatic Asylum two days after Lady Meddleson's soiree.

Lady Duxbury had acted quickly as soon as she received the name of the solicitor. Between the haste of Mr. Brogan's petitions to the court and Lady Duxbury's bribes encouraging signatures of approval to be applied quickly, Eleanor had only been locked within those walls for five days.

Once Lady Duxbury had notice Eleanor could be collected, she summoned Lavinia and Rose to help convey Eleanor home, each telling their family they were out for a picnic at Richmond Park on the outskirts of London.

The carriage now rolled to a stop and the asylum loomed over them like a great beast waiting to swallow them whole. The breath caught in Lavinia's throat and she suddenly felt rooted where she sat, paralyzed by terror.

She had written in her notebook that morning, scrawling her fears of this place in such a swift hand that the words were scarcely legible. But filling a thousand books would not purge her anxiety of asylums, the great nightmare that had haunted her for the better part of her life.

A gloved hand came to rest on Lavinia's shoulder. "You may remain in the carriage if you prefer," Lady Duxbury said gently.

In truth, the countess had not wanted Lavinia and Rose to come at all. They had insisted, determined to be there for Eleanor, to be a welcome, loving embrace after her release.

Through Lavinia's research, she knew how the sane were imprisoned with murderers and thieves as well as those who were truly mad. How some establishments sheared women's hair to their earlobes, like what had been done to Lavinia's grandmother, supposedly to discourage lice. Still, others fared worse, subjected to experimental procedures that were more torture than curative.

Lavinia drew in a fortifying breath and slowly exhaled.

If Eleanor could endure what transpired in those cold walls, Lavinia could summon the strength to walk inside.

"I want to go," Lavinia replied firmly. "I'm fine."

Lady Duxbury hesitated before nodding and alighting from the carriage. She'd worn a black silk dress, her hair in an elaborate style beneath a costly black bonnet. Her appearance was both severe and stately, marking her a force to be reckoned with.

Rose followed behind Lady Duxbury with Lavinia emerging last, the trio led by Lady Duxbury's brutish butler. The walkway toward the whitewashed building was choked with wild nettles.

The women waited before the double doors with Davies protectively in front of them like a wall of muscle, his feet braced wide beneath his broad frame. A click echoed in a metallic lock and one door swung open.

Behind Davies's wide back, Lady Duxbury grasped Lavinia's and Rose's hands in a desperate, quick squeeze.

Only then did Lavinia realize that despite the confidence Lady Duxbury displayed, she was also frightened.

The nurse who opened the door led them inside. Davies entered first, head lowered, glancing left, then right, his body tensed like a man prepared for battle, appearing every bit the pugilist he once was. The June morning was cool, but the shadowed interior of the building was cold as ice.

A scream tore from somewhere in the depths of the building and Lavinia started.

In the distance came a series of answering cries and shouts, a frenzy set off by the scream. The sounds reverberated off the chipped and peeling walls, echoing at them from all angles, until their cries resounded within Lavinia's skull.

Despite the chill, her palms went hot. Tingling. Her breath came fast. Her heart pounding.

No.

Not here.

Anywhere but here.

She could not fall prey to hysteria at the threshold of such a place.

A hand slipped into hers, drawing her away from the brink she was precariously tipping over. Lavinia focused on the pressure of the gloved fingers threaded through hers.

She looked up to find Rose offering her an encouraging smile.

The shuffle of feet snapped their attention to the door at the right where a man with a full white beard entered. The nurse went to him, spoke in a low tone, then departed without looking back. Two more nurses followed behind the man, a bedraggled patient between them. One Lavinia scarcely glanced at.

Then stopped.

Looked again.

And her heart cracked open.

Eleanor was held upright between the two nurses, shuffling on feet that did not seem to work properly, one encased in a dingy black boot, the other in black kidskin embroidered with roses. Her shoulders were hunched in defeat, eyes lowered, her once golden-wheat hair now lank where it hung in her face like river weeds.

Lavinia had never seen Eleanor in anything other than silks or velvets or other costly fabrics, all sewn by a renowned modiste. Now her slim frame was draped in a coarse brown dress that was far too large for her. The sleeves fell over her wrists, drooping halfway down her small hands, and the back of her skirt dragged on the ground, catching on her clumsy steps.

Lavinia remained where she stood, frozen with horror, unable to pull her eyes from the stunning transformation made by only five days' time. Rose's hand in Lavinia's went slack.

Davies rushed into action, sweeping Eleanor into the protection of his arms, away from the two nurses. Her limbs swung limply and her head lolled against her chest as he carried her to Lady Duxbury.

"What have you done to her?" the countess asked, her voice raw with shock.

The doctor did not appear at all ashamed of Eleanor's appalling state. "Her behavior was uncontrollable and required treatment."

"She was stolen from her home and separated from her child." Harsh notes of anger replaced Lady Duxbury's astonishment. "What would you expect of a woman in such a situation?"

"If you are here to collect her," the doctor replied in a bored drawl, "I suggest you do so before I forget the favor I owe Mr. Brogan. You were lucky to enlist his aid." The dim light caught the lenses of his glasses, obscuring his eyes. "You will not continue to be so lucky if you do not depart the premises with expediency."

Davies lowered his head, pinning the doctor with a menacing glare. Even with Eleanor in his arms, he cut a threatening figure.

Lady Duxbury studied the doctor for a long moment, then

finally said, "Come, Davies." She spun away, leading them from that nightmarish place into the June sunshine.

The shadows chased at their backs like nefarious beasts and the screams and cries resumed once more, echoing in the distance.

Lavinia fled the building, practically dragging Rose behind her, their hands still clasped.

Davies gingerly settled Eleanor into the carriage, against the far wall. Her body slumped, her head nodding as if she lacked the strength to keep it upright. Lady Duxbury touched the small hair brooch at her breast, fingers trembling. She entered after Davies unfolded his large frame from the carriage and Lavinia and Rose followed inside behind her.

Lady Duxbury took Eleanor's hands between her own. "Eleanor, what did they give you?"

The beds of Eleanor's nails were purple blue from cold.

"Para . . . parrrr . . . Parald . . ." Her words emerged in a slur, her head bobbing with the effort to speak.

"Paraldehyde?" Lady Duxbury suggested.

"Yes." Eleanor's head dipped forward first, then fell back and did not move again.

Lady Duxbury shot an angry glare back at the asylum. "We'll see to her." Her eyes gleamed dangerously. "We'll nurse her back to health . . . and then we'll make him pay."

And Lavinia knew very well who the countess meant by *him*.

Cecil Clarke.

CHAPTER FIFTY

Mrs. Eleanor Clarke

A HAZE CLOUDED ELEANOR'S THOUGHTS, opaque and nebulous like the heaviest of London fogs, like the smoke swelling over the numerous factories. Time hung in her mind, simultaneously interminable and ephemeral all at once.

Yet, somewhere beyond, there was a calm voice, soothing hands.

How long since she'd experienced either?

An ache welled in her throat, but she did not want to cry. She had wept too many tears already.

There had been roughness and threats and cold—so, so much cold—and fear and sorrow. And there had been that repeated sharp prick at her arm and the weight that settled over her like lead, leaving her thoughts thick as the gray gruel she forced herself to swallow at mealtime.

She'd tucked inside herself, cocooned in thoughts of William, of seeing him one day, of hope. Of the boot. The boot. *The boot.*

That rose-embroidered black boot sitting in the mud.

"Yes, the boot was delivered," a benevolent voice said.

Eleanor blinked her eyes open and found herself in a room

with buttery-yellow walls and a thick, soft blanket with Queen Anne's lace stitched around the border. The pillows at her back were thick as downy clouds and the mattress beneath cradled her body in a way that made her never want to leave.

"Ah, good, you're awake." Lady Duxbury sat at her bedside, the nearby table laden with a box of tinctures and herbs, as well as an empty teacup.

"Where am I?" Eleanor couldn't stop staring at the room, feasting on the beauty, the expanse of her surroundings, the *cleanliness* of it all.

"My townhouse here in London," Lady Duxbury replied. "I've had my solicitor rent a home in Suffolk under his name so it cannot be traced back to me. Your husband will not be able to find you there. You will go as soon as you are able to withstand the journey."

Eleanor shook her head and the residual fog in her mind rolled around, leaving her nauseated. "William. I can't leave him with Cecil."

"If you return home, your husband may send you right back." The seriousness of Lady Duxbury's expression left fine lines pinching between her brows.

"But my son," Eleanor said resolutely. "I cannot leave him."

Lady Duxbury closed her eyes slowly, the way one does when in pain. "I know," she said quietly. "But I cannot in good conscience suggest you return home."

"You know better than most that I cannot leave my child." Eleanor looked up at the countess, letting her eyes plead her case.

Lady Duxbury sighed softly, resigned. "I do. Perhaps you can wait until morning?"

Through the window, dusk was settling over the sky in a pale blue filter, the setting sun burning in its depths like an ember.

"I cannot. Already Cecil may have hired a new nurse. I must go at once."

"Can someone else collect William?" Lady Duxbury asked.

The ache of longing in Eleanor's empty arms for her son became unbearable. Never in her life had she known such pain as the separation from her child.

"I want my son," Eleanor cried in exasperation.

Lady Duxbury was not put out by her explosive reaction. She merely nodded in understanding. "Very well. But when you go . . ." She reached into the open wooden chest on the bedside table. Its interior was separated into small cubbies that housed various glass vials. She withdrew one filled with an amber liquid. "This is an extract of nightshade. Half the vial will incapacitate him. The entirety of the contents are fatal."

Eleanor opened her mouth to protest, but Lady Duxbury handed her the vial anyway. "Just in case."

Resigned, Eleanor curled her hand around the small glass tube, which sat cold and hard against her palm.

"I have a dress that should fit you and will have my maid attend to your hair so you can return home." Lady Duxbury rang for the maid and carefully folded the leaves of the box together before snapping it shut with a great brass clasp. "Davies *will* be joining you. A hired carriage is at your disposal, not only to take you home, but to drive you to the rented residence once you have your son."

Eleanor started. "My maid, Bennett. Cecil had her arrested for thievery. She was trying to protect me . . ."

Lady Duxbury patted Eleanor's hand soothingly. "My maid inquired after your disappearance and heard she was sent to debtor's prison. My solicitor freed her the next day. She is waiting in Suffolk for you."

Eleanor blinked back her tears of gratitude. "Thank you. Thank you for everything." She did not elaborate, but she knew Lady Duxbury understood. The books, the empowerment of their friendship, the knowledge that there was a world outside of obedience, and the confidence to navigate it. The opportunity for a new life. For freedom.

"I would not be the woman I am now without you." Emotion left Eleanor's voice thick.

Lady Duxbury pulled her hand from Eleanor's and smiled. "You would have found the woman you are now with or without me."

Eleanor did not agree. But before she could protest, Lady Duxbury swept from the room to allow Eleanor to prepare for her return home to collect William.

And to finally face Cecil once and for all.

CHAPTER FIFTY-ONE

Mrs. Eleanor Clarke

ELEANOR WAITED ON THE STEP OF HER HOME'S front entrance like a visitor, cast in the cloak of night, her bones practically vibrating with a heady mix of anxiety and fear and anticipation. Davies stood at her side like a sentry.

The door swung open and the butler, Niles, stared at her in shock. As if seeing a ghost.

She didn't wait for Niles to speak, but used the element of surprise and pushed inside. Once over the threshold, she glanced around the austere coldness of her home. The gleaming marble staircase, the openness of the space that caused every sound to reverberate back in an endless echo.

"You cannot be in here," Niles cried out, trying to push Davies outside.

Davies gave an intimidating snarl and shoved back, sending the smaller man scuttling backward.

"Mrs. Clarke has returned, sir," Niles called toward the study. "And brought a brute with her."

Davies nodded to the stairs and Eleanor rushed up the first two steps as the door to Cecil's study flew open.

"Do not let her up there," Cecil bellowed. "Or it will be your job."

Even as he spoke, Davies rushed forward, intent on stopping Cecil while Eleanor collected William. Niles raced after her with surprising speed. She grabbed her heavy skirt, drawing it away from her feet as she clambered up the stairs.

A sickening thunk came from downstairs, the sound unmistakably meaty. Eleanor glanced over her shoulder in time to see Davies crumple. Cecil dropped the granite bust he'd been holding, letting it thud to the floor.

But she could not stop staring at Davies, the man who had come to protect her, whom Rose had once claimed was one blow away from death.

Had Cecil killed him?

Niles's skinny arms caught Eleanor, his grip tight with wiry strength. "Forgive me, ma'am . . ."

That snapped her from her stupor and she writhed in his grip, trying in vain to pull away.

Cecil stalked up the few stairs Eleanor had succeeded in climbing and reached for her, jerking her forward with such aggression, her arm was nearly wrenched from its socket. She stumbled down several stairs before catching herself on the railing.

"Niles," Cecil ground out. "Throw that man back in the carriage and send him home with a warning to Lady Duxbury to cease meddling in my affairs."

Cecil half dragged Eleanor down the stairs. Lady Duxbury had been right. Eleanor had not been ready. But while she ought to have waited until she was stronger, everything in her cried out for the son she feared never seeing again.

Her gaze flicked to Davies, who hadn't moved. With a helpless cry, she wrenched against Cecil's grip. He twisted her arm behind her back and pain shot through her, stilling her efforts.

They stopped before the partially open study door.

"Before you leave, Niles," Cecil said in a breathless growl. "Inform the rest of the staff they may retire to bed. Their assistance will no longer be required this evening."

A chill scraped down Eleanor's spine.

Niles hesitated before offering a perfunctory, "Very good, sir."

Cecil shoved Eleanor inside the study and slammed the door behind him.

He prowled around her, taking her in.

A shiver trembled in Eleanor's marrow, but she refused to allow her fear to rattle free.

She had endured much in these past few days, including the possibility of a life without her son.

Never again.

Eleanor would not be intimidated. Not when she'd been stripped to her bare skin before the probing eyes of a nurse. Not when she'd been injected with a vile concoction that robbed her of thought and consciousness, souring her breath and her spirit. Not when she'd been chained to a wall and left to the mercy of icy showers, sputtering and choking.

She would not be intimidated.

She would not go back.

And she would *not* leave without her son.

Her fingers found the vial in her pocket, a talisman, a promise of safety. And though she was still unsure if she meant to use the poison or not, she was no longer afraid to do so.

"How the devil did you escape?" Cecil demanded.

She didn't answer, hoping he would step closer. Hoping he wouldn't grab her too hard, so she might have a chance to reach for her hatpin . . .

He edged closer, a bully set on intimidation. Just as she'd expected.

He was so near. One more step.

Her breath came fast at her boldness, at the thought of the sticky residue of nightshade coating the point of the hatpin, a precaution in case her rescue of William was unsuccessful. Now she was thankful for her foresight and hoped the poisoned pin would be enough to let her escape with her son.

Cecil's footsteps clicked on the hardwood floor, slow and menacing until he was practically on top of her.

She whipped the hatpin from her bonnet, but as she drew her arm back, Cecil snatched the weapon from her hands and snapped it in half, sending the ruined pieces pinging uselessly to the floor.

Whatever playful nature he'd exhibited before now darkened with a crazed fury. "How did you escape?"

"I'm leaving you, Cecil," she said. "And I'm taking William."

"And what power do you think you have to do so?" he bellowed.

"Knowing that I can't live my life like this anymore. Knowing that I don't want William to become like you."

Cecil lowered his head like a bull about to charge. "You think I'll let you just leave?"

She stood as tall as she could and met his eye. "I will not give you a choice."

Scoffing, he walked several paces toward his desk and splashed liquor into his glass from a crystal decanter. His throat quivered as he swallowed a mouthful, then slammed it to the table's surface with an audible smack. "I'll tell you what I'm going to do."

Turning away from the desk, he paced toward the window. Abandoning the drink.

Eleanor's fingers glided over the smooth glass vial.

He rounded abruptly and returned to his glass. "I'm going to send you to another asylum, one of significantly lesser quality, where you'll disappear in a wave of madness, washed out of sight where no one will ever see you again." His eyes gleamed as he lifted the drink to his lips. "And you'll never have a chance of reuniting with William again. I'll make sure of it this time."

"No."

"No?" He snorted. "You act as though you have a choice."

"I do."

"You don't." The color was back in his face, high and livid.

Her hand curled around the vial with such force, she feared she might snap the glass. "You can send me anywhere you want and I will always find a way to escape. I will always find a way back to my son."

He charged her, his fist sailing through the air with a speed she'd grown accustomed to in the years of their marriage. Her arm flew up, blocking the strike so the blow collided with the bony flat of her forearm.

Cecil roared and this time when his fists flew, there was naught Eleanor could do but wrap her arms over her head, protecting herself, the little vial still locked in the cushion of her palm.

Breathless, Cecil backed away, huffing, his face pink and damp from exertion. "I could kill you," he said in a low voice. "I could kill you right now and everyone in this house would turn a blind eye."

A chill prickled over her aching skin. He was right. His money had swayed Niles and Dr. Gimbal and countless others. Just as it would when slipped into the pocket of an asylum director.

She staggered to her feet, uncertain when during the onslaught she'd fallen to the ground. Her heartbeat radiated in her wounds, thundering with determination, the pulse becoming a chant in her mind.

Never again.

Never again.

Never again.

"Go to bed, Eleanor." Cecil leaned against the desk, pausing to swig his glass. "And don't you dare think about leaving. I'll have a footman posted by your bedroom door, as well as every bloody door in this house that leads outside."

As he spoke, he pulled a box of dates off the shelf by his desk—the box Lady Duxbury had sent to bribe him into allowing Eleanor to go to Rosewood Cottage.

How had that only been a week ago?

Eleanor stood her ground, refusing to leave as he commanded.

Not when she hadn't emptied the vial into his drink. Not when he might pace away again and give her a scant second to deposit its contents into his brandy. She tucked her hands behind her back and discreetly pulled the stopper free.

"I said go to bed," he thundered. "You daft woman, do you not ever listen? Bloody hell, *go to bed.*"

She'd flinched at the explosive volume of his command. The reaction was ingrained in her after so many years of abuse. Even still, she remained in place, silently begging him to turn his back. Just for a moment so she could pour the vial into his glass.

Cecil aggressively plucked a date from its nested pocket and tossed the dried fruit into his mouth. His eyes bulged suddenly and he gave a thick choking sound.

His hand curled around his neck, face reddening as a rasp croaked from his lips.

He staggered toward her, hand outstretched.

She stepped back and he pitched forward, falling to the floor at her feet.

He writhed, still reaching for her with one hand, the other clutched at his neck. His face went from red to purple, the room filling with the strangled sounds of his obstructed breathing.

She took another step back, just out of reach of his flailing arm, and stoppered the bottle.

There would be no need for the belladonna after all.

"You're right," she said in a voice loud enough that anyone listening to their conversation might hear, a mask for the retching, stilted gasps coming from the floor. "You're right, Mr.

Clarke. I haven't been an obedient wife. I shall do as you bid now and go to bed."

His struggles slowed and he lay there motionless, save for one spasm that made his body twitch.

She turned from where he lay facedown on the hardwood floor. "Good night, husband."

Then she walked toward the door slowly, her steps measured to ensure there was no life left in him. Only then did she exit the study and close the door firmly behind her.

Part of her was desperate to return to Lady Duxbury's to see to Davies's welfare. But a larger part of her knew she had to remain home, to act surprised at the inevitable news the following morning.

She went to William first and pulled his sleep-warm body into her arms, soothing his little grunts of protest until he lay his head on her shoulder, asleep once more. In that moment, she savored every part of her son, the weight of him in her arms, the scent of the clean soap in his hair and the familiar smell of little boy sweat.

She gasped a quiet sob and hugged him to her, this precious child that she would do anything to protect.

That she *had* done something to protect.

With him in her arms, she returned to her bedchamber and slept with him curled at her side in the plush comfort of her own bed, no longer fearing the ruthless interruption of Cecil turning her dreams into a nightmare.

Her eyes fell closed and a soft rap sounded at her door.

Eleanor bolted awake, blinking in surprise at the cracks of golden sunlight limning the curtains. How long had she been asleep?

It had seemed only a minute.

William lay with his legs tucked under him, bottom in the air, his cheeks flushed from his slumber.

Before she could question if she was hearing things, the gentle knock came again.

Her heart slammed in her chest, her pulse echoing in every fresh bruise. She slipped carfully from bed so as not to wake William and rushed to the door.

The head housekeeper stood in the doorway, her back straight as a rod, her face drawn and pale. "Ma'am, forgive me for waking you. Your husband . . ."

A moment of fear washed over Eleanor.

What if he was still alive? What if she'd been mistaken when she left him there?

Eleanor gripped her hand in a fist. "What of him?"

"Forgive me, ma'am." Her maid averted her gaze from Eleanor's battered face. "There's been a terrible accident . . ."

EPILOGUE

Lady Duxbury

LADY DUXBURY OPENED THE DIARY, THE SPINE so new, its leather creaked with the effort. A blank page stared up at her, ripe with possibility.

Anything might become of a fresh page. It might be transformed into a book of poetry for someone like Lavinia. It might provide the design for a new nursery for someone like Rose. Or it even might detail the start of a new life for someone like Eleanor.

But for Lady Duxbury, this blank page represented the start of a journey, a means by which to make her thoughts heard in a world deaf to women's voices.

March 1896

My tutelage of the women last year was most effective. Offering repressed women the opportunity to enlighten themselves with empowering literature and creating a private setting allowed for trust, and lifelong friendships, to grow.

Lavinia has recently announced her engagement to the talented and respectable Mr. Wright, who was integral in assisting us with Eleanor's emergency last year. Not only is Lavinia still writing poetry, but she is often asked to read her work aloud as entertainment at social events. And if gossips are to be believed, both Lavinia and her handsome fiancé are quite active in the new suffrage movement that has been sweeping London.

I suspect the two shall enjoy a happy union like Rose and her husband, a fine couple reunited through the bond of love and the arrival of their first child, a lovely daughter whom Rose has decided to name Clara. It is an honor to have my godchild also be my namesake.

Even with a new child, Rose has taken on a leadership role with the Society for the Advancement of the Poor and has employed several recipients of the charity within her home. Included among those is Sam, the brave boy who brought me Eleanor's boot, no longer skinny and scruffy, but happy, healthy and fiercely loyal to Rose.

Eleanor is also finding joy, her face light despite the shadow of her widow's weeds. But then, I know exactly how freeing black lace can be. I suspect when she casts off her mourning, her wardrobe will be filled with all the colors of springtime. She visits often, her son filling the silence of my home with his laughter and play, and simultaneously filling the long-dormant emptiness in my heart.

As for myself, I am not unchanged. In helping these women, I searched deep within myself, to know what I needed to heal so that I might better aid them. Through their friendship and support, I have discovered a strength I did not know I had. In time, I allowed both Rose and Lavinia to read my diary as Eleanor once did. What felt too open and vulnerable in the past is now comfortable among my dear friends. We all have our wounds, and our friendship is the balm that has let us begin to heal.

I think Elias would be proud to see what I've accomplished, that I heeded his counsel and found an endeavor to pursue, one that fills the void his loss left behind.

What started with books and freedom became a sisterhood. Women ought not tear one another down, but encourage and support one another. For together, truly great things may be achieved. And together, we are now stronger—our happiness realized, our voices heard.

Young Lavinia once asked me if I should want to find love again. I think not.

I have purpose. What I have done with several women, I can do for more. Through those efforts, I am fulfilled.

The women of England will no longer be silent in their screams, their suffering no longer unheard.

I hear them, and I mean to do whatever necessary to save them.

Lady Duxbury set aside the fountain pen and stroked a hand over Otis's sleeping body in her lap as she considered her words on the page, the careful scroll of her handwriting. Her penmanship was far more sophisticated than the hasty scrawl of her youth. Allowing Eleanor to read her past had been a great risk. One that might have caused much damage should she have proven untrustworthy.

But Lady Duxbury had become a good judge of character over the years—a skill born of failure and hard lessons learned. She knew Eleanor would find strength and comfort in those pages.

She regretted nothing.

Not even giving Eleanor that vial, though whether she'd used it or not was uncertain. Lady Duxbury never asked after its contents.

A woman must do whatever necessary when the world put their back to her, leaving her to fend for herself. Lady Duxbury was certainly in no position to judge.

A knock sounded at the door to the library, though it was hardly necessary when the door stood open.

Lady Duxbury had spent far too much of her youth locked behind a door to ever abide one being closed.

If the house did not truly belong to the new Lord Duxbury, Edgar's second cousin, she might have had them all pulled from their hinges. But he was a young recluse, happy to reside in the country and allow her the use of this house unimpeded. Likewise, he did not challenge the generous jointure Edgar had left her in his will.

Davies cleared his throat and Otis lifted his head in irritation before hopping from her lap.

"Forgive me, my lady." Davies entered the room. A slight scar bisected the arch of his right eyebrow, a mark left by Eleanor's former husband. The blow had taken several days to recover from with Davies having sustained so many head wounds in the past. But recover he had, and woke all the more determined in his efforts to protect Lady Duxbury and the women of the Secret Book Society.

Lady Duxbury smiled at him now, waving him in. "You needn't ever seek forgiveness for doing your job, Davies."

He offered a serious nod of understanding, though she knew he would still apologize just as profusely the next time he interrupted her. "Lady Pempton is here to see you."

"Lady Pempton?" Lady Duxbury recalled the woman whose invitation to the Secret Book Society had been sent out the prior year along with the others. The woman who had not come.

And now she was here.

Davies extended a calling card to Lady Duxbury. The thick card stock was snowy white with Lady Pempton's name inscribed upon it. On the back was a neatly written message.

If I am not too late.

Lady Duxbury smiled softly to herself. It was never too late, and she would never turn away a woman in need.

"Send her in," Lady Duxbury advised.

Davies turned away to see to the request, leaving Lady Duxbury alone. She touched the brooch over her heart, the lock of Elias's hair over the locket housing George's portrait. She would honor the memory of her love by continuing her work to help women, and she would honor George's memory by ensuring every mother could protect her child.

As the sound of footsteps approached, Lady Duxbury stood, glancing out the window as she waited. Snowdrops had begun to push up from the frozen ground, their buds white with the promise of spring.

Lady Duxbury turned as Lady Pempton entered the room, her blue-green eyes overly large in her timid face. She offered a nervous smile. "I'm not too late to accept your invitation, am I?"

"Absolutely not." Lady Duxbury smiled. "Allow me to formally welcome you to the Secret Book Society."

★ ★ ★ ★ ★

AUTHOR NOTE

AS A LOVER OF BOOKS, I WAS HORRIFIED TO learn that women in the Victorian era were discouraged from reading. While literacy rates were higher toward the end of the nineteenth century than at the beginning, women were often relegated to reading texts meant to mold them into better mothers and wives. Books like *Mrs. Beeton's Book of Household Management* were practically mandatory reading. But when it came to novels, women were often discouraged—if not restricted—from reading. It was thought that books created a distraction from women's roles as mothers and wives and made them contrary when they dared develop opinions that differed from their husbands, fathers and even sons.

This is illustrated in *The Reader of Novels* by Antoine Wiertz, painted in 1853, depicting a female reader lazily lying in bed in the nude (because books were believed to lead to promiscuity in young women) as a nefarious person cast in shadow pushes another book her way.

Women were often restricted in so many ways in this era and had little control; sometimes all they had a say in was what they wore. This particular aspect was one that I explored with Eleanor's character, emphasizing the choice of her clothing to illustrate how very small her area of freedom truly was.

But women had more to worry about during the Victorian era than having their reading materials restricted or living with few personal liberties. Being afflicted with "hysteria" could have a woman sent to a lunatic asylum. Hysteria was the most frequent diagnosis for women in this time period and covered a lengthy list of symptoms including (but not limited to): depression, anxiety, melancholy, being overly excited, being too angry, being difficult or disagreeable. Yes, you read that right— being difficult or disagreeable. In fact, sadly, it was far too common for women who needed to be "set aside" to end up in a lunatic asylum for "hysteria."

One story I found in my research was a lightning bolt of inspiration for this story. In a Cinderella-esque tale (that is not a love story), a woman's husband was having an affair with her niece. When she protested, she was conveniently sent away to a lunatic asylum, freeing up her husband to continue the affair. On the way to the asylum, the woman spotted a boy on the side of the road and threw him coins, begging him to inform her friends of her fate. When asked how they would know he told the truth, she pulled off her shoe and threw it from the carriage. That real-life story of the shoe saved the woman whose friends were able to enlist the aid of a solicitor who specialized in helping women in such situations.

The ease with which women could be sent to asylums and the ready diagnosis of hysteria has been something that has long fascinated me about the Victorian era. But then, so much of this time period fascinates me. Writing this book allowed me to explore so many aspects of this part of history.

Like book societies. Books were very incredibly expensive and not available to everyone. It was not uncommon for people to pool their money together to purchase books to share (and for poorer classes, this extended to newspapers as well). The idea of book societies creating an opportunity for people to read books they otherwise could not was a lovely inspiration for this book.

I have also long been intrigued by the art of floriography—using flowers to convey meaning. This was especially popular during the Victorian era and I jumped into the concept. Please note that any flower or a plant written into this book has been done for a reason. Either the flower or plant says something about the scene itself or about the character. While doing my research, I noticed there were inconsistencies with books on floriography, so I used one particular book to make it easy for readers to see which meaning I wanted the flowers/plants mentioned to convey. If you would like to look up the flower/plant meaning for this book, please refer to *Floriography* by Jessica Roux.

Another aspect I want to mention here in the author note is hatpin fighting. Technically hatpin fighting really caught on in the twenty-first century; however, hatpins were used in the late 1900s. I made hatpin fighting happen a little earlier for the purpose of this story. This was admittedly indulgent on my part, but I enjoyed exploring the concept and have no regrets.

As with all my novels, I mention many books within this story. A list of those books can be found in the reader's guide for *The Secret Book Society*, along with book club questions and interesting facts, on my website: madelinemartin.com/book-clubs. Also, I love to do Zoom chats with book clubs, so feel free to reach out!

Please note that while I have done extensive research on these topics and try to be as accurate as possible, I did not live during this time period and some mistakes may have been made.

If you've ever felt judged by what you read. If you've ever felt like you don't belong. If you've ever worried that you aren't good enough. If you've ever longed for someone to truly understand you. Know that you are among friends here, and you are cordially invited to the Secret Book Society.

Bookishly yours,
Madeline Martin

ACKNOWLEDGMENTS

THERE IS SO MUCH GRATITUDE IN MY HEART for the amazing people whose expertise, support and love have gone into this book.

Thank you so much to all the wonderful readers who read this book. Without you, *The Secret Book Society* would never have come to life. Thank you for the hours you devote to reading my stories and for sharing with friends and writing reviews. Your support means more to me than I could possibly say.

Thank you to the incredible team at Hanover Square Press who make it possible for me to publish my books: to Peter Joseph and Grace Towery for their great suggestions and edits, to Leah Morse and Brianna Wodabek for being such a powerhouse in marketing and publicity to make people aware of *The Secret Book Society* being out in the world, and to Eden Railsback for the many times you always save the day. Thank you also to the cover design team for such a stunning cover—I think this one might be my favorite (but I love them all). And thank you to Kathleen Carter for always being such a cheerleader of my work and working so hard to get this book seen by everyone. And an enormous thank-you to my agent, Kevan Lyon, for always believing in me and always being in my corner.

I'm so grateful to have a team of family and friends supporting me as well. Thank you to John, who wrangles teens and cats while I'm on deadline and traveling, and for listening to endless amounts of historical details that I enthusiastically (possibly over-enthusiastically?) share. Thank you to my parents and brothers for always being so proud of me and for reading my books, and to my mother, who has read every book I've ever written and is always the last person to read it before it goes to print. And thank you to my girls, who inspire me to always be better. Thank you to my bestie, Eliza Knight. I cannot imagine doing this without you. Thank you to Tracy Emro for being such a huge part of every one of my books and for all your fabulous suggestions. Thank you also to Susan DeFreitas, the book coach who I worked with on this book. What you taught me during the writing of this book will stay with me forever. And thank you also to Darlene Michel for her last-minute read of all my books to catch any little slips.

Thank you to my amazing agent sisters, the Lyonesses, for always being a sounding board and for all your unending support. To my reader group, who takes the time to be there for me and is always so enthusiastic for my book ideas, for always being so supportive.

A huge thank-you to the librarians and booksellers who carry my books and recommend them. Book people are the best people, and you create magic with the world you manage. I'm so grateful to you.

To all the book bloggers, reviewers and bookstagrammers. I'm in awe of you for the number of books you read and the passion you so beautifully convey. Your eloquent praise, your stunning pictures, your passion for reading—they are so integral to the book community, not only for authors, but also readers. Thank you for sharing my books and for all the books I've read and loved by your recommendation.

I'm truly grateful to have so many to thank.